Was Ethan there? Was he in the cottage with her? None of what happened to Emily was the way she'd seen such things depicted in movies. The sense that something of Ethan remained in their home came to her in small, insignificant ways she barely noticed at first, or brushed aside as exhaustion or imagination.

It wasn't until there'd been several incidents that she began to wonder about them. On one day, she'd be sitting drowsily on the deck and suddenly feel a lingering touch on her cheek, then raise her hand to find nothing there. The next day she might walk through a room and reply to a remark she'd clearly heard addressed to her. Déjà vu, she decided, or perhaps a fragment of remembered conversation.

And often at night, as she prepared for bed, she was aware of a whisper of a breeze, as though someone had stepped out of her way as she passed. An open window somewhere or imagination or…

Dear Reader,

Although *The Secret Dreams of Emily Porter* is my first book to be published, and my first romance, I actually wrote my first novel at the age of nine—thirteen hundred pages of closely lined notebook paper about a nine-year-old gun-toting cowgirl and her pet collie, who live on a Wyoming ranch and fight crime and injustice. Mercifully, however, the manuscript of this epic appears to have been lost.

In college in California, I majored in journalism and English, and eventually married my psychology professor. After college, though, I somehow drifted into art instead of journalism, and spent thirty years as a professional artist before returning to my first love—writing.

My husband and I have one beautiful and talented daughter, and three beautiful and talented grandchildren. We live in suburban New Jersey now, with two aging cats.

I hope you enjoy the book, and Emily's journey to happiness.

Sincerely,

Judy Raxten

The Secret Dreams of Emily Porter

Judith Raxten

HARLEQUIN®

TORONTO • NEW YORK • LONDON
AMSTERDAM • PARIS • SYDNEY • HAMBURG
STOCKHOLM • ATHENS • TOKYO • MILAN • MADRID
PRAGUE • WARSAW • BUDAPEST • AUCKLAND

ISBN-13: 978-0-373-65420-8
ISBN-10:   0-373-65420-0

THE SECRET DREAMS OF EMILY PORTER

ABOUT THE AUTHOR

The talented Judith Raxten has been writing for much of her life, although this is her first book in print. The manuscript for *The Secret Dreams of Emily Porter* was a finalist in the Everlasting Love "epic romance" contest in 2006. She lives in New Jersey with her husband and two cats. You can reach her by e-mail at jrer@earthlink.net.

For Gene, and for Jess,
with love.

Prologue

Maine, 2006

Was today an ending or a beginning? Emily wondered, trying to ignore the echo of her own footsteps on the bare floors as she walked through the empty cottage for the last time. In checking the rooms for anything Sam and Josh might have missed, all she'd found were two of Sam's old glass marbles. When was it he'd been so fascinated by them? The summer he was six, maybe?

"See how they're all different?" he'd inquired solemnly, holding each new marble up to the sun the way a jeweler scrutinizing precious gems would. "You know—like snowflakes are?"

Josh had spent hours teaching him the rules of the game, but Sam was only interested in the swirl of light and colors. Before long, that childish fascination with light and color had grown into a passion for photography, and now, Sam was graduating from the University of California, Berkeley, with a degree in film and cinematography. Two days afterward, he and Jess, his bride of six months, would leave on a long-delayed honeymoon to Mexico.

Aside from the two forgotten marbles and the patches of dust the two men in Emily's life had somehow overlooked, there was nothing left in the cottage to pack. The cardboard box she'd brought from the house in town would go home empty. The small shell was in the exact spot on the fireplace mantel where it had lain for years, but she knew that Josh hadn't forgotten it. He'd left it there for her. The shell would be the final thing to leave the beach cottage—the last tangible memory of everything that had happened here—the heartbreak and the boundless joy.

Emily heard a car pull into the driveway, and glanced out the window to see Josh standing in the yard, looking toward the sea. For several minutes, she watched, but didn't call to him. Today of all days, Josh, too, would be thinking about endings and beginnings.

At fifty-eight, Joshua Lundgren was still almost as lean and tanned as he had been the day he first came to the cottage, three years after Ethan's death. Only a slight thickening at his waistline and the inevitable crinkled lines around his eyes betrayed the passage of those twenty years—that, and the few strands of gray that had begun to appear in his pale blond hair.

She watched a while longer, then opened the window and leaned out.

"Hi, there."

Josh turned and waved. "Hi, yourself. I stopped the mail, locked up the house and disconnected the washer hose—as ordered. The dog's at the kennel and the bags are in the car. Both of yours are probably fifty pounds overweight, by the way. So much for packing light." He smiled. "Are you ready to go?"

"Just about. But it's lucky for you I didn't bring a broom, buster. You guys forgot to sweep up in here after you moved the furniture out."

Josh grinned. "We didn't forget. We were male bonding. You can't expect two guys who haven't seen each other in months to think about housework. Not when they're sharing a touching father-son moment."

Emily rolled her eyes. "Well, darling, when the Hendersons complain about the dirt, I'll let *you* explain all that touching business about male bonding. Oh, did you remember to pack the photo albums? Jess has been begging to see Sam's baby pictures."

"So I heard," Josh said, chuckling, "but Sam says to tell you that if you show her the naked ones, you're in big trouble." He motioned toward the beach. "Don't forget to close that window when you finish in there. There's a storm blowing up."

Emily shut the window, locked it and the back door, then joined her husband in the small yard. When he encircled her waist with one arm and pulled her close, she let herself melt against him, aroused by that same girlish lightheadedness she always felt when he kissed her like this. After all these years, Josh could still make her knees weak when he put his mind to it.

"Last chance," he asked softly. "Are you sure you want to go through with the sale?"

Emily nodded. "I'm sure. Besides, escrow's closing tomorrow afternoon, and Mrs. Henderson told me their movers will be here from South Carolina on Thursday."

"So let them sue us. I want you to be certain about this."

"I am, darling. I promise." Emily sighed. "It's been wonderful spending weekends and summers out here, but with Sam and Jess planning to live in Los Angeles, and us in the big house in town, how often will anyone come? I can't bear thinking of it standing empty. Houses are meant to be lived in. You've always said that yourself. No, it was time to sell, and the Hendersons seem like really nice people. She's going to use the boathouse as an art studio, the way I did till we bought the gallery."

"Did you warn her about the spiders—and the weather?"

"I'm not *that* dumb," Emily said, laughing. "I'll let her first Maine winter be a surprise, the way it was for me."

"Okay, then. As of tomorrow afternoon, this house will officially belong to the Hendersons. Until then, it's still ours." He began toying with the top buttons of her blouse. "We've still got three hours until our flight takes off, you know."

She slipped her arms around his waist. "That's all very well, but in case you've forgotten, there's no furniture left inside. And here I thought I'd be the only one to get all weepy and sentimental."

"Sentiment has nothing to do with it. I think it's the idea of all that freedom we're about to have. No kids, no rock music, no houses to build—just you and me with lots of time on our hands and nobody in the next bedroom. I thought you might want to get a head start. You know, a little practice as we enter our golden years?"

"Stop fishing for compliments, darling," she teased. "You've never needed practice at that sort of thing, but you *do* need to allow for airport traffic. Besides, after packing boxes for days, these old bones are too stiff to roll around on a hard oak floor. Try saving all that boyish energy for San Francisco. I hear the Palace Hotel has beds in every room."

"Suit yourself, but as it happens, I have two very soft down sleeping bags in the trunk." He winked. "It wasn't easy cramming them in, either, with all those suitcases."

They made love in the empty living room, with the smell of pine boughs and salt air drifting through the open window, and caught the flight to Los Angeles with only four minutes to spare.

On the plane, while Josh dozed, Emily stared out at the clouds and thought back to when Sam was a baby. It was just the two of them in the cottage, then—a new widow afraid of life, and a lonely little boy who needed a father.

Then Josh had come—to make her start living again, and to be the father Sam needed so badly. And today, she knew that Ethan would be happy for her, and as proud of his son as she and Josh were. She slid her hand deep into the pocket of her skirt to touch the little shell, then closed her eyes and tried to remember it all from the beginning.

Chapter 1

There had been a thunderstorm that night, too—the night more than twenty-five years ago when she first met Ethan Douglas. The day had been unseasonably warm, with the kind of cloudless, dazzling blue sky that gave no forewarning of the sudden Maine squall that was about to sweep in off the bay and alter the course of Emily Porter's life.

Emily had never believed in predestination, but that evening's sudden downpour made everything that happened afterward seem more like fate than mere coincidence. After one of her twice-yearly visits, Emily's widowed mother was returning to Los Angeles the following day, and in preparation for her flight home, she'd spent that morning in the beauty parlor. There were few things more annoying to Helene Porter than having a new hairdo ruined by rain, so if the storm had blown through a few minutes earlier, the theater tickets would have ended up in the trash, and mother and daughter would have whiled away their last evening together watching television and dining on frozen pizza. They wouldn't have ventured out into an almost biblical deluge to a play neither of them really wanted to see, and Emily's life would have remained exactly as it had been for the past three years—safe, predictable and lonely.

Emily had discovered the tickets in her mailbox two days earlier—a joke gift from her best friend and former college roommate, Maggie Beckman. "I know you're going bonkers after a full week with Mom," Maggie's accompanying note read, "so take these and have an unforgettable evening of great theater, my treat!"

The play was a revival of *A Streetcar Named Desire,* performed by the theater arts department of the high school where Maggie taught American literature to kids whose idea of classic drama was TV's *Starsky and Hutch.* It was a measure of how grateful Emily was to be spared another evening alone with her mother that she hiked the three blocks to the nearest pay phone to call and thank Maggie for the reprieve. (It was a full week until payday, and the telephone company had declined—for the second time that year—to wait any longer for their money.)

"Em!" Maggie cried. "I was kidding! If Tennessee Williams ever gets wind of what we've done to his masterpiece, he'll probably sue. Blanche's Southern drawl is pure South Boston, and the kid playing Stanley Kowalski is a gangly basketball nerd with pimples and zero talent. I have to show up to provide moral support, sweetie, but you don't."

"Too late," Emily said wearily. "I already told Mom we'd do something special on her last night. I can't even afford a movie, so it's this play of yours or another enchanted evening like last night. I made popcorn, then sat through another lecture about my many shortcomings."

"You could get her drunk," Maggie suggested, only half in jest.

"No, thanks. She gets morose when she drinks, and starts weeping about how good old Dennis would *still* take me back, prince among men that he is, if only I'd ask him 'nicely.' Mom would know this, of course, because she's been stalking him ever since we got divorced. She skulks around some pricey grocery store in Malibu, waiting for him to show up, then pops up in the organic veggie aisle like an escaped lunatic, claiming she just happened to be in the neighborhood."

"Try reminding her of what the son of a bitch did to you—the bruises, the black eyes. Hell, what about that time he broke your wrist?"

Emily sighed. "Let's face it, Mag. Mom adored Dennis. She's never going to believe he did those things. He dumped wife number two last month, and now she's begging me to call him and 'make up.' She's not going to stop until I die, or until Dennis does. Even then, she'll probably show up at the funeral with a humongous wreath of white carnations, apologizing to the corpse because I didn't appreciate him while I still had the chance. Whenever she brings up the subject of Dennis, I remind myself that in a couple of days, *both* of them will be more than three thousand miles away. Tomorrow morning, she'll be on a plane back to L.A., and I can relax and have my usual post-visit breakdown."

Emily could hear her friend's disapproval in the uncomfortable silence that followed. Her steadfast refusal to stand her ground and demand her mother's respect was an issue she and Maggie had argued about many times before.

Maggie adroitly redirected the subject. "That reminds me. Did the flowers I sent get there? The ones from this new guy you made up? Ethan Whatshisname?"

Emily laughed, grateful for the change in subject. "You're a lifesaver, Mag, and your timing was perfect. When the doorbell rang, we'd already been over my weight, why I never get what she calls a 'decent' haircut and why I live in—quote—'a deplorable slum.' I keep telling her this neighborhood is considered artistic and bohemian, like Greenwich Village, but I don't think she's convinced. Maybe it's the roaches, or the drug dealer who moved in upstairs last week. The flowers distracted her— for a few minutes, anyway. No wonder I'm always so broke, though. I'll bet I've sent more flowers and candy to myself than any other woman in the known world!"

At least once during each of her mother's visits, Emily conspired to have flowers delivered—not to Helene, as might be expected, but to herself. The bouquets were usually accompanied by a prettily wrapped box of candy or a small but conspicuously expensive gift, and always included a faintly amorous note from one of Emily's devoted, thoughtful—and totally fictitious—suitors.

Emily's mother was always suitably impressed, but the

elaborate ruse had proven expensive and sometimes embarrassing. The only florist within walking distance of Emily's apartment building was a seedy storefront operated by an aged busybody who showed more interest in the private lives of her customers than in the wilted merchandise she offered for sale. Curious about Emily's practice of sending floral tributes to her own address, the old woman had recently begun to open and read the enclosure cards. At that point, Maggie volunteered to make the flower purchases.

"Now the old hag thinks *I'm* your secret admirer," Maggie observed. "But you'd rather look like a popular lesbian than a dateless wallflower, right?" Emily laughed weakly, but agreed.

Emily told herself that the flowers were a vital prop in the ongoing minidrama she had written to comfort her overanxious mother. Helene often confided to friends that Emily had walked away—for the flimsiest of reasons—from an excellent marriage to a wealthy husband. And now, her beloved but misguided only child was floundering in a morass of her own making, with no husband, no prospects and no future.

And so, in an attempt to relieve her mother's fears, and coincidentally to improve her *own* image, Emily had begun to invent things. Small, innocent things, at first. A boyfriend here, a job promotion there, and before long, she had become a skilled and convincing liar. In the three lonely years since she'd left California, Emily had invented a creative, financially rewarding career, a host of amusing friends, and when necessary, another adoring suitor given to sending flowers and candy.

Having been raised a proper midwestern Methodist, Emily wasn't especially proud of the complicated web of lies she'd woven, and she knew that someday, when she least expected it, her house of cards would collapse. In the meantime, though, she had persuaded herself that the lies were only a stratagem for survival—a tactic that was both practical *and* altruistic. For, in spite of their many differences, Emily understood that Helene's continual nagging was well meant. Annoying and sometimes maddening— but well meant.

There had been five nonexistent suitors so far, each with an extensive biography and résumé. All of the men were designed to suit Helene's taste and not Emily's, so it went without saying that they were always financially well-off, employed as middle- to high-level executives and predisposed to marry in the very near future. Since Helene Porter had never exhibited much faith in either her daughter's taste or her allure, Emily had learned to avoid using the words *handsome* or *attractive* when describing her imaginary suitors. She found it safer to say that they were "presentable." Regrettably, each of the five had eventually turned out to be—in some tragic and irreparable manner—flawed.

Until a few months ago, all had gone well with the subterfuge. Like most mothers, Helene Porter believed herself to be an excellent judge of her child's character and truthfulness, which meant she didn't credit her normally submissive daughter with sufficient imagination or cunning to lie well. Even so, Helene had recently begun to wonder— aloud—why she was never introduced to Emily's boyfriends before they disappeared into boyfriend history.

Inventing the newest man had always been an amusing diversion, but with Helene becoming more insistent, Emily had decided, four months earlier, to put an end to the parade of fictitious suitors. The deception and the guilt had become emotionally exhausting and increasingly difficult to manage. But then, she had foolishly allowed herself a last "fling." Not another executive, this time, but someone creative—in the arts, maybe. When she told her mother about this so-far nameless "creative" person, the reaction on the other end of the line was predictable—and shrill.

"Creative? Dear God, not some artist, I hope! You of *all* people should know they're all drug addicts!" (Emily was an artist by training and disposition, but a minimum-wage, part-time employee at a discount store by necessity.)

Realizing her error, Emily changed course. "Calm down, Mom. He's not an artist." Her mind raced through the possibilities, discarding a musician as even less appealing to her mother than an artist. "He's…he's in the theater, sort of."

"An actor? Emily, where do you *find* these people? Actors are horribly vain, and most of them never make any money."

Emily was close to panic. She usually had a prepared script when she invented a man. "He's not like that. He's… Well, he's a little older."

"Old!" her mother wailed. "Oh, dear God! How old?"

"Not old, more like…retired, you know? As a matter of fact, he's not acting anymore." Emily had suddenly remembered something that might save her—for the moment.

"Retired! Unemployed, more likely. What's his name?" Helene asked suspiciously. "Have I ever heard of this person? Has *anyone?*"

Frantically, Emily dropped to her knees and fumbled under the coffee table. Somewhere in the clutter of out-of-date magazines was a book of photographs she had bought months earlier. She found it buried under a pile of old *Newsweeks*.

"Ethan Douglas," Emily said quickly, dusting off the cover. "His name is Ethan Douglas. He lives here in Maine and he used to be an actor, but now he takes pictures." She sat with the book open in her lap and turned the pages slowly, moved once again by Ethan Douglas's hauntingly lovely black-and-white photographs of Maine's rugged coastline. "Very good pictures, actually," she murmured, pausing at a breathtaking, two-page panorama of the snow-bound West Quoddy lighthouse. "Some of the best I've ever seen."

"If he was an actor, why have I never heard of him?" Helene insisted.

Ethan Douglas probably hadn't made a film in fifteen years, but he had been a fine, well-respected actor. Not exactly a household name, but respectable. Emily decided he would do nicely. "He hasn't made a movie in a while, but he did several excellent westerns, and…"

Helene moaned. "You're mixed up with some movie *cowboy?*"

Emily swore under her breath. "Two of them were classics, Mom. You remember *The Trail Home,* I'm sure, and he made that really great mystery, *City Full of Strangers.* And he starred in a TV series, *Thatcher, P.I.* Well, after he retired, he became a photographer."

Helene had begun to cry.

"Does he make a living?"

"He's very comfortable, Mom, I promise." Emily checked the copyright date of the book, praying it was current. She would need time to dump Ethan Douglas, and if his name popped up in the obituaries first, the game would be over.

And then, almost four months to the day after that conversation, before Emily could arrange Ethan Douglas's graceful exit, Helene had arrived for a visit. They'd gone out to see the horrendous *Streetcar Named Desire,* and Emily's house of cards had dissolved in an unexpected cloudburst.

It was a four-block walk to the high school, and both Emily and Helene were soaked to the skin by the time they arrived. Later, with the play mercifully over, they struggled up the crowded aisle toward the exit, damp, rumpled and eager to get out of the stifling auditorium and find a cab. Emily was lost in thought as they neared the doors, fighting not to lose ground in the surge of babbling and ecstatic parents.

"Look, darling," Helene cried. "They're signing autographs."

"I'm thrilled, Mom," Emily growled. "Could we keep moving, please? Who the hell would want their autographs? My God! They've just savaged a jewel of the American theater!"

But Helene had stopped in the middle of the aisle to point toward the stage.

"Is that who I think it is?"

Emily rolled her eyes. "Well, if it's Tennessee Williams,

these people are in big trouble, that's for sure." She glanced up, blinked once and looked again, this time in disbelief. Ethan Douglas—in the flesh—was standing on the stage, surrounded by the youthful cast. The play's male lead was accepting Douglas's handshake with an awed, buck-toothed grin. As Maggie had predicted, Stanley Kowalski was wearing a pair of grungy, high-top basketball sneakers.

"It's him," Helene exclaimed. "I know it is! I recognize him from the back of that book you showed me. I thought you said he was in London!" Helene's voice resonated with accusation and open suspicion.

Emily tried very hard not to throw up. "I did. I thought…I mean, I *think* he said he was going this week-end, but maybe it was…"

Helene was staring at her. "Well, for heaven's sake, darling, aren't you going to take me up there to meet the man, at least?"

Emily went pale. "No, Mom! He's really busy. He's… he's working! I'll call him later and—"

"Don't be silly! Have you two had a quarrel or what? Why don't I just go up there and introduce myself, and—"

"No!" The scream was louder than Emily had intended, and several people turned to stare. "You wait here! I'll go…I'll go get him…talk to him," she stammered. "You wait right here, and *don't* move!"

Emily darted away into the crowd before Helene could protest. In the grip of a sickening panic, she elbowed her way through the mob, each step bringing her closer to the stage and to the utter humiliation that waited there. Turning back to motion to her mother, Emily threw up her arms to suggest frustration at her inability to reach the stage. Then, hoping her short stature would make her difficult to see, she milled about in the crowd, desperately trying to buy time and to think of a way out of the mess she'd made.

After rifling through the clutter at the bottom of her purse, she found a scrap of paper and a pen and began to write. Oddly, the outrageous words came easily, and she scribbled them down as quickly as they popped into her head. Then, clutching the note in her hand, she shoved her way relentlessly down the aisle, moving ahead before she lost her nerve. When she reached the steps, she saw that Douglas was still standing on the stage, chatting with the short, squat young woman who'd played Blanche. Emily stood frozen, certain that she was going to be sick. Only the knowledge that Helene was watching impelled her to climb the short staircase to the stage. As she took that first step, Emily knew in her heart that Anne Boleyn and Mary, Queen of Scots, had probably approached the execution block with more enthusiasm, but there was no turning back.

Chapter 2

Only a minute earlier, a group of people had stood between Emily and Ethan Douglas, but now, this hideous moment seemed to be playing out in slow motion, like a protracted death scene in a bad movie. The crowd on the stage had melted away, leaving her standing before him, alone and trembling. Even from the depths of her terror, Emily could feel her mother's steady gaze on the back of her head. It was now or never. She took a deep breath, and without a word, thrust the note into Douglas's hand.

He was much taller than she'd expected, looking down at her with an expectant half smile. An autograph, of course! He thought she was asking for an autograph. Without pausing in his conversation, he took the scrap of paper and started to sign it, then glanced at it, more carefully. Was he shocked? Irritated? Maybe even frightened? Was this damp, wrinkled woman a lunatic—a deranged stalker? He cocked his head quizzically for a moment, and then smiled. Their eyes met, hers wide with fear, his with what might have been amusement.

Her note, in its entirety, read, "My name is Emily Porter. I have exactly fourteen hundred and eighty-four dollars in the bank and no criminal record. If you will kiss me, right now, in the most realistic way you know how, I will donate every last penny of that to your favorite charity. I'll explain this bizarre request later, and be indebted to you for the rest of my life. I don't believe I'm insane, and I have no communicable diseases of which I am aware. I will understand completely if you choose to have me arrested or committed, but you can count me out as a fan."

For several seconds, he said nothing at all, studying her with what Emily took to be puzzlement. Suddenly, her knees went weak, and an image flashed across her mind— a vision of herself being hauled off in a straitjacket, before her mother's horrified eyes. And then, in what felt like a dream, Ethan Douglas took her into his arms, pulled her against his chest and kissed her on the mouth, very, very hard. It was a long, deep, thorough sort of kiss, and he lifted her slightly off the floor in the process. From what Emily could remember about being kissed, this one was extremely believable and well worth fourteen hundred and eighty-four dollars—if she'd had it. When he set her on her feet again, she noticed several of the people near them staring with undisguised curiosity. From below, on the floor of the auditorium, three or four cameras flashed.

"Oh, God!" she groaned. "I'm sorry! That's probably going to be in the school paper!"

Douglas grinned. "Better than the *National Enquirer.* So, tell me, did you do this on a dare? Lose a bet? Or was it an initiation of some kind?"

Emily shook her head. "Worse than that. It's my mother. Over there, near the exit. I…"

He shaded his eyes to look across the crowd. Helene was easy to spot, waving both arms above her head, and he waved cheerfully back.

Emily gathered her courage and attempted an explanation. "I told my mother that… Well, that I sort of knew you." The words that tumbled out of her mouth sounded ludicrous, even to her.

Douglas smiled again. "Well, now you do." For the first time, Emily noticed his slate-blue eyes and the light brown hair going ever so slightly gray at the temples. The photo on the back of the book hadn't done him justice. At forty-eight, Ethan Douglas was still an astonishingly attractive man.

Emily took a deep breath and tried to regain control of her shaking hands. "Look, Mr. Douglas, I really can't thank you enough for this, and I know you must think I'm some kind of… Anyway, I'll just go away now and disappear, and I swear I'll *never* bother you again! *Ever!* Thank you, from the bottom of my heart. You've saved my life."

"Is there someone else you'd like me to kiss?" he asked affably. "A baby, perhaps?"

She flushed. "No, honestly. Thank you. You've done enough."

"Your mother's coming this way, you know—steaming toward us like a German U-boat, actually." Placing both hands on her shoulders, Douglas spun Emily around to look.

"Oh, dear God!" Emily cried. She darted down the steps, turned to blow him a wildly overacted goodbye kiss, and plunged headlong into the crowd, frantic to intercept Helene before she got any closer. Suddenly, she felt a strong hand on her elbow.

"I'm curious," Ethan Douglas said, smiling broadly. "I'd like to meet your mother. Is she anything like you?"

Emily froze. "No! She isn't! And please take my word for it, you don't want to meet her. I'll send the check to your hotel or agent or whatever. *Please!* She's almost here! Oh, shit!" Emily wailed, unable now to halt the impending disaster. "How could I know you'd show up in a dump like this?"

The question didn't require an answer, and in any case, there was no time. Helene's perfectly coifed, unnaturally bright red head was bobbing closer, just a few yards away now.

"Okay," Emily gasped, gripping Douglas's arm in one last effort to save herself. "Here's the deal! You and I are engaged and you're supposed to be off in London, doing something or other! I was going to break up with you in a few days and then—"

Douglas glanced up to check on Helene's progress. "Maybe you should just tell me her name. And a bit about us, like where we met? I'll wing the rest. You've got maybe fifteen seconds, so start talking."

"I'm a starving artist," she whispered frantically. "Divorced three years ago. I live in a rattrap a few blocks from here. My mother's name is Helene Porter. She's always bugging me about my love life, or lack of it, and she's never heard of you, so I kind of…" Emily shook her head dolefully. "Okay, look. I know it was stupid, but the thing is, I made you up."

Douglas frowned. "Actually, you didn't make me up, and there probably are a *few* people left who've even heard of me."

And then, like a cloud of locusts or a plague of frogs, Helene Porter was upon them, but Ethan Douglas didn't miss a beat.

"Mrs. Porter!" he boomed. "I'm so glad to meet you at last!" He embraced Emily's mother warmly, kissed her on both cheeks, then slipped his arm around Emily's waist and kissed *her* on the mouth again, with what seemed to Emily a bit more realism than was absolutely necessary. "What luck, running into the two of you like this! I was scheduled to be in London tonight. I didn't even have time to call Emily when my plans changed. How long are you in town?"

"Why, I'm afraid I have to go home tomorrow, Mr. Douglas," Helene gushed, still flustered by being kissed by a genuine ex-movie star, even one she *didn't* quite remember.

Douglas took her hand. "Well, we can at least have dinner together. There's a terrific little Italian place near here called Emilio's. Em and I eat there every time I'm in town. Right, darling?"

When he kissed her, Emily tried to ignore the sensations the repeated kisses had begun to arouse in her. She nudged his arm. "Please!" she whispered. "You don't have to do this!" She turned to Helene. "Really, Mom, Ethan has to catch a plane tonight. Some other time, maybe. Right, *darling?*"

Douglas smiled. "Come on, Em, I'm not going to miss a chance to have dinner with your mom. There'll be another flight tomorrow. Wait here a minute, and I'll tell the people I'm with to go on without me." With that, he disappeared, back into the crowd.

After dinner and cocktails at Emilio's, Ethan Douglas drove them home. They were no sooner inside than Helene made her apologies and went in to bed, exhausted after one too many Manhattans and two hours of scintillating Hollywood insider gossip.

"I made most of that up, of course," he admitted to Emily as they sat at the kitchen table over a cup of coffee. "I knew Elizabeth Taylor and Richard Burton well enough to say hello to, and I had lunch with Steve McQueen a couple of times while he was on the next soundstage doing interiors for *The Great Escape*. The truth is, I don't really know anything about the business anymore, or even who's still who in Hollywood. When I came home to Maine twelve years ago, I bought a house, quit for good and never looked back."

"Then what were you doing at that awful play?" Emily asked. "These things usually draw adoring family members, not celebrities—even former celebrities."

"Herb Denning was my agent for fifteen years, and young

Mike Denning—tonight's Stanley Kowalski—is Herb's grandson. I'm afraid it's going to take more clout than Herb's got to find that kid a job in Hollywood, though. I've probably seen worse acting, but I can't remember when." He glanced down the hall at the closed bedroom door. "Okay, now that the coast is clear, tell me something. What would you have done if I'd turned down your offer tonight?"

Emily grimaced. "Who knows? Hopped a bus some-where—to Peru, maybe, or Bangladesh? Dyed my hair, become a Hare Krishna?" She looked down at her coffee cup. "May I ask *you* something, now?"

"Sure. Ask away."

"Why did you do all this? Are you really that nice a guy, or do you just have a soft spot for needy misfits?"

"More curious than nice, I'm afraid. I've had my share of odd experiences with fans, but tonight was a first. Do you do this a lot, like a scavenger hunt, maybe, or a hobby? Or was it genuinely a one-time event?"

Emily raised her right hand. "One-time, I swear to you! Mom's going home to L.A. tomorrow, and once she's safely out of range, I'll write to her and tell her we broke it off."

"Damn!" he said. "Was it something I did? Forgot your birthday? Ran over your cat? Anyway, you can't break up with me yet. You still owe me for tonight, remember?"

Emily flushed. "I know. Now, about the money…"

"No. Something else."

"Oh." She laughed nervously. "I see. Well, here's the thing. If it's my…uh…sexual favors we're discussing here, I may as well confess right up front that I've never been much good at playing hard to get." The nonsense pouring out of her mouth was making Emily cringe with embarrassment, but somehow, she couldn't stop herself. "I should warn you, though, you'll probably be disappointed. You're not into anything weird, are you? Bondage, opium, wife-swapping, white slavery? Do you even *have* a wife, by the way? What about—"

Ethan Douglas came to her rescue once again, and interrupted her babbling. "No bondage, drugs or white slavery, and no wife at the moment. Don't be insulted, but all I want you to do is have lunch with me tomorrow, and dinner."

She stared. "That's it? That's all you want?"

When he smiled again, Emily was relieved to see that he wasn't laughing at her. "We'll both know more about that tomorrow, *after* we've had lunch—and dinner, of course. But unless I miss my guess, there's going to be a *lot* more I want from you."

Emily blushed. "Well, okay, but lunch will have to be your treat," she said. "Dinner, too. I donated all my money to charity, if you remember. Which charity, by the way?"

Douglas frowned. "It's a school upstate for wayward young women who accost strange men and force their favors on them."

She lowered her eyes, suppressing a smile. "Are there many cases like that?"

"I certainly hope so," he said, chuckling.

In a sudden change of subject, he glanced around the room. "You said you were an artist. Is this where you work?"

Emily shrugged. "Yes. When I work. You might be shocked to learn this, but there seems to be a glut on the market right now—of what you kindly refer to as my 'work.' I've sold exactly three paintings in the three years I've been here."

"Would you mind showing me a few of them?"

"Do you have a strong stomach?"

He didn't smile. "I'd really like to see them." Emily hesitated briefly. The request sounded sincere, though, and lacked the usual note of artificial politeness, so she got down on her hands and knees and searched underneath the couch until she found two large, dusty canvases—her most recent. Douglas held them up to look closely, then propped both paintings against the couch and stepped back to study them more carefully.

"They're very good," he said finally. "The seascape, particularly."

Emily cocked an eyebrow. "So now you're a qualified art critic *and* an actor?" She could hear the sarcasm in her voice, but he didn't seem offended.

"No, but I *am* a fairly well-heeled member of the art-buying public, so I wouldn't be too quick to write me off, if I were you. I've got a place north of here, on a strip of beach like the one you've painted. You've got everything just right—the late-afternoon light, the color of the water and especially the loneliness of… No, that's the wrong word. It's the solitude and the quiet. Most of them have too much going on—abandoned boats, seagulls, pounding surf, you know what I mean?"

She nodded. It was an observation Emily had made herself about many of the seascapes she saw in galleries.

"Thank you," she said grudgingly.

Once again, he didn't smile. "You're welcome."

Emily hesitated before speaking again. "I bought your book," she said softly. "Last year. Your photographs are wonderful. I should have said something earlier—told you I'd seen them…knew about them. I don't know exactly why I didn't. Jealousy, maybe."

He looked at her curiously, but it was a while before he replied. "I'm glad you liked them," he said finally.

Emily thrust the canvases hurriedly back under the couch and stood up. "Would you like another cup of coffee?"

"It'll have to be quick. I've still got a long drive up the coast in the rain."

While Emily got the coffee, Ethan sat and waited, and when she returned to the living room, he was leafing through her copy of *Maine: The Changing Seasons*—his book.

She set the coffee cups down. "That wonderful little beach house in the fog is my favorite. Page seventy-two."

He paused for a few seconds, then nodded. "Mine, too."

The rain had begun to slash against the windows more insistently, so they finished their coffee quickly. When he got up to leave, he asked for her phone number.

"I'm sorry," she said. "I don't have a phone."

"How do you get by without a telephone?"

Emily flushed. "Well, I *had* one, but then there was this little dispute with the phone company," she explained, hoping to conceal her embarrassment with humor. "They have this obsession with getting paid."

"I see. Well, since I'm considering forgiving that promissory note of yours, you're about fourteen hundred and eighty-four bucks richer than you thought. Get a phone. You're going to need it."

"Well, that's the problem, you see," she confessed. "I'm dead broke. If you'd actually taken that check to the bank, it would've bounced sky-high. I was sort of hoping you'd let me give you the money slowly, like in a long series of very, *very* tiny installments."

Douglas shook his head disapprovingly. "In that case, it looks like you owe me a lot more than just lunch and dinner."

"I bring home one hundred and eighty-six dollars a week," she said as she walked him to the front door. Outside, the noise of the rain was getting worse. "Let's see. It'll take me about…" While he looked in the closet for his jacket, she attempted to calculate the exact amount on her fingers.

"Seventy-four weeks, at twenty bucks a week," he said.

Emily sighed. "Oh. That's a long time to wait to collect a bill, I guess."

He smiled. "Yes, but I'm an unusually patient bill collector." He took her elbow and pulled her close, then kissed her hard and deeply. She returned the kiss eagerly, making no effort this time to conceal her feelings and secretly hoping that in the heavy downpour, Douglas's car wouldn't start. It started on the first try, so she consoled herself by going to bed with his kiss still warm on her lips—and a lunch date for the following day.

The next morning, after seeing Helene off at the airport, Emily found a yellow notice hanging on her doorknob. The outstanding phone bill had been mysteriously paid and her phone reconnected. Two minutes after she walked in the door, it rang. Ethan, asking where to she wanted to have lunch, and dinner, and if she might be interested in a "no strings" houseguest for the weekend. Emily accepted instantly, then dashed off to give her disorderly apartment the six months of thorough cleaning it needed—in the two meager hours she had.

Chapter 3

Emily had never been swept off her feet before, and her first heady, whirlwind week with Ethan left her breathless and confused—and wary. It had been almost fifteen years since his last movie, but Ethan Douglas was still decidedly handsome. He was slender and well muscled, and the rugged good looks she remembered from his early films showed only a minimal degree of wear. In meeting new people, he was charming and self-assured, putting them at ease as readily as he had Emily. He was educated and widely read, and though apparently very well-off, he never made an issue of money, as Dennis always had. He spoke at least three languages that Emily knew of, and she suspected that he'd visited most of the exotic capitals of the world more often than Emily had been to nearby Boston.

All of which added to Emily's nervousness. This sophisticated and attractive man, who could have been with almost any other woman in the world, had spent an entire week courting *her*—plump, awkward Emily Porter—in the most tender and considerate manner imaginable. When she resisted going to elegant restaurants or clubs, he deferred to her wishes, then seemed pleased with the simple picnics or long walks that she preferred. Cinderella herself could not have asked for a more idyllic interlude.

But Emily didn't believe in fairy tales, and she'd learned from experience that when things seemed too good to be true, they usually were. Even as she luxuriated in Ethan's romantic attentions, she remained watchful for signs of rejection—a rejection she knew wouldn't be far away.

Emily wasn't unattractive. Small and reasonably pretty, she had dark brown hair, green eyes and straight teeth. Her skin was fair and clear, and since her divorce, she rarely wore makeup, explaining when friends asked that it made her feel silly and dishonest. At thirty-one, her figure was nicely proportioned but determinedly plump, a longstanding problem she chose to accentuate by buying her clothes too large and relentlessly drab. Protective coloration, bordering on invisibility, she joked—like the shy, soft brown mourning doves she fed every winter on her fire escape. Until now, all of this had suited her nicely.

She'd dropped out of college in her final year, but read voraciously, and was blessed with a natural curiosity that usually disguised her lack of formal education. Unlike Ethan, she was shy and ill-at-ease with people she didn't know, and tended to avoid them. Possessed of a generally pleasant and compliant disposition, Emily was slow to anger or take offense, and when confronting awkward social situations, she deflected criticism by using humor and a quick wit to point out her flaws before anyone else could beat her to it. This self-deprecating humor disarmed critics, and led people to regard her as wryly amusing and perceptive. But for Emily, there was a deeper purpose to this behavior than saving face. It reassured her of her own unworthiness. She'd learned a long time ago that feeling unworthy made accepting failure easier and spared her the tiring and ultimately useless struggle to succeed.

Among her many protective mechanisms, though, the most indispensable to Emily was one she seemed to have been born with—an almost intuitive animal sense of when it was time to turn and run. She had already come to care deeply for Ethan Douglas, and she knew it would break her heart when he tired of her. From her perspective, the crucial thing in ending any relationship was self-preservation. Loneliness and heartbreak were old and familiar companions, and she knew she could survive those wounds again if she had to, but when the affair with Ethan Douglas was over, Emily wanted very much to be the first to back away.

On the morning following the disastrous play, he'd taken her to lunch at a small café on the wharf, where they sat and talked until late afternoon.

"I think they're hinting that we should leave," he suggested, when the staff began to reset the tables. "Where would you like to have dinner tonight?"

"I'm not really hungry. We could just go back to my

apartment, and maybe call out for pizza or Chinese later? If it's okay with you, of course."

He grinned. "My grandmother always told me to look for a woman who was a cheap date."

Emily smiled. "Well, then, you've come to the right place."

Back at her apartment, Emily went to the bedroom to change clothes, and when she emerged in jeans and a sweatshirt, Ethan was nowhere in sight. She found him in the kitchen, washing the embarrassingly tall pile of dirty dishes she'd left in the sink for two days.

"I'm sorry," she apologized. "I was in a rush and couldn't get to those. But please, you don't have to do that."

"There was a big roach sitting on top of the pile," he remarked amiably. "I was afraid he'd fall in and drown."

Emily sighed. "That's all right. There'd still be maybe twenty million of his relatives left. I've learned to live and let live, as long as they stay out of the Oreos." She sat down at the table to watch him work. "You're that kind of guy, aren't you?" she asked.

He dropped a clean plate into the rack. "I'm not sure. What kind of guy is that?"

"You know, the neat, well-organized kind, who never leaves dishes in the sink or drops his underwear and socks on the floor."

Ethan thought for a moment. "There *was* once, back in 1955, I think, but I was having a very bad week."

"You were in the army, I'll bet. Or the marines?"

"The navy. Get a dish towel and dry."

"I don't own a dish towel. I always just let them drip. Only obsessive-compulsives dry their dishes."

"I'll try to remember that. Anyway, I don't know about you, but I'm getting hungry again. Do you keep anything to eat in this house?"

"Are you sure you want to risk it? I'm not insured."

He smiled. "I'll take my chances."

Emily opened the freezer with a flourish. "Okay, let's see what's on the menu." She rummaged through the jumble of packages, most of them so thick with frost that they weren't readily identifiable. Finally, she pulled out a flat, squashed box and scraped off a chunk of ice to read the expiration date. "Aha! We have frozen pizza! Of course, it probably would've been better if we'd opened it back in…" She looked again at the date. "Back in 1978. Okay, never mind the pizza."

She flipped the pizza box back in the freezer and searched again. "How about a giant pretzel? I get these really big pretzels at the Dollar Store—a buck for two boxes, including these cute little packets of salt." She wedged her hand into the very back and pulled out an irregularly shaped, rock-hard mass. "Then again, we could have…" Emily looked at the lump closely. "How does some fabulous leftover guacamole strike you? *Muy sabroso, no?*"

Ethan took the lump and turned it over in his hands. "Is it supposed to be this color?"

"Search me. It was my friend Maggie's. We dragged it home in a doggie bag from Pancho's Taco Palace."

"When?"

Emily shrugged. "I can't remember exactly. A couple of years ago, maybe. Pancho's closed down last year, though—some sort of disagreement with the health department. You know, now that I think about it, it might even have been *three* years ago. Right after I moved here."

Ethan tossed the package back to her. "I think I'll pass on the guacamole. So, you're not a big shopper."

Gratefully, Emily closed the freezer door. "*Au contraire!* I hate shopping, but when I finally go, I buy so much at one time, I forget what's in there. Kind of scary, really. You don't want to look in the vegetable keeper, take my word for it."

Ethan walked into the hallway and retrieved her sweater from the coat rack. "Come on, I'll take you to dinner. I can't afford a long hospital stay."

"Don't get snotty," she said. "I did warn you."

"Your good deed for the day. Now, what do you want to eat?"

"How about Chinese?"

As they went out the front door, Emily turned to him and smiled sweetly. "So, this is our second date already?"

"Nope. This is purely self-preservation. On our *second* date, I'm planning to take you back to Emilio's, for old time's sake. You know, white tablecloths, candlelight and wine, no vermin?"

Emily spent much of that first weekend apprising Ethan of her faults, her blemishes and her limitations—always in a humorous manner, of course. He played along by sitting on her frayed couch and listening attentively, nodding or shaking his head in sympathy as she cheerfully catalogued her lackluster record in college, her string of low-level, dead-end jobs, and her failures as an artist and a wife.

On the evening of the second day, while she was in the middle of a long and intensely boring discussion of the many excellent reasons she'd rarely dated in high school, Ethan had heard enough. He interrupted the monologue in midsentence by placing one hand firmly over Emily's mouth and telling her, very politely, to shut up. Then, without another word, he swung her into his arms and took her to bed. The weekend was over, and the love affair had begun.

What Emily had most wanted for her first time with Ethan was to seem at ease and in control, maybe even to be charmingly seductive. But after a marriage lacking in physical pleasure, followed by three years of self-imposed celibacy, she'd forgotten how to be seductive, if she'd ever known. Emily had always imagined that sex was like tennis, a game requiring regular practice with a capable partner. Dennis had insisted she learn tennis from the pro at their country club, but after two years of awesomely expensive lessons, Emily still played like a beginner. Now, as Ethan carried her into the bedroom, Emily had already concluded that if anything was going to happen between them, the first serve would definitely have to come from *his* side of the court.

Even her choice of clothing was ill-suited to seduction. That morning, without thinking, she'd put on her only "dressy" blouse—a birthday gift from Helene that had spent its first three dusty years languishing at the back of Emily's closet. The mock-Victorian confection featured a row of tiny pearl buttons that extended from her throat to her waist, and undoing them proved to be time-consuming. Emily immediately apologized.

Ethan merely smiled, told her once again to shut up, then kissed the hollow of her neck and began working his way down the row of pearls. Finally, taking the hem of the blouse in both hands, he tugged it off over her head, popping off most of the buttons. Emily would continue to find them in unlikely places around the room for weeks. She had already begun to apologize for the oversized safety pin holding her bra strap together when he pulled both straps down and took her left nipple in his mouth.

Emily closed her eyes then, surrendering to the almost forgotten sensation of a man's hot, insistent mouth on her breasts, his lips tugging firmly but ever so softly at her nipples. As he removed her skirt, Emily lay on her side, watching dreamily as he drew her panties down over her hips and slipped them off. Her budget hadn't allowed for panty hose, making the process simpler and mercifully shorter, since she was growing more uneasy by the moment about what was expected of her in all of this. When he'd finished undressing her, Ethan slipped one hand between her thighs, parting her legs.

At this juncture, Emily moaned as convincingly as she knew how, then reached down to stroke his erection for what she imagined was an acceptable period of time. She writhed a little as his fingers explored her, the way she had always writhed at this point in the proceedings. After doing these things in the correct order, she closed her eyes, lay back and waited. If Ethan was surprised at how little foreplay she had required, he made no comment about it.

The next few minutes were extremely pleasant, and Emily enjoyed them thoroughly. At times, in fact, she had difficulty remembering when to make the appropriate sounds and movements. Whatever Ethan was doing to her was becoming more and more distracting.

But when it was over, Emily felt as she always had after Dennis made love to her—oddly depressed and lonely. She thanked Ethan, and he kissed her again, then lay for a long while with her in his arms, caressing her in ways that made it hard for her to think about what would come next. When he rolled over and sat on the bed next to her, Emily stiffened, knowing he was about to glance at his watch and say something like, "I didn't realize it was so late. I suppose I should be getting home." And at that point, she would have to say something in return. Something cheerful that would save her pride and conceal her disappointment until he was safely out of the apartment.

But he didn't say those words—exactly. He took her hand, turning it slowly in his as he spoke.

"I'll admit to being a little out of practice, but offhand, I'd say something was missing from that, wouldn't you?"

Emily blushed, and swore to herself. She must have left a step out. Her well-honed defenses went up at once, and she attempted wide-eyed innocence. "I'm…I'm sorry," she stammered. "I don't understand." The blush was genuine, if nothing else.

But Ethan wasn't buying it. He patted her once on the hip, kissed her again lightly, and began to look for his clothes.

"Acting used to be my business, remember? I don't

know where you learned all that, but take my word for it, your performance will never get you an Oscar."

Emily sat up abruptly and then, for the first time in her life, slapped a man across the face. She regretted it instantly and apologized, then sat rigidly, with her back against the headboard, fighting a ridiculous impulse to cry.

"Do you want to tell me what happened?" he asked softly. "I'm always open to a little friendly advice, you know—or criticism."

Emily said nothing, too humiliated to answer.

Ethan sighed. "Okay, I'll tell you what. I'm going to put my pants on and go home, and let you think about everything for a couple of days. You've got my phone number, and you can call me when…if you want to talk." Now that he'd finally said the words she'd been dreading, Emily was somehow relieved. He would leave and it would be over. Life would go on, as it had before.

And then, very suddenly, Emily realized that for the first time in longer than she could remember, she wanted something enough to try to hold on to it. Maybe even enough to embarrass herself. She yanked the sheet up over her breasts.

"My God, you're arrogant!" she cried, wiping her eyes and nose with a corner of the sheet. "Why is it that all good-looking men think they're a gift from the gods? This fabulous prize we imperfect women should be thrilled to compete for? Those clumsy and insecure women like me, the lonely ones, the… Well, okay, let's just call it like it is—the fat ones!"

Ethan found his pants. "In the first place, I don't think you're fat. I'm sorry if what I said hurt your feelings, and I can see now that it did. You surprised me, that's all, and I've never had much patience for people who lie to me— about anything. After these past couple of days together, I'd like to think you wouldn't *need* to lie to me, certainly not about *this*." He gave the mattress a small, meaningful pat.

While she was listening to him, Emily's eyes had drifted southward from Ethan's broad shoulders to the dark thatch of hair on his chest, aware once again of that same familiar tug in her belly whenever she looked at him.

He began to put on his jeans, and Emily tried not to focus on the lean, hard curves of his flanks and the taut sinews at the back of his thighs as he bent from the waist. Something low in her abdomen twisted again, and she drew in her breath as he pulled up the zipper.

He took his shirt from the back of a chair, and began buttoning it as he started out of the room.

"Please," she said. "Don't leave yet."

He stopped in the doorway and turned to face her. "Why?"

Emily's courage failed her. She blushed ferociously and drew the covers up over her head.

"I don't know." Muffled by the bedding, her voice was small and morose.

Ethan walked back to the bed and sat down on the edge. "Sure you do." He reached under the sheet and caressed her thigh. "But you're going to have to say it."

There was a strangled sound beneath the covers. "You're going to make me grovel, aren't you?"

He grinned. "Could be. You said a couple of pretty nasty things a few minutes back, you know, and I haven't been slapped by a woman since I left high school."

Emily groaned. "All right, I'm an idiot. Could we just forget it—what I said? I'll make it up to you, I swear."

Ethan chuckled. "How? Cook me a real dinner, maybe?"

The lump in the covers growled. "Yeah, sure! Try again, pal. I can change, but Rome wasn't built in a day, you know. Start with something easier."

"Like what?"

She pulled the covers from her head. "Maybe we could just go back to where we were before you got in a big huff and…"

"*Who* got in a huff?"

"I'm sorry," she said softly. "You're right. I'm a jerk and I've ruined the whole weekend, but please don't go home. Not like this."

"No more lies, and no acting?"

She made a face. "I guess not, since you tell me I'm so bad at it. But if you'll remember, I warned you right at the beginning that you'd be disappointed."

Ethan smiled. "Did I say I was disappointed?"

The things that happened next were things Emily had once known about, but had done without for more years than she cared to admit. The act of love with her husband had been little more than a responsibility—one that came with a lengthy book of rules and expectations, and Emily had learned early in their marriage to defer to his wishes or risk being made to feel foolish and unattractive. Dennis knew best. To suggest dissatisfaction would be an affront not only to his to his to his pride, but to his superior expertise and prowess. If she failed to enjoy what happened between them in bed, it was understood that it was her failure, not his. Soon, she'd discovered it was easier to fake her own pleasure than to argue.

Ethan pressed her backward onto the bed, leaning forward to kiss each nipple in turn. Then, with exquisite slowness, he moved down the length of her body, his warm mouth and gentle fingers exploring every inch. Emily closed her eyes as he traced one last, slow circle around her navel with his tongue before spreading her trembling legs to probe deep into the lush recesses of her body that ached for his touch. She twined her fingers in the tangled bedding and submitted to the opulent swell of sensation, her moans of pleasure at last genuine. Powerless to stop, she gave herself over to the delight that had eluded her for so long, and to wave after wave of shuddering spasms that left her weak.

When it was over, and when the trembling had subsided into small, rippling tremors, Emily began to cry. Ethan gathered her in his arms.

"I'm sorry," she murmured.

He chuckled softly. "*Now* what are you sorry about?"

"I couldn't…w-wait," she stammered.

Ethan leaned down to kiss her breast and slipped back into bed beside her. "Could you give me a little credit here, Miss Porter? We've got the whole night ahead of us, and I promise you you'll be paying back that little favor in full."

In that one instant, Emily knew that she was falling in love with Ethan Douglas.

And that was both unexpected and frightening.

Chapter 4

The following morning, Emily crawled out of her rumpled bed, took one look in the mirror above her dresser and stumbled to the bathroom. The aroma of freshly brewed coffee and the damp towel hanging neatly over the shower rod told her that Ethan had already bathed, and that he was now puttering around her messy kitchen unsupervised, but before she could intervene, major repairs to her appearance were definitely needed. She showered and washed her hair, chose the most alluring oversize sweatshirt she could find in the chaotic closet, and sprayed herself with a quick mist of cologne.

Once in the kitchen, she found that last night's dishes had been put away. There was an empty mug sitting next to the full coffeepot, but no sign of her houseguest. She helped herself to coffee and went looking, and found Ethan sitting outside on the rusted fire escape that passed for her porch. He was inspecting a row of dead geraniums—her garden.

"I'm guessing gardening's not your favorite pastime," he said as she opened the rickety screen and came out to join him.

"Yeah." Emily picked up the nearest pot. "Everybody told me you can't kill geraniums, but I just kept at it till I got the job done. I'd give them a decent burial, but I'm not sure they're completely dead. I'm already a geranium murderess. I'd hate to be accused of burying them alive."

He took the pot from her. "Trust me. Geraniums don't get much deader than this one."

Emily sat down next to him, and sighed. "So you're a whiz at gardening, too, right? As well as housekeeping, making great coffee and…well, other things."

Ethan smiled as he set down the deceased plant and took her in his arms. "What other things?"

She blushed. "I forget. It's funny, too, because it was on the tip on my tongue when I woke up, but now…" Before she could finish her sentence, he kissed her. Emily wrapped her arms around his waist and laid her head on his chest.

"Can I ask you something?" she asked quietly.

"Sure."

"Would you have asked me out if you hadn't met me first?"

"Run that by me again?"

"I mean, if I hadn't…you know, done what I did at the

play? Gotten you all tangled up with me? If you'd just seen me, another chubby wallflower standing alone at a singles' bar somewhere, would you have asked me out—at first sight?"

"No."

Emily dropped her arms and moved away from him. "Well, thanks for being so honest—I guess. But you could've thought about it for a minute, you know. Instead of answering so fast and cutting me to the quick."

"I didn't have to think about it. I never ask out women I meet in bars. I've never been in a real singles' bar, for that matter."

"Now you're hedging. You know what I mean. Would you have been attracted to me?"

"Yes, I would have. Of course, I didn't know then that you can't cook, but you've got everything else we arrogant, god-like men look for in a woman—a nice personality, a good sense of humor—and a fine mind, of course." He pulled her closer and slipped one hand up under the sweatshirt to her still-naked bottom. "And the terrific ass doesn't hurt, either."

"You have a lovely way with words, Mr. Douglas, and you lie *far* better than I do. Probably all those years on the silver screen. But, for your information, I actually *can* cook a little—when forced. My husband was crazy about French restaurants, so I took all these lessons in *nouvelle cuisine.* I could go in there right this minute and whip you up something French. French toast, maybe? French fries? French dressing?"

Ethan laughed softly, and slid his other hand under her shirt to fondle her breasts. "What do you think?"

She grinned. "Later, maybe?"

"*Much* later," he agreed. He took her hand and led her back inside. "Maybe by lunch. Let's see how it goes."

It went better than Emily could possibly have imagined.

"How about making this an extended weekend," Ethan suggested later that afternoon. "I have to see my publisher in Portland tomorrow about the new book. I know you probably have to work, but if you can manage some time off, I thought we could spend a couple of days just bumming around the city and…"

Emily was already rummaging in the closet, and a moment later, she tossed a battered suitcase onto the bed. "Of course," he continued, watching with obvious amusement as she dashed to the bathroom to grab an armful of toiletries, "it's not that urgent, so if you *really* can't take the time off, I'll juggle a couple of things, and we can go next week."

"Stop trying to wriggle out of it," Emily said. "You invited me, and now you're stuck with me. Anyway, I won't get fired. It's too hard to get suckers to work for what they pay, as it is. But I'll call someone to cover for me, just in case. The rent's paid up for the month, and I'm assuming you're going to feed me all weekend, right?"

"You're a free spirit, Miss Porter."

Emily stood on tiptoe to kiss him. "Not free, by a long shot. I'm planning to eat like there's no tomorrow," she promised cheerfully. "When I dine out, it's usually at the kind of place that hurls food at you from a drive-through window. Now, what do I need to pack? Keeping in mind that you're looking at maybe twenty-five percent of my wardrobe. That's clean, anyway."

"I'd like to take you to a couple of good restaurants, so maybe something a little dressier?"

Emily pointed to the line of sweatshirts and jeans in her closet. "Dressy, huh? Okay, your choice—Save the Whales, or No Nuclear Proliferation."

"Well, blue's your color. Let's go with Save the Whales. It looks like we'll be doing some shopping in Portland."

She shook her head. "I hate shopping. Besides, I'm still broke, and now I'm temporarily unemployed."

"No problem. I'll take care of it."

"Thank you, Ethan, but… Well, meals and lodging are one thing—two things, I guess—but…" She flushed. "I'd rather not, if you don't mind." She turned back to the closet and pulled out several items. "I'm sure I can find something in here that won't embarrass you."

Ethan took her chin in his hand and tilted her face up to his. "I'm sorry. I didn't mean to—"

"Don't worry about it." She selected a flared black poplin skirt and a white cotton blouse from the pile. "Anyway, it just so happens that I have business near Portland, too, so I should probably try to dress for success. I put a couple of paintings on consignment with this little tourist trap near the harbor—the Cozy Nook Gift Shoppe, with an E, naturally. Maybe I'll drop by and dust off what I have languishing there. If you've got the time, of course."

"I've got the time. So, business hasn't been too brisk at the Cozy Nook?"

Emily grimaced. "Would you shop for *your* fine art at a dump called the Cozy Nook?"

"I know a couple of galleries in the city that might take a look at your work."

Emily stuffed everything into the suitcase and slammed it shut. "Nope," she said breezily. "I already have a fabulous career that keeps me *way* too busy—stocking shelves and manning the snack bar at my local Shop-a-Lot."

"Don't do that," he reproached gently. "You know you're good, and so do I. You just need to work at it. Look, Em, I don't want to upset you again, but I could help you out, you know. I'd like to."

"I'm not cut out to be a kept woman, thanks. I tried that once, and the price was five years with Dennis. Besides, a woman has to guard her reputation. Remember that old book, and the movie, *Back Street?* The heroine came to a very bad end, if you recall, and all because of her lax moral code. She starved to death. I'm sure there's a lesson there somewhere."

Ethan shook his head in frustration, but laughed, nonetheless. "Okay, I won't ask again."

Emily sighed. "Well, you don't have to go and get fanatic about it! Keep asking. I feel my moral code getting laxer every day. Tell you what. I'll let you start by picking up the tab for just a few things—at some of the places I usually shop. Okay?"

"Good. What are they?"

"Salvation Army, Goodwill. You know, all the best places."

They checked in to a suite with a spectacular view of Casco Bay and spent the afternoon in the marble hot tub, making love until the harbor lights began to twinkle in the distance. Skipping dinner at the restaurant where Ethan had made reservations, they dined instead on pretzels and tiny bottles of premixed margaritas from the honor bar. Afterward, Emily lay in Ethan's arms in the sumptuous king-size bed and tried without success to remember a time in her life when she had felt happier.

Alone wih Ethan, Emily always felt comfortable and at ease. After that first awkward evening at her apartment, the crippling shyness she'd lived with for most of her life had begun to fall away. Now when Ethan touched her, she was able to respond with a healthy, unbridled lust that both surprised and delighted her.

It was when they *weren't* alone that her demons re-emerged.

Dennis Lockhart had been a successful investment counselor when she married him, and an attractive man, as well—"Prince Charming," Helene had gushed when they were introduced. During her five years as Prince Charming's plain and disappointing wife, Emily had grown accustomed to being reminded of her inadequacies, and very little had happened since then to reassure her.

On her first "dressy" evening with Ethan, at an expensive restaurant in Portland, Emily was quick to notice the curious glances of other women. The kind of sleek, elegant women whose sophistication showed in their demeanor, and with whom Emily knew she had nothing in common other than hormones. She could still remember similar looks when she was out in public with Dennis, and although it might have been her imagination, Emily chose to take from these women's glances the same unflattering inference she had then. *What could such an attractive and obviously successful man possibly see in someone like her?*

She and Ethan had already ordered but barely finished their salads when Emily complained of a headache and asked him to take her back to the hotel.

They drove home the following morning, after Ethan had finished his business with his publisher and she had checked in at the Cozy Nook. No sales, of course. When Ethan seemed lost in thought and said very little on the trip home, Emily feared she knew why. It was late afternoon when they got back to her apartment, and once he'd taken her suitcase inside, he didn't stay long.

"I've got a lot of things to take care of this week," he began.

Emily felt her stomach muscles contract. "I understand. Actually, I'm probably going to be really busy myself," she lied. "I promised Maggie I'd help her wallpaper her bedroom."

Ethan nodded. "I'll probably have everything wrapped up by the weekend. So, if you're not too... Well, I thought you might like to come up to my place and stay for a few days—maybe for the whole week—if you can get away, of course. I've done a lot of work on the house since I bought it, and I'd really like to know what you think."

Emily closed her eyes and willed herself not to cry with relief. "I'll tell Maggie some other day."

"Great. I'll call you tonight, and we'll work out a good

time for me to pick you up. Pack light, by the way. This'll be just your kind of visit. No frills and a lot of frozen dinners. You're being drafted to help me paint the deck. Oh, one other thing." He grinned. "There's not much hot water in the house. We'll probably have to rough it, and share showers." After a quick kiss goodbye, he walked back to the car and drove away. Emily stood on the front steps and watched until the car turned at the end of the street and disappeared.

He hadn't said anything specific, but Emily knew this week would be important for both of them. Things were moving so rapidly that she'd been thrown off balance, but her instinct to flee was strong. By this time, though, Emily had reason to believe she was in love. There would be no going back to the safe hiding place she had crawled into three years earlier.

"I don't bring just anyone up here," Ethan said, turning off the county highway onto a narrow dirt road. "I can't take the criticism." After he'd picked her up on Friday afternoon, they'd driven more than a hundred miles up the coast and passed through the small, quaint village of Dunlin Cove. Now, all Emily could see on either side of the rutted gravel road were dunes, and ahead of them, a deserted stretch of beach. "You say beach house to most people, and they imagine a three-story mansion out on the tip of Long Island. I'm hoping *you'll* look at the place through an artist's eyes, and see its inner beauty."

Emily smiled. "That bad?"

He laughed. "It's old and pretty small."

"I like small houses," she said. "Big ones are unknowable. The house in Malibu—Dennis's house, really—was this big sprawling glass thing, sort of ersatz Frank Lloyd Wright, with six bedrooms and a lot of uncomfortable modern furniture. When we moved in, I sat in each room for at least half an hour every day, hoping to make it feel like home, but it never did. I used to wander around like an idiot, trying to remember where I'd left stuff. Finally, Dennis installed an intercom so we could talk from room to room. Maybe it would've been different if we'd had kids—you know, to fill it up, but…" She let the sentence trail off.

He stopped the car and looked over at her. "You didn't want children?"

For a long moment, Emily didn't answer. "I can't have children, Ethan," she said quietly. "Dennis and I tried for almost two years. After that, I began to see that a baby would be a bad idea, with… Well, with the way things were."

"And how were 'things'?" he asked pointedly. "I don't want to pry, but you haven't said much about him."

Emily laughed, hoping the laugh didn't sound as bitter to him as it did to her. "The less said about Dennis the better. Besides, is there anything more boring than the gory details of someone else's divorce?" She looked around. "Excuse me, but as I liked to whine at age six, are we there yet?"

He drove on, and soon, as they came up over a low rise, the open deck of a gray clapboard house appeared, tucked between two rolling dunes. Ethan stopped the car about a hundred yards away and got out to open Emily's door.

"You're making me walk the rest of the way?" she asked.

"Sorry, but this house is like some of the aging actresses I used to work with. She likes to be seen from her best side. Especially the first time." He took her hand and they walked through the tall grass and across the first of several low dunes until they arrived at a worn plank walkway that circled up the beach toward the house.

"When it was built, this boardwalk ran all the way to the beach," Ethan explained. "The lady of the house could push a baby carriage the length of it without getting her long skirts in the sand. Well, what do you think? Humble, no?"

Emily stopped and stared in wonder.

"It's that beautiful cottage on the cover of your book," she said softly. "And again on page seventy-two. This is where you live?"

"I'm afraid so."

She squeezed his hand. "It's even more beautiful than your picture."

"Thank you. Although Mother Nature probably deserves most of the credit. Not just for the location, but for being kind enough not to blow it out to sea."

The little house was a strong, sturdy New England seaside cottage in the purest sense, simple and graceful of line. The beach side and the deck were built out on sturdy pilings, but the rear sat solidly on higher ground, sheltered between the dunes. Constructed of naturally aged gray clapboard, the cottage boasted a slightly pitched roof of weathered shingles and tall windows framed in white.

Each window was equipped with wide, faded-blue storm shutters. A no-nonsense house, built to survive a gale.

"It's not humble at all," she breathed. "It's…it's lovely. No, I take that back. This is the sort of house a Quaker whaling captain might have built a hundred years ago, and he wouldn't have used a trite, wimpy word like 'lovely.' Maybe admirable, or commendable."

Ethan was obviously pleased. "Actually, it *was* built by a retired whaling captain. All I know about him is that his name was Enoch Birdsong and he probably hailed from Grand Manan Island. But you're the first to call old Enoch's house admirable or commendable. I usually hear things on the order of *rundown* and *ramshackle. Dilapidated,* now and then—and my personal favorite? My agent once referred to it as a 'doddering, feeble sinkhole.' Of course, that was right after he fell through the deck where it had rotted out and broke an ankle."

"You know too many prosaic and humdrum people," Emily declared stubbornly. "This little house has praiseworthy lines. It's hardy, and built to last."

"Well, you're right about its age, anyway. It's been here for over a hundred years, and there's a stone boathouse at the back that's even older. An old fisherman's hut, they tell me. But whatever you and I choose to call it, the state of Maine calls it prime beachfront and taxes it accordingly, and the local Realtors seem willing to overlook its faults. *They* describe it as adorable, quaint or charming. Sometimes enchanting. Take your pick."

"You're not thinking of selling it!" she cried.

He laughed. "I only think of selling it when the barometer starts to fall. And don't worry. People aren't exactly lining up to buy it—not since the last hurricane blew through and took out a couple of my nearest neighbors. It's too far from town and off the road. Off the sewer line, too, but that's another story. Another *expensive* story."

"It's withstood over a hundred years of hurricanes, right?" Emily asked. "So why not another hundred?"

"Hurricanes, maybe. Termites and flood, I'm not so sure. Still, it's home, if you don't mind a leaky roof and freezing all winter. Now, would you like to see its praise-worthy interior?"

"Tell me you don't have a lot of modern Scandinavian furniture."

"I don't have modern furniture, Scandinavian or otherwise. Everything in the place is about as beat-up and well-seasoned as I am. Most of it's what my mom and dad had in our house when I was a kid, and I've refinished a lot of yard-sale stuff I got when I moved here twelve years ago. Come on. I've got a surprise for you."

"What kind of surprise?" Emily asked, but when Ethan only smiled mysteriously, she clutched his hand tighter. They walked the remainder of the way hand in hand, and as they climbed the stairs to the deck, Emily ran her fingers over the worn banister, feeling somehow that she was coming home.

Chapter 5

Ethan hadn't exaggerated. The house was furnished simply, with a mixture of antiques, beautifully refinished older pieces and a curious collection of nautical gadgets and ship models.

A battered baby grand piano sat in front of the large window that faced the ocean. Emily opened the lid and played a few bars of Mozart.

"It has a lovely tone."

Ethan laughed. "I'm glad you play. I took what turned out to be a lot of thoroughly wasted lessons on that piano when I was a kid. It'll be nice to have someone using it other than me."

Before the fireplace stood a tall, very old bow-backed rocking chair. "My great-grandmother's," Ethan explained when Emily remarked on it. "All the 'wee bairns o' the clan Douglas' have been nursed to sleep in it, me being the last of the line. The rest of the house is what the magazines call eclectic."

Emily heard only part of what he said. She had just noticed the large painting over the fireplace. Ethan stood back, smiling, and watched her reaction.

"It's mine!" she exclaimed. "My painting of the Cape Neddick Light!"

He laughed. "Cape Neddick, yes, but it's not yours anymore. It's mine, and I've got the receipt to prove it. I found it at this peculiar establishment down the road called Aunt Somebody or Other's Cottage of Crafts and Curiosities."

Emily groaned. "Aunt Polly's. Okay, so how much did you pay the old biddy for it?"

"Four hundred dollars."

"You were had. I traded it to that white-haired thief for forty-three bucks' worth of art supplies over a year ago."

"It's worth every penny and more. I wanted to get in on the ground floor, before the rush. You're going to be famous someday."

Emily sighed. "From your lips to God's ears, as my grandmother always said, but don't hold your breath. It looks nice hanging there, though—in the privileged company of your own terrific photographs."

She paused while Ethan opened the curtains on the front window. "This is why I bought the place," he explained. Emily came and stood before the wide, mullioned window. The view across the dunes and to the ocean beyond was astonishing.

She glanced to either side. "You must not get a lot of neighbors dropping by to borrow eggs and sugar."

He nodded. "We got hit pretty hard two years back, and three other houses down the beach blew away. I was lucky. I lost the deck and some of the windows, but the house came through all right. Most of these places were intended as summer cottages, not meant for all year. After your first winter here, you'll see what I mean. This house has defied the odds for more than a hundred years. Which is either good or bad, depending on how you look at it. It may be running out of time and have a date with destiny."

Emily had heard the remark about her "first winter," but tried to attribute nothing to it. She ran her hand over the smooth gray stones of the fireplace. "I don't care what anyone says. This house will live forever."

Ethan folded her in his arms. "Nothing lives forever, Em. I've worked my tail off for twelve years fixing this house up, and replacing what the wind keeps ripping loose, but if it gets swept out to sea tomorrow, I'll remember every last plank and shake and stone, and how much I loved living here. Then I'll pack up what *hasn't* blown away and move somewhere else—with central heating."

Emily laughed. "So much for sentimentality. And I thought you were a poet." She turned back to the window and marveled again at the breathtaking view.

"This house was what I needed when I left Hollywood," Ethan explained. "A good place to hide out—to get my head together and figure out what I wanted to do with the rest of my life." There was a small pause. "In these past two weeks I think I've finally figured that out, Em—what I want to do with the rest of my life, I mean. And you're a big part of it." Emily didn't turn around, and didn't ask what he meant. She tried to focus on the gulls sweeping along the surface of the water, but her heart felt as though it had missed several beats.

After a moment, Ethan reached for her hand. "We'll talk later. Now for the rest of the tour. I thought we'd drive into town for dinner. There's a pretty good seafood place at the docks. I made reservations for seven-thirty." He checked his watch. "It's four-thirty now. Three hours should give us just enough time to have a look around the bedroom."

They never made it to the seafood place on the docks, and settled for canned soup, stale crackers and a bottle of red wine in front of the fireplace. Afterward, Ethan threw the sofa cushions on the floor and made love to her by firelight. The fire had burned down to a cluster of faintly glowing embers before they went to bed.

The following morning, he nudged her awake, a cup of coffee in his hand. "Get up, and come for a walk on the beach. I need to tell you something."

Emily turned a sleepy eye on him. "Like?"

"I've kept a secret from you, and it's time you knew the whole truth," he said. "I don't live here alone."

"You don't live here alone," she repeated groggily. "Okay. Well, after these past few days—last night in particular—I'm not going to believe you're gay, so there must be another woman who stays here, right?"

He looked at her warily.

Emily sat up in bed. "I'm not blind, Ethan. There's long

hair all over the couch, and in the car. A very *old* woman, is she, and going bald, maybe?"

He grinned. "You know."

"I know there's a long-haired gray dog that hangs around here—or one hell of a big cat. Where is she—or he?"

"It's a she, and I left her with some friends. She's too big to haul around with me when I go out of town, and she gets suicidal when I leave her in a kennel. We'll go over and pick her up tomorrow, and you can meet my best friends in the world, Kate and Matt O'Connell. Oh, and the dog's name is Sarah—as in Bernhardt. Half Old English Sheepdog and the other half drama queen. I guess it's rather late in the game to ask if you like dogs."

"I love dogs. Better than people, usually. I found a couple of long gray hairs on my pillow. So, two questions. Does this other woman sleep in the bed, and will she be jealous?"

Ethan thought for a moment. "She's not the jealous kind, but you may have to fight her for the pillow."

The morning stayed rainy and damp, and Emily and Ethan shared a late breakfast of croissants and coffee by the fire, made love again, and then spent most of the day talking. It was early evening by the time the rain stopped and they ventured out for their walk along the beach. Ignoring the cold, they sat on a blanket on the wet dunes and talked, then watched the moon shining on the ocean for another two hours.

As they started back to the house, Ethan bent down to pick up a small shell from the sand.

When he laid it in Emily's palm, the shell caught a beam of moonlight, and its color seemed to change from iridescent pink to gold, and then to a pale lavender.

"It's beautiful," Emily said. "What kind is it?"

Ethan shook his head. "I don't know. There's a book about shells in the house somewhere. I'll look around for it."

Just before they reached the cottage, Ethan took Emily in his arms and asked her to marry him. Emily put her head on his chest, and didn't answer at first.

"You don't know much about me, Ethan," she said softly. "Are you sure?"

"I've never been more sure of anything in my life, Em, but I know that everything has happened pretty fast, and I want you to be as certain as I am. There's still the issue of our age difference. And I know you'll want to talk to your mother first, and maybe Maggie."

Emily didn't need to talk to anyone. She knew she was in love with Ethan Douglas, and wanted to spend the rest of her life with him. The time had come to take a second chance at living. It was the idea of marrying again that frightened her.

Emily returned to her apartment just long enough to introduce Ethan to Maggie, give notice to her landlord and quit her job. When she began the tedious job of packing up everything she owned for the move to the beach cottage, Maggie came over to help, and to ask nosy questions.

"All right," Maggie began, munching on a stale donut while they emptied Emily's cabinets. "In the last week,

I've had two dinners, a long chatty lunch and conducted an uninterrupted one-on-one interrogation of your dream man. I subjected him to the usual exhaustive battery of tests, during which he showed remarkable patience, and which he passed with flying colors. I have found absolutely *no* detectable flaws in the man, except that he's crazy about you, which doesn't really qualify as a fault. So, when do I get to be a bridesmaid?"

Emily hesitated. "I don't know exactly. We'll talk about it when you come up to visit next month."

Maggie shot her friend a suspicious look. "The hell we will. We'll talk about it now. I'm not your mother, Em. I can always tell when you're bullshitting me. Out with it!"

Emily dropped wearily to the couch. "It's just that both of us are going to be so drained after we get all this crap moved in," she explained. "We won't be in any mood to start planning a wedding. As far as I'm concerned, we can get married at City Hall, or in the back of the damned moving van, but if we don't throw some sort of wedding extravaganza, Mom's never going to accept it and stop calling me in tears. Besides, when Ethan gets a load of all the junk I'm planning to stuff into that wonderful little house, he'll probably change his mind. Where did all this stuff come from, anyway?" she wailed. "I've only been here for three years. Are you sure you can't use a few pieces of heirloom furniture, like this fabulous Nixon-era couch, or some more pots and pans? Mom keeps sending the stupid things, hoping I'll learn how to cook."

"I don't need any pots and pans, and you're stalling,"

Maggie said firmly. "Spit it out, kiddo. What's up with you and the matinee idol? And while we're on the subject, why aren't you wearing an engagement ring?"

"All right. I told Ethan I didn't want a ring. Not yet, anyway. They just get stuck on everything. And all that's 'up,' as you call it, is that I'm not ready to set an exact date. What's the big rush?"

"And what does Ethan think about all this?"

Emily sighed. "He says I'm stalling."

"Ha!" Maggie cried. "I knew I liked the man the minute I set eyes on him. Take some advice from a two-time loser, sweetie. Grab this guy while you can. They don't get any better."

Emily nodded. "I know that. Mom still calls twice a day, informing me that he's too old, of course."

"Do you care about that?"

"Honestly? I never even think about it. He's brought it up a couple of times, but I don't see the problem. It's not like I'm eighteen. I know what I want."

"Well, then marry the man, dummy! What if he gets bored with waiting and starts looking around for company?" Maggie winked slyly. "It happens. He could meet some willing lady while he's out walking the dog. That's where I found my first husband. What will you do if he starts mooning over some gorgeous young thing he meets at the grocery store?"

Emily smiled sweetly. "I'll rip out his heart and lungs and roast them over a slow fire, how's that?"

Maggie laughed. "Good answer. It shows you're learning. Well, whatever you do, I wish you'd do it fast. I'm not getting any younger, and everyone says a wedding's the best place to meet decent, eligible men. I'm not sure I've ever dated a decent, eligible man, come to think of it, but the change would be nice. Besides, I'm dying to give you a wedding shower. You know, where people you hardly know come and eat all the free food and give you a lot of pots and pans?"

"Thanks, Maggie, but I really don't need a wedding shower."

"Sure you do. It's a rite of passage. Female bonding. You sit around playing smutty games, then everyone gets wasted and puts bows on top of your head and screams every time you open a package with another toaster. Then the male stripper shows up. What's not to like?"

Emily rolled her eyes. "Sounds lovely. I can hardly wait."

Emily called Helene two days before the final move to the cottage, and listened for nearly an hour while her mother complained again about the age difference between Emily and Ethan and detailed every failed live-in arrangement she'd ever heard or read about.

"I raised you better than that," her mother complained. "And besides, it never works. Men aren't like us. They get bored when you make things too easy for them. After all, why should a man want to buy the—"

Emily groaned. "If you say one word about cows and milk, Mom, I'm going to hang up. Anyway, I've got to go. I've got a million things to do. Ethan and I packed boxes all weekend, and I'm *still* not even half done. The moving people are coming the day after tomorrow."

A few days later, Ethan was out and Emily was unpacking boxes in the cottage's cluttered living room when Helene called again. Emily settled comfortably on the plaid couch with Sarah at her feet and prepared for another lecture, but Helene was nearly hysterical.

"Emily, tell me the truth! Are you all right? Is *he* there?"

Emily frowned. Even for her mother, the desperate tone was peculiar. "I'm fine, Mom. What's the—"

"Is he there with you?"

"Ethan? No, he's at his lawyer's office, changing some insurance thing. He won't be home till later tonight. Why? What's wrong?"

"Thank God I got hold of you in time. I've just found out something terrible!"

"Mother, would you please calm down!" Emily implored. "Take a deep breath, and tell me what's—"

"It's horrible, Emily! I just got off the phone with Dennis, and…"

Emily groaned out loud, but Helene rushed breathlessly on. "Don't be that way, Emily! You know how much Dennis has always cared for you and worried about you. When I called and told him about this Ethan Douglas person you're involved with, he—"

"Damn it!" Emily shouted into the phone. "Why the hell would you—?"

Helene gasped. "Emily, stop speaking to me like that and *listen!*" She paused for a moment, possibly for effect, then hurried on. "You know that Dennis knows some very important people in the movie industry, right?"

"Dennis knows what he reads in the *National Enquirer,*

at the damned supermarket!" Emily fumed. "And I'd appreciate it if you'd—"

Helene took a deep breath and triumphantly spat out her news.

"Dennis says it's common knowledge in Hollywood that this Ethan Douglas had something to do with murdering his wife! He was never convicted, but *that's* why he ran off to Maine all those years ago!"

For one moment, Emily seemed to stop breathing. *Wife?* She gained her composure quickly, and spoke as coldly as she could.

"You're being ridiculous, Mother. I'm hanging up now, and next time you have one of your little chats with my son-of-a-bitch ex-husband, do me a favor and leave me out of it!" She slammed the phone down before Helene could answer, then purposely left the receiver off the hook. Right now, she didn't want to talk to her mother. She wanted to talk to Ethan. But first, she needed to think.

The longer Emily thought, the angrier she became—not at Ethan as much as at her own blindness and stupidity. What kind of moron moved in with a man she hardly knew? A man she'd never even *asked* about his past? And how long had he expected to keep this from her? She phoned the lawyer's office and left a terse message for Ethan to call her back, then went to the kitchen and took out the bottle of Scotch he kept there. She sniffed the top, gagging at the odor, then tipped her head back, held her nose and swallowed as much as she could in one gulp. As the scalding liquid settled in her stomach, Emily retched. Lying on the kitchen floor, her head cocked to one side, Sarah watched curiously as Emily rushed to the sink to wash away the taste with a glass of tap water. One of the dog's rarely visible eyes peeked out through the mass of floppy gray hair, and when Emily glanced at her, Sarah wagged her tail tentatively.

"Mind your own business," Emily grumbled. Minutes afterward, still carrying the Scotch, she backed Ethan's red Jeep wagon out of the sandy yard, and turned onto the beach road.

When Ethan arrived home two hours later, he found a bewildering, partially legible note from Emily on the kitchen table, three hysterical phone messages from Emily's mother and another two from Maggie. He'd finished reading the note for the third time when the phone rang again. A Miss Emily Porter had been picked up in the parking lot of a local bar, in a damaged vehicle registered to him. There had been a complaint filed, as well. Over the phone, the message sounded like "running over a dwarf."

A trooper from the state police delivered a bedraggled Emily to the front door soon after that, along with an irate note from the owner of the bar and a towing bill from a garage in the village. Emily politely thanked the trooper, then staggered to the living-room couch and fell facedown into the pile of cushions. Ethan signed the necessary paperwork, agreed to call the complainant and saw the officer out.

When he went back into the living room, Emily was trying with very little success to stand up.

"You know the place out on the highway?" she asked, slurring her words just slightly. "The one with all the neon beer signs—Lucky Chucky's?"

Ethan nodded. "I know the one. Is that where you…" He glanced down again at the papers to check his facts. "Where you ran over the…three-and-a-half-foot 'dwarf'?"

"Plaster," she groaned. "Maybe concrete? He felt like concrete when I hit him, that's for sure. His name is Chucky—the dwarf, I mean. Well, it *was* his name, anyway. Chucky, just like the place. You know the one—he's holding up this really big hamburger?" She tried once again to stand, wobbled precariously, and sat down quickly.

When Ethan bent down and lifted her off the couch, Emily pressed her face against his neck and kissed a spot just below his ear. "I was mad at you," she said morosely.

"I know. It took me a while to figure out your note. Maggie called. Your mom's been on the phone to her, too, so I've got the gist of what happened. We'll talk about it when you're feeling better. Maybe sometime next week, from the look of things."

Ethan helped her to the bedroom and sat her on the edge of the four-poster to get her undressed. Emily teetered dangerously.

"You're not much of a drinker, are you?" he asked, keeping one hand on her shoulder to stop her from falling off the bed. "You couldn't have had a lot to drink at that dump. You weren't there long enough."

"I got an excellent head start. Before I got up the nerve to go inside, I sat in Chucky's parking lot and drank most of that dark stuff with the funny name. I think it's gone bad, by the way. It tastes awful." She burped, and Ethan chuckled.

"Sorry about that, but swilling thirty-eight-year-old single malt whiskey probably isn't the best way to begin your drinking career. Aside from everything else, it's expensive. I'm guessing you guzzled down around seventy bucks' worth of Strathisla cask 1182 before you took out the dwarf."

"Are you mad?"

He smiled, and began turning down the covers. "About the Scotch? No, I'm not mad. Am I going to be when I pick up the car?"

"It's possible," she said glumly. "*Now* you're going to start yelling, right?"

He shook his head. "No, Cinderella. I think I'll just let nature take its course. Pretty soon, when all that fine malt liquor meets up with all the cheap beer, you're going to start paying the *real* price for staying so long at the ball, and I can promise you won't like it."

Apparently feeling less remorseful now, Emily slipped her arms around his neck, but Ethan pulled away, kissing the top of her head.

"Not tonight, Cindy. It threatens my masculine pride when a woman passes out in the middle of being made love to."

Emily giggled. "I wouldn't do that." She hiccupped once, and passed out.

Chapter 6

The next afternoon, Emily woke with her head throbbing and her stomach in full revolt. Still pale and unsteady on her feet, she made her way carefully to the kitchen. She'd spent most of the previous night on the bathroom floor, while Ethan held her head and provided a steady supply of cold towels.

"I can't believe there are people who do this all the time," she mumbled hoarsely. "If I live through today, which I doubt, I swear I will *never* take another drink!" She flopped down on a kitchen chair and took a cautious sip from the coffee Ethan set before her.

"Can you eat something?" he asked.

She groaned and held up a hand. "Oh, God, no! Please!"

Ethan sat at the table across from her. "So, the bar hopping didn't go too well."

"I wouldn't say that, " Emily said defensively. "I met many lovely people and I learned to line dance. Oh, and I may have agreed to marry someone named Earl, who claims to be a long-liner from Long Beach, which he tells me is *not* in California, as I kept insisting, but somewhere or other in Massachusetts. What is a long-liner, by the way? Anyway, Earl doesn't have a lot of teeth, but he's a whiz at pinball." She put her head down on the table. "Oh, Ethan!" she moaned miserably. "I am *so* sorry about the car!"

Ethan grinned. "They called with the estimate this morning. You're grounded—until you're forty, give or take a couple of months. And no *Lawrence Welk* or *American Bandstand* for six weeks—at least."

There was an uncomfortable silence while Emily sipped her coffee. After a few minutes, Ethan began to tell her about his wife.

"I should have told you right away," he said quietly. "About Diana. It was partly ego, I guess, but I assumed you already knew the story. Anyway, you shouldn't have had to find out the way you did. I was wrong, and I'm sorry."

Emily shook her head. "It's all right. My own fault, really. I've never been a big fan of gossip columns. Is that why you left California and came here?"

"Not entirely. I'd had my fill of everything, actually. I was never cut out for the life there. When I met Diana— my wife—I was just out of college and doing stage work in New York when I could get it. I had the second lead in an off-Broadway revival of *Anna Christie* when we got married, and she was out of work. Diana was good, but she had a lot of trouble getting work. She was so damned beautiful, I think a lot of casting people figured she was all looks and no real talent. She was ambitious enough for both of us, though. When I got the offer to do my first movie, I wasn't especially interested, but we moved to Los Angeles anyway to give it a shot. Diana could always smell money.

"We were all right at first, and after that film did okay, the money got to be pretty good. By the second year, I think we both knew it was a mistake—the marriage, I mean. But Diana wasn't about to give up—not until she'd found a sequel, anyway. The next year, she did." Ethan leaned back in his chair and rubbed his eyes. "His name was Armando Arranjeuz-Carrillo, a small-time bullfighter she met while I was on location in Seville. The bullfighting business must not have been too good, though, because even before we'd wrapped up the shooting, Armando had decided he'd rather be Diana's personal manager, so he gave up the bullring—or maybe it gave *him* up. Anyway, one night Diana came to me and explained that she'd finally found the excitement she'd always needed. The next day, they took off on what Armando described as a publicity tour—to kick off Diana's new movie career. I flew home alone to pay the bills and send cash whenever she ran out.

"It didn't last long. Four months later, he left her for a fifteen-year-old waitress he'd 'discovered' in Barcelona. Diana OD'd on sleeping pills and jumped—or fell—from a twelfth-floor hotel balcony in Madrid. She was almost six months pregnant."

"Was the baby yours?" Emily asked softly.

Ethan didn't answer immediately. "I never knew. I guess there were ways to find out, but at that point it seemed… Anyway, I got the call from Armando in the middle of the night and flew out first thing the next morning, but by the time I landed in Madrid he'd already taken off. It turned out he had a wife and three kids he hadn't mentioned to Diana *or* to the waitress. I dealt with the authorities and the paperwork, and then took Diana back to New Hampshire—where her parents lived. By the time I got back to L.A., every gossip rag in town was saying she'd committed suicide because I wouldn't take her back."

"Was that true?"

He shrugged. "I think it had more to do with the bullfighter and the baby, but who knows? At that point, I still loved Diana and I think she knew it, but she never asked to come back. I'd gotten pretty tired of all the screaming and flying crockery by that point, so I can't say what I would've done if she'd wanted to try again. It wouldn't have worked, though. Diana wanted a lot more glamour and celebrity than I had to give. She'd always wanted to be 'in,' and all I wanted by then was to get out."

Ethan finished his coffee and twirled the empty cup on the table. "The papers played it up as a tragic love triangle, of course—the ones that didn't openly suggest I'd hired someone to push her off that balcony. In any case, the scandal was terrific for business. My next two films cleaned up at the box office, and there were even rumors of an Oscar nomination—which didn't pan out. For years afterward, though, that was always the first question anyone asked me in an interview. Was there something more to my wife's death than a suicide? And by that time, I'd about decided it *was* my fault. Finally, when I'd had enough, I sold the house in Brentwood, said goodbye to a couple of good friends and came here.

"I know it came as a shock, Em. My only defense is that I was sure you'd heard the story and were too polite to ask. I knew we'd have to talk about it sometime, but now… It was stupid and inconsiderate, and I'm sorry. I guess that doesn't help much, but it's all I can say now."

Emily shrugged. "It doesn't matter. I didn't really believe all that murder crap Mom was spewing, but you're right. A dead wife was a shock. That's what comes of not reading the old copies of *People* at the beauty salon, I guess." She sighed. "Of course, the last time I was inside a beauty salon was when Dennis was on his mission to turn me into Grace Kelly."

"Grace Kelly?"

"Yeah, dumb, huh? Dennis had a very big thing for Grace Kelly. That probably explains my feeble-mindedness—all the noxious chemicals he had me dunked in to make me a sun-streaked blonde. I'm sure it's no surprise that the venture failed. I looked like I had this permanently attached fright wig, but Dennis seemed happy and at least I didn't go bald."

Ethan reached across the table and took her hand, then turned it over to kiss the inside of her wrist. "Now that you've heard about the skeletons in my closet, isn't it time you told me more about yours—about Dennis?"

"Dennis is old news. He's not worth talking about. Why

can't we forget all the ex-spouses in this house and move on? It's over."

It had been a difficult day, and while she was grateful that Ethan wasn't pressing the issue for the time being, Emily knew it was far from over.

Emily was feeling mildly better by evening, so they drove across town for a previously arranged dinner with Ethan's old friends, Matthew and Kate O'Connell. She'd already visited the O'Connells in their big old house twice before, and had fallen in love with the couple at the first meeting. When Ethan was sixteen, his parents had died in an accident and Matt and Kate, with no children of their own, had taken him in and cared for him as their own son. Now, they seemed equally ready to embrace Emily as part of the family.

When they arrived, Emily was still a bit under the weather, and her obvious reluctance to eat drew Kate's attention.

"You may as well get that greedy look off your face, Kate," Ethan said, grinning. "Sorry to disappoint you, but Emily's not pregnant."

"I thought no such thing!" Kate cried. "Why on earth would that be any of my business?"

Kate had settled Emily into a soft, comfortable chair and insisted on pulling up an ottoman for her feet.

"And when has that ever stopped you?" Matt gave his wife's ample rear a cheerful pat as he passed. "Sorry, Emily. Kate's been at this midwifing business for close to fifty years, and even though she claims to be retired, same as me, she's always on the lookout for new victims for those medieval birthing methods she practices."

Kate's protest was vigorous and heated. "Medieval, my you know what, Matthew O'Connell! Women have been having babies for thousands of years, and most of the time, they've gotten along fine without the kind of doctors with no common sense and a lot of fancy shmancy degrees. And without the medical-pharmaceutical industry making things more dangerous and downright expensive than they need to be—and don't you forget it!"

Ethan smiled as he explained the familiar argument to Emily. "You already know that Matt used to be the town's best doctor? Well, since he retired—and I use the term *retired* loosely—he's the town's best 'semiretired, sometimes, maybe-if-he-*feels*-like-it doctor.' He has a limited practice now. Mainly the friends he hasn't already killed off, like me, and anybody who still owes him money."

"Anyway," Kate continued, plumping a pillow behind Emily's back, "I wasn't suggesting anything except that Emily looks a bit peaked tonight."

Matt O'Connell studied Emily more closely, then slapped her on the knee. "Peaked, my ass! It doesn't take a 'fancy shmancy' physician or even a backwoods medicine woman like you to see this girl's just plain hungover. Am I right or not?" When Emily nodded her head miserably, he went to the cabinet and pulled out a bottle.

"Can I interest you in a little of what we used to call 'the hair of the dog'?"

"I've sworn off dog," Emily said weakly. "Scottish dogs, specifically."

"Hogwash! Good Scotch is a tonic for the blood," Matthew announced.

Kate touched Emily's hand, and shook her head disapprovingly. "Ignore him, honey. He says the same thing about what he calls 'good' tobacco. He's been telling me he's quit smoking for twenty years, and thinks he's fooling me, but I know better. I can smell it on him every time he comes in from fishing with his cronies."

"The woman's got a nose like a bloodhound," Matt growled. "I only keep her around because she's such a rotten cook. Keeps me from eating too much and wrecking what's left of my liver."

"Well," Kate conceded, "that's the truth, anyway. I never got the hang of cooking, nor cared to, especially."

"We have something in common," Emily said, laughing. "I hate cooking, too."

Kate beamed. "Glad to hear it. I've always told Matthew that if God had wanted women to cook, He'd never have invented the microwave oven."

As they drove back to the cottage that night, Emily leaned back against the seat, smiling.

"They're wonderful people, Ethan."

"None better, and don't let that crusty New England act fool you. Matt's a fine doctor and Kate's as sharp as they come. Before they retired, one or the other of them probably delivered half the babies in this county, and they worked as a team about as often as they did alone. I saw Kate in the kitchen, mixing one of her home remedies for you. Are you feeling better?"

Emily touched her stomach. "It's amazing! I don't know what she put in it, but I drank it down—to make her happy—and now I feel almost normal!"

Ethan laughed. "In my wilder years, I swallowed quite a few of Kate's hangover cures. Matt's always claimed that she's really a witch. He says she goes out after midnight and brews things up in a cauldron or a withered tree-stump—like newts' eyes and toadstools."

It was past eleven by the time they got back to the cottage and were ready for bed. Ethan dragged the reluctant Sarah out of the bedroom and closed the door so they could make love with some degree of privacy. Sarah, as it turned out, wasn't at all jealous, but she did like to watch.

"It doesn't really bother me," Emily decided, the first time they noticed Sarah on the end of the bed observing them from beneath her overgrown bangs.

Ethan scowled. "Well, it bothers *me*. I can't decide whether she's morally offended, unnaturally curious or just grading my performance."

When they'd finished, Ethan got out of bed to let the whining, deeply wounded Sarah back into the room and to close the bedroom window. There was a fly in the room that had been annoying them since they got home. As he reached to turn off the light, the fly buzzed by Emily's ear and landed on the wall above her head. Ethan grabbed a magazine from the bedside table and leaned across her to swat it, but when he raised his arm, Emily cried out, threw her hands to her face and pressed her body against the headboard.

Ethan halted his swing in midair and looked down at

her. "Emily! What in the…" When he tried to touch her, Emily flinched. She regained her composure quickly and apologized, but her face was flushed and her eyes red.

"I'm sorry." She gave a nervous laugh. "I just…"

Ethan took her chin in his hand and forced her to look at him. "You thought I was going to hit you!"

"Of course I didn't." Emily pulled the covers up over her naked breasts, suddenly self-conscious. "When you moved so quickly, I…"

"You what?"

"I don't know. It surprised me, that's all. Why are you making such a big deal out of it?"

"Because it's a very big deal to me when the woman I love, and to whom I just made love, thinks I'm about to punch her in the face."

"Oh, for God's sake, Ethan, I didn't think that! I just… You know what? This is really stupid! Could we drop it, please?"

"No, we can't. It reminded me of something."

"What?" she grumbled.

"It made me think about this dog I adopted from the pound," he said. "Years ago, back in California."

Emily rolled her eyes, then turned over and began plumping her pillow. "Thanks. I'm trying to remember the last time I was compared to a dog. Probably in high school. You really know how to dazzle a girl, darling. Now, I'm tired and I'd like to go to sleep, if you don't mind. You can tell me about your dog in the morning."

Ethan ignored her and went on with the story. "Every time I picked up a newspaper or a stick or just about anything else, the dog would hide under the couch or a bed.

I couldn't get her out, sometimes for hours. I had that dog for eight years. She slept at my feet every night of her life and followed me everywhere I went. She was the most loving, loyal animal I've ever known. I never raised a finger to her, but until the last day of her life, she ran under the bed and cowered if I so much as swatted a fly—exactly like you just did."

He took her shoulder and turned her to look at him. "Did your ex-husband… Did Dennis hit you?"

Emily thought about lying, but didn't. "Sometimes."

"How often is sometimes?"

"What does it matter, Ethan?" she asked irritably. "It was a long time ago. Water under the bridge. Spilled milk. You want a couple more clichés?"

Ethan's voice was firm. "What I want is a straight answer. Did he ever really hurt you?"

Emily sighed. "Define *really*." For a moment, she said nothing else. "It's a long, boring story, and some of what happened wasn't his fault. Not really. Dennis was this very… Well, he was a perfectionist, and frankly, I was a pain in the ass a lot of the time." She laughed—a weak, unconvincing laugh. "You may have noticed that about me. Anyway, once in a while, when I screwed up, he…he lost it, and… It wasn't always a major thing."

"And how often was it 'a major thing'?"

"Now you want all the gory details?" she asked sullenly.

"What I want is to grab the first plane to California and beat the shit out of the son of a bitch," he said grimly. "But for now, yeah, I want details. Like why didn't you tell me about this before now?"

"Why didn't you tell me about your first wife?" she shot back. "Maybe it just didn't seem important anymore."

"After three years, you still duck when a man lifts a hand near you. I'm no psychologist, but that says to me there's something going on, and that maybe it's got a lot to do with why you're so set against getting married again."

"One has nothing to do with the other."

"Do you think I'd ever hit you?"

Emily threw up her hands. "Of course not, but…"

"But you didn't think this bastard Lockhart would, either, right? Not at first?"

"That's not what I was going to say. It's just that… Well, things happen after you've been married for a while." Emily wiped away a tear. "Things change, Ethan. People change. Even when you think you know them, they can change."

"Go on."

Emily cleared her throat. "The real problem was that from Dennis's point of view, I let him down. He was training me to be this model wife, and I could never seem to get it right. At first, I couldn't figure out why he even wanted me. I think I was like a challenge, you know? This lump of clay he was going to sculpt. Liza Doolittle to his Henry Higgins.

"You need to understand that Dennis was very successful, and a lot of other stuff I wasn't. But I was artistic and well-read, and Dennis—who wasn't either—seemed to think I had possibilities. Anyway, I'd just dropped out of college, and I was drifting around aimlessly. You know the type. A tie-dyed hippie wannabe with long, straight hair, peace symbols and Che Guevara posters on the walls. Everything I owned was from India or a Salvation Army store. I'd already figured out I was a failure. Then Dennis came along and started changing everything about me—the way I dressed, talked, the way I did my hair. From 'Poor Pitiful Pearl' to Grace Kelly, in five easy months. That's how long I knew him before we got married."

Emily leaned wearily back against the pillows. "After a while, I started to disappear. I could feel it happening, but I didn't really mind that much. I mean, it's not like I was anything special or interesting, or that I had any better ideas about what to do with my life. Dennis kept telling me that he didn't want a Stepford wife, but he did. And he was mad as hell that he hadn't been able to build one that looked more like Grace Kelly."

During this speech, Ethan didn't take his eyes off Emily's face. "Is that when he started hitting you?" he asked softly.

"Dennis never wanted me to work," Emily continued. "He was very old-fashioned that way, and he always referred to my painting as a 'nice hobby.' He was right. I'd never sold anything, but I kept plugging away at it. Dennis was a fanatic about the house being perfect, but I started rushing through my housework so I could spend more time in this little studio I'd set up in the garage.

"He was insane about having meals on time, too, and he always wanted elaborate dinners, with linen tablecloths and the good china. Pretty soon, I figured out I could call out and have dinner delivered, put *that* food on our own dishes and then squash the takeout containers in the kitchen wastebasket. Clever, huh?

"I got caught, of course, and when I tried to make a joke of it, Dennis slapped me, really hard. It was the first time he'd ever hit me, so I sat there, not knowing what to say. He was so mad, he jammed the garbage disposal with a couple of sterling silver salad forks, and when I tried to help him get them out, he slapped me again, harder. He apologized, but somehow, after that... Well, I kept screwing up, and I guess smacking me got to be a habit with him."

She glanced at the clock on the bedside table. "Is it all right if we talk about this some other time, darling? I'm tired, and I think Kate's wonder cure may be wearing off."

"All right," Ethan agreed. "But I still want to hear the rest, Em. It's obvious that this bum is unfinished business, and you can't shove the whole thing in some dark closet in your mind and ignore it. I tried that with my own mess, and it doesn't work."

Emily stiffened slightly. "I'm not ignoring it, Ethan. Just because I don't go around wallowing in it doesn't mean I'm ignoring it."

Ethan wrapped her in his arms. "You know, Em, it can feel damned good to face down what scares you. Did you ever tell this bastard off? Let him know what you thought of him?"

Emily rested her head on his chest, genuinely weary now. "Not in so many words, but I think he may have gotten the picture after I filed for divorce and moved three thousand miles away. I couldn't have gotten any farther from Dennis without falling into the Atlantic."

"That kind of bully never gets it. He still wants you back, doesn't he?"

"Ah, I see you've been talking to dear old Mom. Well, if he does, it's only because he lost the game. And that's exactly what it was to him—a game. He'd made a bet with himself that he could turn me into this ideal wife, and then, after he'd spent a lot of time and money on the game, he lost." She laughed bitterly. "Dennis always hated losing *anything* he'd paid for, even when he didn't especially like it, anymore—or want it."

Ethan had been asleep for more than two hours before Emily finally gave up and slipped quietly out of bed. She enticed Sarah into the hallway with a hunk of cheese, then closed the bedroom door and settled on the couch with a warm quilt and Sarah snoring peacefully beside her. There was a full moon that night, and from where she sat, Emily could see across the dunes and watch the waves rolling in. But despite the soothing sounds of the ocean, she was unable to fall asleep. Sarah began to whuffle, her feet moving rapidly. Emily smiled to herself. Chasing sheep, maybe.

What Ethan had said earlier that evening was mostly true, of course. Dennis Lockhart *was* unfinished business, along with much of what had happened during their marriage. A period of her life she thought she'd put an end to more than three and a half years earlier, on a rain-soaked pier in Santa Monica, California.

Chapter 7

Over breakfast the next morning, Emily told Ethan about her marriage to Dennis, starting at the very end.

"The day the divorce was final, I walked down to the Santa Monica Pier to throw my wedding ring into the ocean." She laughed at the memory. "At sundown, in the pouring rain. I was looking for some kind of symbolic ending—the sunset of my failed marriage or something. Anyway, I waited until the exact moment the sun began to disappear, then leaned over and tossed my ring off the end of the pier. I watched it sink, really enjoying the idea of how enraged Dennis would be if he knew what I'd done. It wouldn't be losing *me* that bothered him, of course, but the cost of the damned ring. The only reason I didn't toss the engagement ring at the same time was because I'd already sold it to retain an attorney. It wasn't the brightest thing to do, of course. I had no job, no prospects, a little over three hundred bucks in the bank and my last rent check still floating around, waiting to bounce. But I didn't care. I wanted a gesture."

"I'd signed a prenup, but I still came out with enough of a settlement to keep me for a couple of years. I even felt rich, until I got my attorney's final bill. I'd hired the woman because she had a reputation as a pit bull. She never lived up to her reputation in court, but she *was* a good listener." Emily sighed. "You'd be surprised to find out how much a lot of sympathetic chitchat with a pit bull can run you, at a hundred and fifty bucks an hour."

She paused to sip her coffee.

"I figured things out last night, Ethan, and I know why I didn't want to tell you all this. It's pretty simple, really. I was ashamed."

"Ashamed of what?"

"Of myself. For letting it happen and for staying so long after it did."

Ethan shook his head sadly. "Emily, none of what happened was your fault. You have to know that."

"But it was, you see. I wasn't really afraid of Dennis, not terrified like some abused women are. I knew all along that he wasn't the kind to kill me. Dennis would have hated prison. All that lousy food and no place to get his hair styled? Later, when people kept asking me why I hadn't called the police—especially after the last beating, when he broke my wrist—I didn't have a good answer. But the truth is, I never once seriously *thought* about the police, and even then, I think I knew why. It wasn't out of fear of Dennis. Fear would've been easier to admit, and easier to live with. I was embarrassed. Here I was, spouting feminism one day and letting a man dominate and hurt me the next. I was humiliated to have anyone know that I'd become the kind of woman who let that happen—over and over—without doing anything about it. I'd let myself be a victim, and maybe I even *liked* being a victim. It made all my failures so easy to explain away. Everything wrong with me was Dennis's fault.

"What's worse, I did it all to impress people. I only married Dennis to prove to my mother, and maybe to myself, that I could get the 'right' kind of man if I really wanted to. Meaning rich and successful. Oh, Dennis wasn't a CEO of anything, but he was on the way up the ladder. And then, even after I left him and came here? All this time I've been telling myself that the way I lived was showing my independence, when all I've *really* been doing is hiding out, afraid I'd do it again." She stopped then, and sighed. "Does this make any sense at all?"

Ethan smiled. "Yes, and what's more, I think you've just taken that first step we talked about. Congratulations. You're on the way."

Several days later, Ethan shook her out of a sound sleep. "Get up. I've got a surprise for you."

Emily turned her face back into the pillow and groaned. "Go away! It's too early."

"It's ten o'clock," he observed, lifting her head to thrust his watch under her nose.

"That's what I said," she mumbled. "It's too early."

He dragged the covers off and pulled the pillow from under her head. "Now, sleeping beauty. I've got something important to show you."

"Jeez, what a grouch! This had better be good, buster." Emily crawled out of bed and followed him into the yard, where she immediately tripped over the rusted remains of a push lawn mower. The entire yard was littered with piles of broken furniture, ancient plumbing fixtures and several old bicycles.

She yawned. "If you're expecting me to mow the lawn, get yourself another girl. I'm going back to bed. Where did all this crap come from, anyway?"

He pointed to the stone boathouse. "In there, with another six or seven tons of trash. Nobody, including yours truly, has cleaned it in maybe fifty years. They just kept cramming stuff inside. I've been working for two hours. Would you like to grab a broom and help me out?"

Emily yawned again. "Not especially."

"Let me put it another way. Get dressed and find a broom."

Emily kicked at the decrepit lawn mower. "What's in it for me?"

"Since you seem bent on a life of leisure and sloth, I figure it's time to put you back to work," he explained. "When I get all the junk out, the boathouse will make a pretty fair studio. What do you think? There's even a bathroom, if you're not too picky about comfort."

Emily grumbled, but went inside and returned wearing a pair of old jeans and a T-shirt. She peeked inside the dusty boathouse and made a face.

"Not the spacious loft in Greenwich Village I always dreamed of, but I read once that this is how Jackson Pollock got famous. He and his wife had this old shack on their property on Long Island, and it was stuffed to the ceiling with years of accumulated garbage, just like this. So, they cleaned out all the junk and made it into a studio for him. That's where he developed that drippy style and got filthy rich and famous."

Ethan laughed. "Exactly what I had in mind." He handed her a large broom.

"Of course," Emily continued, "after that, he turned into a mean, arrogant alcoholic who beat his wife and killed himself driving drunk." She shook her head. "This is an awful a lot of work you're taking on. You sure you'll have the time, with the new book and all?"

"I've got the time," he said. "What I don't have is cheap, nonunion labor—which is where you come in."

Emily sighed. "I figured."

As Ethan picked up the old lawn mower to add to the trash pile, he hummed a song she'd occasionally heard him singing as he worked.

"An old sea chantey," he told her when she asked about it. "It's called 'Farewell, Spanish Ladies,' and most of the verses are grossly obscene, which, knowing you like I do, I figure you'll probably want to commit to memory."

They worked on the boathouse for the rest of that week, and four days later, it had begun to take on the appearance of a genuine studio. On the fifth day, Ethan stopped early, complaining of a headache.

Emily followed him inside, worried. "That's twice you've begged off because of a headache. I always thought that was a woman's line to avoid sex."

Ethan pretended to think for a moment. "At my age, my mind could be going, of course, but I don't remember avoiding sex. Have I been?"

Emily grinned. "Well, certainly not that I've noticed, but you've been out there in the sun all day. You've earned some time off. Go take some aspirin and watch the news, and I'll finish up the caulking. But don't blame me when the window falls out."

A few minutes later, she wandered into the living room and found him resting on the couch with a wet rag on his forehead.

"No better?"

"Much better. I was getting ready to come back out."

"Too late, slacker. I'm done. I may never walk upright again, but I finished it." She sat down on the couch next to him. "Does Maine have any poisonous snakes or spiders?"

"Probably. Did you see any, or is this another excuse to stop working?"

"I don't know if they're poisonous, but I saw a couple of spiders big enough to swallow a poodle, and there's a huge black beetle that's got Sarah cowering in a corner. I was thinking maybe something bit you. Why don't you call Matthew and get it checked out?"

"Matthew's a quack, and a *retired* quack, at that. Twenty years ago he told me to quit smoking, and I did. Then, after

I'd been spitting nails for five weeks, lusting after another cigarette, I find him puffing away on this big, fat cigar. So, he tries to convince me that after a certain age—coincidentally the exact age he was then—that 'it' won't have time to catch up with you. How's that for sound medical advice?"

He sat up and pulled her close to him. "While I was lying here, I came up with a great idea."

Emily smiled. "And here I thought you were tired."

"Get your mind out of the gutter. No, my idea was that we drop everything we're doing, drive to Bar Harbor and put the car on the ferry across to Nova Scotia for a few days, while it's still warm. Then just drive around, doing whatever we want, stopping when we feel like it."

"That sounds a lot like a honeymoon," Emily observed softly.

"Unless you really want a big wedding—and I've got the feeling you don't—we could get married in Bar Harbor. I know a couple of terrific little inns right on the water where we could stay for a few days, and then take the ferry over to Yarmouth. Or we could get a cabin and poke around Acadia Park for a while. It's beautiful this time of year. I know your mom wants a big wedding, but Matt and Kate will understand, and let's face it, Maggie just wants us to get it done."

"Mom will survive," Emily said. "I had a big wedding the first time, and we all know how that turned out. There were two hundred and fifty people on the guest list, only eight of whom Mom or I had ever met. Dennis paid for the whole circus himself, so he could direct every scene. I had a dress that cost more than my college tuition and a cake the size of a VW. There's even a full-length movie of it somewhere."

Ethan took her hand and kissed it. "Okay, then. This time, it'll just be you and me. Give me the word, and…"

Emily laid her head on his chest and waited while he slipped his arms around her.

"Would you be mad if I said I wanted to take a little longer to decide?" she murmured. "You know, time to think about… Well, about everything?"

Ethan's voice was gentle, but she could hear the disappointment in it. "Take as much time as you need, Em. I'm not going anywhere."

Two days later, Emily was walking on the beach near the cottage, waiting for Ethan to return from town, when she glanced up to see a heavyset man standing on the deck and peering in the large window. Visitors, or even passersby, were rare this far from town, so she strode briskly back toward the cottage, dropping some of the driftwood she'd been collecting along the way.

Just then, the man appeared to notice her, as well, and he came down the steps to the beach.

He started across the dunes in her direction, waving and moving clumsily in the sand. An off-islander in city shoes, Emily thought, smiling to herself. When he was within a hundred yards of her, Emily stopped abruptly and took a deep breath to compose herself. The man approaching was Dennis Lockhart—forty to fifty pounds heavier than when she'd last seen him, but his bearing was unmistakable.

When he was close enough, Dennis opened his mouth to speak, but Emily cut him off. "What the hell are you doing here?" she demanded, hurling the last of the driftwood onto the sand. Dennis looked surprised at her hostility, and then annoyed.

"Your mother asked me to come," he explained. "I was in Boston on business. I had to fly into Bangor and rent a damned car, then I got lost. I've been all day getting here."

Emily glanced at her watch. "Bangor's about a hundred miles from here. If you turn around right now and catch a late-afternoon flight, you can be back in Boston for dinner."

"I want to talk to you, Emily." His voice was stern, and for a second, Emily felt as she always had when he used that tone with her—intimidated. Amazingly, the feeling passed quickly. Dennis was nothing to her now—less than nothing.

"Well, I don't want to talk to *you*, Dennis. What I want is for you to go back to California and stay out of my life. You can tell my mother I'm fine. Hell, Dennis! You couldn't stand her when we were married, and now you're bosom buddies?"

Lockhart stared at her and shook his head in disapproval. "You've changed, Emily."

"Thank you. Finally, after all these years, a compliment. I'll be sure to put that in my diary. Now, go away."

Dennis ignored her. "He's not here, is he?"

"Why? You want another shot at breaking my arm without witnesses?"

"That was a filthy lie, and you know it!" he shouted.

"Fine," Emily said coldly. "I'm a liar, and you're trespassing. This beach is private property. Get off it."

"Helene tells me you're actually planning to marry this old actor you're involved with."

Emily moved deftly around him and continued walking up the beach to the cottage, with Dennis right behind her. When he grabbed her arm, Emily whirled around and slapped him as hard as she could.

"I'm…I'm sorry, Dennis," she stammered, flushing. "I didn't mean to…"

Emily recognized the controlled rage in his eyes, but when he made no move to retaliate, she pushed past him again, to the foot of the deck stairs. As she walked, she was aware of a curious feeling of exhilaration. She pointed around the back of the house. "You can go out that way," she said. "I assume that's where you parked."

He nodded, but stood his ground. "I'm not going anywhere. I want to talk to him—this Douglas person."

Emily laughed, in spite of herself. "No, you don't. Just leave, now, Dennis, and I promise not to tell him you were here."

"You're not seriously planning to live in a place like this?" He waved his arm to indicate the cottage, his voice dripping with contempt. "Doesn't this old has-been have any money? God knows, he made enough second-rate films."

Emily turned and smiled. "No, Dennis, the old has-been is marrying me for my money. You know, the vast financial settlement I got after our divorce? And he didn't make 'films,' Dennis. He made movies. Good, honest ones, not pretentious, nouveau-fake French crap… No, *excusez moi*. I misspoke. I meant to say, French *merde!*"

At that moment, Ethan opened the back door and came

out onto the deck. He leaned over the railing and applauded Emily's speech.

Emily turned to beam up at him. "You're home!" she cried.

Ethan walked to the edge of the deck. "And just in time, it looks like." He pointed at Dennis. "So, who's the fat French guy?" In that instant, Emily loved him more than she'd ever thought possible. She came up the stairs, hooked her arm through his and kissed him lightly.

"Ethan, this is my ex-husband, Dennis Lockhart, who was about to leave."

Dennis started up the steps after her. "I'm not leaving until I talk to you, Douglas, and to my former wife. I still feel responsible for Emily's welfare, and her mother and I have heard some ugly rumors that—"

Ethan stepped in front of him. "The lady said leave, Mr. Lockhart, and I think she means it. I wouldn't mess with her if I were you. She's got a hell of a temper when she gets riled."

"And you're planning to throw me off the property, is that it?" Dennis challenged.

Ethan glanced at his watch. "Not yet. You've still got thirty seconds. After that, Emily goes after you with a broom, unless I beat her to it."

Dennis glowered, but backed down one step. "Very funny, and very courageous of you, Douglas," he remarked sullenly. "Considering you're six inches taller than me."

"Yeah, but as you just pointed out, you're a whole lot younger," Ethan said affably. "And you've got at least fifty pounds on me, with that gut you're working on. Too many

French pastries is my guess. Still, if you'd rather take a couple of swings at an old guy like me, instead of Em here—the way you're used to doing—I'll give it my best shot."

Dennis's face went red with anger. "Did she tell you that?"

Ethan's voice was hard. "She didn't have to. I know the type. Now, get going, asshole, and don't come back. If you've got something to say to either of us, put it in writing. We've got a mailbox *and* a garbage can."

"And a vicious dog," Emily piped up, indicating the snoring Sarah.

Ethan grinned. "Right. I forgot about the vicious dog."

Dennis clenched his fists, and for a second, it seemed as though he might actually take that swing at Ethan, but instead, he turned and stomped down the stairs. They heard him scrambling up the slope, slipping in the sand and cursing at every step. Two minutes later, the roar of a powerful engine came from behind the cottage, followed by the sound of gravel scattering as Dennis's car tore out of the yard.

Ethan shook his head. "There goes the driveway. I wondered when I came home who we knew that drove a big silver Jaguar."

"That one's a rental, but Dennis always bought big, fancy cars. Mom says he's ordered a…I can't remember the name. Oh, yeah, an Espada. Is that expensive?"

Ethan chuckled. "Just a little. Of course, some thirty-five-thousand-dollar Lamborghini Espada would probably look like junk parked next to a six-year-old Jeep with a big dent in the rear fender—from running over a concrete dwarf."

As they walked into the house, Ethan took her hand.

"That took guts," he said. "I'm proud of you."

Emily flushed. "Not really. I should've done it years ago."

"And today you did."

"With you standing there, ready to beat the crap out of him."

"Don't kid yourself. I saw the whole thing. You didn't need me, and he knew it."

"Okay," she said, beaming with pleasure. "You're right. I wasn't intimidated by him anymore. Does that mean I've grown up?"

"It means you've put him where he should've been a long time ago—in the past. Now, what'll we do to celebrate?"

"I've got an idea." Emily looked down at their clasped hands and blushed. "Why don't we go to bed early and act out all the love scenes from your movies. Maybe update a few of them, from 'PG' to 'X.' And you know what else I was thinking?"

"Probably, but please keep in mind how little sleep I've had lately, with this boathouse project of ours."

Emily smiled. "I was thinking you could rest up in Nova Scotia, maybe."

"You mean it?"

"Yes, but these places you're thinking of had better not be fancy. I don't have anything to wear. I'll be half-naked as it is."

He smiled and kissed the tip of her nose. "I wouldn't have it any other way. What about leaving this coming weekend?"

"This weekend will be perfect. Now I'm going out to my unfinished studio to paint something, if you don't mind."

"Good. With what this studio is costing, we're going to need to be a two-income family. Go to work." He smacked her on the rear end and walked away, humming the first few bars of "Farewell, Spanish Ladies."

Chapter 8

Several days after Dennis Lockhart's unwelcome visit, Emily and Ethan drove to Bar Harbor, where they stayed at a charmingly run-down old bed-and-breakfast until they could get the necessary blood tests and paperwork. That weekend, they were married in a diminutive white wooden church they'd found while exploring the roads outside of town. The elderly Reverend Edward Dinwiddie, who performed the ceremony, spoke with a noticeable Scottish accent and bore a strong resemblance to Dickens' Mr. Pickwick. When Mrs. Dinwiddie—a plump, spry lady of some eighty-six years—discovered that they had no family with them, she insisted on baking them a "simple little wedding cake." Mrs. Dinwiddie boasted that she owned every wedding and bridal book ever published, and after a quick glance at the crammed bookshelves in the bright, sunny Dinwiddie kitchen, Emily believed her.

Hester Dinwiddie's "simple little wedding cake" turned out to be an ornate fantasy in three tiers, festooned with clusters of hothouse roses from the Reverend Dinwiddie's own greenhouse. The newlyweds shared the cake and a crystal pitcher of freshly squeezed lemonade with their hosts on the Dinwiddies' enclosed summer porch overlooking Penobscot Bay. And when she learned that Ethan and Emily had no hotel reservations for their wedding night, Mrs. Dinwiddie offered the use of the turn-of-the-century guesthouse that sat at the back of the garden.

"A nice bottle of champagne would be lovely now, I know," Mrs. Dinwiddie confided when her husband left the porch briefly. "But Edward doesn't allow spirits on the Sabbath. Any other time, either, for that matter—the old goat!" She laughed heartily, and poured fresh glasses of lemonade.

"Are you sure he won't be bothered, then?" Emily asked. "By a couple of strangers staying in his guesthouse?"

"Oh, Edward hasn't anything at all against sex," Mrs. Dinwiddie explained matter-of-factly as she helped herself to another wedge of cake. "He quite likes it, actually, even at our age. All six of our children got started in that bed. It's a very lucky bed, you know."

As they undressed that night, Emily eyed the elderly brass bed cautiously. "Lucky bed, huh? What do you think she meant? Lucky just for getting pregnant, or…?"

Ethan grinned and turned down the antique wedding-ring quilt. Underneath was another handmade quilt and a soft, downy featherbed. "I guess we'll have to take our chances and find out. What do you say? Are you feeling lucky, Mrs. Douglas?"

Emily slipped her arms around his neck. "Never luckier, and never happier."

The following morning, they said goodbye to the Dinwiddies, then drove the car onto the ferry to Yarmouth. They sat in one of the comfortably enclosed observation decks for the three-hour voyage and watched not the normally splendid view, but heavy rain and thick fog.

"So much for the lucky bed," Ethan grumbled. "I'm sorry about the weather, darling. It's not turning out to be the picturesque honeymoon I promised you."

Emily snuggled closer in the wide chair they were sharing. "I didn't come for pictures," she said softly. "It's easily the best honeymoon I've ever had. Who wants to waste a lot of time outdoors, anyway?"

Ethan grinned. "Not a big nature-lover, eh?"

"It has its moments, but give me bad weather, a roaring fire and a good book any day."

"A good book?" He raised an eyebrow.

Emily blushed. "Okay, so skip the book. Why don't they have cabins on these things?"

"You can't wait three hours?"

"I can probably wait," she said, letting her hand wander down the inside of his thigh, "but I don't have to like it. How far is the hotel from where we land?"

After ten days spent exploring Yarmouth, Halifax and the Bay of Fundy, they returned home, stopping first at the

Dinwiddies' to collect their frozen wedding cake and the couple's best wishes. They arrived at Matthew and Kate's in a drenching rain, and stayed to share wedding cake and congratulatory champagne before heading back to the cottage with Sarah. While Emily and Kate prepared dinner, Ethan and Matt went into the family room. Ethan put a fresh log on the fire, and Matt lit his pipe and got comfortable in the worn leather recliner beside the hearth.

"Well, I don't have to ask if you had a good time," Matthew called out to Emily, winking broadly. "I can tell by the slump in this man's shoulders that you've about worn him to a frazzle." He slapped Ethan on the knee. "'Course, it could be all that driving, but I keep telling you, my friend, young women and old wine'll take it out of a man every time."

Ethan laughed. "Thanks, Matt. Go ahead and run an old guy down in front of his new bride. If you knew the project I've got in store when we get home, you'd—"

"I saw it," Matthew interrupted. "Me and Kate drove out there a couple times to check on your place after that big blow last weekend. We noticed all the junk piled up behind the house. You're tearing up the boathouse now, are you?"

"Ethan's making me a studio," Emily explained from the kitchen. "To paint in."

Matthew shook his head. "Yeah, well, you just see he doesn't overdo it. This man gets some damned thing in his head, and then he doesn't know when to stop, or how to just go about it easy."

Ethan yawned and flopped onto the couch. "Do you get the feeling that Matt thinks I'm over the hill?"

"No such thing," Matt growled. "But I told you after that business two years ago to slow down a little, hire yourself a contractor if you need one and let—"

Emily had stopped what she was doing, and come into the family room. "What business, two years ago?" she asked quietly. She looked at Ethan. "Is there something I should know about?"

"Nothing," Ethan said, pulling her down on the couch with him. "Matt's been out of the doctoring business too long. Now he makes all his friends patients, and forces his advice on them whether they want it or not. A very good, very *expensive* neurologist in Boston told me I was fine."

"Neurologist, hell!" Matthew snapped. "Just because he's got a few more initials after his name and charges six times what anybody else does doesn't mean he knows about a patient he's only seen one damned time in some fancy, high-rise office!"

"Two damned times, actually," Ethan corrected him. "And six thousand bucks' worth of tests, all to find out I probably had a pinched nerve. Six weeks of physical therapy, and it went away."

"Are you sure?" Emily asked, looking from Ethan to Matthew and back again.

Ethan nodded. "I'm sure. But if you want me to use that as an excuse to let you do the rest of the painting, just say the word. Now, can we eat and go home? Sarah's itching to christen that brand-new rug you insisted on putting down."

The next morning, Ethan woke to find Emily already up and busily painting the back door. She greeted him cheerfully and handed him a second paintbrush. "I've been thinking. After we've finished the boathouse project, we could probably do some work on the cottage ourselves. It might be fun. I think I'm really getting the hang of this home repair stuff."

Ethan dropped the brush back in the paint can. "No, thanks. I did that twelve years ago. I hesitate to bring this up—repeatedly—but I'm not getting any younger. Since you're having such a great time, we'll go ahead and sand and paint by ourselves, but we need a contractor for the big stuff. I had a guy out here a while back to give me an estimate. Josh something-or-other. He came highly recommended, and seemed to know a lot about these old places. It's kind of late in the year to start now, but come spring, I'll call him. By summer, the place will be the envy of all our neighbors." He glanced down the empty beach. "If we had any."

He took Emily's brush and kissed her, then put the brush in the can and wiped a spot of paint from her cheek. "Besides, all this 'home repair stuff,' as you call it, is beginning to look like a stall to me. We've already invested a bloody fortune in that boathouse. When it's finally ready, I'm going to chain you to the wall out there, so you can start painting something besides doors and windows. Sell a mural or two to Peggy Guggenheim, like Jackson Pollock, and make me a *rich* old man."

Although the boathouse looked ready by the time winter arrived, Emily soon discovered that even with the space heaters they'd bought, the new studio was too cold and damp to use for longer than an hour or two a day.

"Come spring, I'll get someone out here to add insulation and install some kind of heating system," Ethan said as he set up Emily's table by the fireplace. "For now, though, I plan to lie around on my duff all winter, and watch you work."

They passed the coldest days that first winter sitting in the living room together, close to the fire. Ethan was doing the final work on the new book, and Emily puttered busily about with brushes and paint tubes, pretending to paint. But much of their time was consumed with talking—learning all those things about each other they hadn't yet discovered.

When the weather permitted, they took a thermos of coffee and a blanket and spent their days on the beach. While Ethan took a camera and searched for interesting pictures, Sarah lumbered around the dunes, digging an endless series of holes in pursuit of mysterious and unseen prey, but always came back to them disappointed and muddy. Emily sat on the blanket and tried her hand at drawing with pen and ink. But mostly, she found herself watching Ethan, and when he wasn't looking, she did a series of sketches of him.

Although the cottage was warmer than the boathouse, it was still chilly, and Ethan added yet another item to the list of things to do "come spring."

"Matt calls this place the 'Meat Locker,'" he observed, adding more logs to the fire. "But I never really minded the cold, and it *did* keep overnight guests to a minimum." He looked across the room at Emily and smiled. "Funny how I used to like that."

They fell into the habit of eating dinner in front of the big stone fireplace and ended many evenings making love on the deep shag rug before the blazing fire. When it rained heavily, the power often failed, and on those nights they piled extra quilts onto the antique four-poster for warmth and went to bed early. Then they lay in the dark and talked, listening to the rain pelting the cottage's increasingly frail roof.

"There is absolutely nothing more romantic than being in a soft, warm bed on a cold night with the sound of rain on the roof," Emily whispered into Ethan's ear. But Ethan was less moved.

"Romantic now, maybe. By morning, every bucket I set out will be overflowing. I found six leaks in the living room and kitchen tonight, and that's just since last year's patch job. Come spring, we'll need a new roof. You sure you don't want to drive into town tomorrow and look at a new house? Something built after Wilbur and Orville Wright—maybe with central heating, modern plumbing and a roof that doesn't require sleeping in a raincoat?"

She snuggled deeper under the covers. "Never! We're going to live in this cottage until we're old and gray and they come to carry us off to the home."

Ethan yawned. "Suit yourself, but when you step out of bed into a frozen puddle, you can't say you weren't warned."

In late March, with the boathouse warm enough to work in during the day, they drove to Bangor and found an art supply store.

Emily stood and gawked at the astonishing range of materials. "I don't know what to look at first," she admitted.

"Start with an easel," Ethan suggested. "You can put it in front of the big window, after I scrape ninety years of dried paint off the glass. How about this one?" He pointed to an enormous wooden framework. Emily looked at the tag and yelped.

"How about my old card table?" she whispered. "Did you see the price on that thing?"

Ethan glanced at the price tag. "Don't worry about it. If that's the one you like, take it." He walked around the sales floor and returned, pushing a rolling chair toward her. "You need a chair, too. This one goes up and down."

"I have a chair," she said.

"No, you have *my* kitchen chair, and I want it back. Sit down and try this one."

"It's over three hundred dollars!" she cried. "And that easel you like so much is almost six hundred. I can't let you spend a thousand bucks on all this. I'm not likely to make a cent for a year, maybe longer. Okay, let's face it. Maybe never. The stuff I've still got hanging at the Cozy Nook and sweet old Aunt Polly's isn't exactly flying off the walls."

Ethan motioned to the salesman. "I'm ready for lunch. Decide which ones you want, or I will. When we get home, I'll figure out a few interesting things you can do to pay me back. Then again, you could just stop feeling guilty about every dime you spend. I read somewhere that's what most wives *like* to do—spend their husbands' money. Look at it this way. I'm giving you the chance to start supporting *me*."

The new furniture and supplies were delivered three days later, and while Ethan assembled the chair and what she would always think of as The Six-Hundred-Dollar Easel, Emily put away her art materials and scraped the last of the paint from the big window overlooking the ocean.

She stepped back to study the completed room. "Everything is beautiful. Like a real studio."

Ethan smiled. "For a real artist." He kissed her once and walked out, but then called over his shoulder. "Paint something! We need the dough."

Emily set the big easel in front of the window and began to work again—slowly and unsurely at first, not even certain what she wanted to paint. It came back slowly, and her initial efforts were driven more by guilt about what Ethan had spent than genuine artistic passion. Finally, though, her first painting in almost two years began to take shape—a small likeness of the stone boathouse itself.

"It's not too bad," she said, cocking her head to look at it again as she showed it to Ethan. "But when I look at it again, I can see that the whole thing is crooked."

He chuckled. "It's a great painting and it's not crooked. The subject is." He picked up a metal T-square and handed it to her. "Go outside and stand at the edge of the yard, and check it out with this. You'll see what I mean."

She came back inside laughing. "You're right. I thought it was me. More repairs?"

"This thing's not worth fixing. I think you're stuck with what we've got. Just try leaning a little to starboard whenever you paint."

Before long, Emily felt the urge to paint returning, and she began to work again. When she had finished ten canvases—mostly seascapes—she placed them with a small gallery in Bar Harbor.

"Maybe this town will be lucky for me," she said as they pulled out of the gallery's parking lot. "It was once."

Two weeks later, the gallery called. They had sold five of the original ten.

Ethan took her to dinner to celebrate, and on the drive home, brought up a subject Emily had thought was closed for her.

"You liked my last couple of ideas pretty well," he said. "You know, moving here, then marrying me. Starting to paint again. Now I've got another one. Not right away, of course, but maybe next year sometime?"

"And what might this idea be?" she asked warily.

"I thought we'd ask Matt for a couple of names—specialists we could talk to—and see about producing an heir or heiress to this lavish estate we're building."

"I can't," she said simply.

"How sure are you of that?"

Emily shrugged. "Well, I was married for five years, and for most of that time, I didn't do anything to keep from getting pregnant."

Ethan was silent. "Did you ever see a doctor?" he asked, at last.

"Only one, and he was kind of indecisive. He suggested a couple of possibilities, but when things started getting worse between Dennis and me, I quit trying. I still didn't do anything to prevent it, though. It was like I was playing

Russian roulette, or maybe leaving the decision to God. Anyway, Mrs. Dinwiddie's lucky bed didn't do the trick, so if you're really serious about producing that heir or heiress, we may have to try a lot harder."

He smiled. "Well, the part about trying harder sounds good—say three or four times a day, in between all these construction projects we've started, and your painting?"

On the rest of the drive, they discussed names for the as-yet-unconceived child.

"We'll name him after you if it's a boy," Emily said firmly.

"I've never really liked the name Ethan. I always envied the kids with simple names, like Sam. Mom loved music, and she hoped I'd turn out like the biblical Ethan, a singer who played 'musick, psalteries, harps and cymbals.' Which accounts for the name *and* for the five years of wasted piano lessons. What if it's a girl?"

"Maybe Hannah?"

"That's good. Biblical names are always best. Reliable. Let's name the poor kid Ezekial or Zebulon. Maybe Hepzibah for a girl? What about Jochebed?"

Emily threw a folded road map at him.

When summer was in full bloom, Ethan set out to look for new photographs, and used the trip to show Emily the Maine he loved, from one end to the other. They packed camping equipment, made a place for Sarah in the back of the Jeep, and spent four glorious weeks on the road.

"Our second honeymoon," Emily laughed. "Even before our first anniversary."

And somehow, between the second honeymoon and

Emily's painting, the elaborate plans to remodel the cottage got put off again—until spring. They had been unable to recontact the carpenter Ethan had spoken with— the one he obviously wanted for the job—but with fall approaching, he decided one morning in early September that they had already delayed too long in getting to the irritating job of sanding and repainting the cottage's worn shutters.

"Everything else will wait until I can reach this Josh guy again," he said at breakfast. "All I get when I call is a recording that says they're closed until further notice. Next week, I'll drive into town and see what's going on, but in the meantime, those shutters and window frames won't wait. I want them to have a fresh coat of paint when they blow away again this winter. You ready to start?"

Emily yawned. "Do we have to do it today?"

"Yes, after I go out and make those adjustments you wanted on your easel. If we finish early enough, I'll take you to dinner and a movie."

The job of painting the shutters took longer than expected, and by midafternoon, they still hadn't finished. At around four o'clock, Ethan put one final brushful of blue paint on the next-to-last shutter, then dropped the paintbrush back in the can and sat down on the steps.

"Not fair," Emily cried. "I've already done the last window frame. The shutters are yours. That was the deal."

Ethan grinned. "So sue me. Cut an old guy some slack, will you? My head's killing me. Too many fumes, I guess. Sorry, but I've had it for today, babe. I'm going in to take a shower and sack out for a while. After you're done there, we'll try for that dinner and movie."

"Looking like this?" Emily asked, displaying her paint-spattered shirt and jeans. "I don't think so. Go ahead and lie down, you rat. I'll find something in the fridge for dinner and I'll even cook it. Woman's work is never done." She put her own brush away and came over to sit next to him. "You look terrible, by the way," she said fondly, wiping a smear of paint off his forehead.

"Thank you," he said. "You, on the other hand, look like roadkill. What's all the red from? Last time I checked, our window frames were white."

"I used the leftover enamel from the boathouse door to do a bunch of flower pots I found under the house. I'm going to try my hand at planting more geraniums."

"God help them," he said with a grin. He stood up then, and kissed the tip of Emily's nose. "I love you, you know."

Emily smiled. "I know. I love you, too, and that's why I'm going to be a wonderful wife and finish the last shutter for you. Go shower and get some rest, and decide what you want for dinner." Then, Ethan went inside the house and Emily went back to painting her flower pots—and the last blue shutter.

It was an hour before Emily put the finishing dab of slate-blue exterior enamel on the shutter and closed the paint can. It was almost dark now, and she desperately needed a hot shower and a nap, so she slipped off the old long-sleeved shirt she'd stolen from Ethan's closet and tossed it in the plastic trash bin on the deck. Ethan hadn't turned on the lights, and the house was cool and dark. He was still asleep on the bed, so she walked through the bedroom into the bathroom on tiptoe, trying not to wake him, and closed the door as she started the shower.

Ten minutes later, Emily emerged from the steaming shower rosy-skinned and warm. A glance at the clock on the bathroom wall told her they were about to miss the evening news, so she dried off quickly, wrapped herself in a big towel and went to wake Ethan.

He was still asleep, and after debating for a moment, she decided to let him rest. It was unusual for him to nap during the day, so she knew that he must have been exhausted. It had been a long week, and Emily was tired, as well. Suddenly, the idea of dinner seemed too much. She fished out a flannel nightgown from her dresser drawer, slipped it over her head, then very carefully pulled down the covers on her side of the bed. Hoping not to wake him, she crawled into bed—and accidentally kicked his leg.

Ethan didn't move.

Later, she would torture herself with regrets. If she had gone inside when he did, if she had skipped the long shower. If. If only…

It took the ambulance almost forty-five minutes to get to the cottage from town. During that time, Emily sat on the bed next to Ethan, holding his head in her lap and weeping. She kissed his face again and again, knowing in the part of her mind that was functioning clearly that there was no need for the ambulance to hurry. But there was still a part of her that hoped she was wrong, and that somehow, he was still alive. She'd tried CPR at first as well as she could remember how, but even as she worked over him, she knew it was useless. Ethan was gone. But as she waited those endless minutes for the ambulance to arrive, she began to pray to a God she wasn't sure she believed in, begging Him over and over and over—to please, please, let her be wrong.

Chapter 9

There would be no funeral. Ethan hadn't liked funerals, nor did Emily. They had both enjoyed strolling along the silent walkways of the old Quaker cemetery outside town, holding hands and reading the worn headstones, and Ethan had often remarked that being buried in such a place wouldn't be a bad way to spend eternity. But in the end, Emily was persuaded by something he'd said to her on her first visit to the cottage.

"I always liked the idea of being buried at sea, the way they used to do it two hundred years ago. Someone says a quick Bible verse and then tips you over the side with a final salute and a cannonball tied to your feet. On the other hand, I've been happier here than anywhere else in the world, so I'd settle for being scattered on this beach, too.

Everyone should end up where they've been the happiest while they were still alive. Of course, if I ever come back as a ghost, it'll have to be in the cottage, so I can finish up all the repair jobs I never got around to."

They'd both laughed about it then, but when Emily signed the papers for cremation, she knew in her heart that she'd done what Ethan would have wanted. His ashes would be scattered at the evening tide along the beach he had loved so well, just below the cottage—except for the small portion that Emily would spread on the roots of the rebellious white rosebush he'd tried to train around the doorway for twelve years, without success.

They would have celebrated their first anniversary in three weeks.

The autopsy had shown that Ethan's death was an intracerebral hemorrhage—caused by what Matthew called an AVM—a congenital defect that had probably lain undetected for years. Everyone assured her that there was nothing she could have done, but it would be years before Emily stopped asking herself the same painful questions about all of the small, sad details of that last day. She knew without asking that Matt blamed himself for not having insisted on a further exploration of the episode Ethan had suffered several years earlier.

The memorial was quiet and simple. Aside from the O'Connells, Ethan had no family other than two distant cousins with whom he'd never kept in close touch. Herb Denning and his wife flew in from California, along with Ethan's editors from Portland and New York, and a number of people from town. Maggie's brother Alan, an attorney and longtime friend, came—then stayed to help Emily go through the masses of paperwork that threatened to over-whelm her.

The phone rang constantly, and after the newspapers picked up the story, several magazines asked for inter-views, which Emily politely declined. Two of them, however, made mention of the "scandal" during their requests, and Maggie took the phone and turned the air blue with obscenities as she detailed what they could do with their "filthy, rotten yellow rags." It was the only time anyone heard Emily laugh during that first difficult month.

Flowers and tributes arrived—mostly from California, but a few from New York and London, and two from a playwright and a writer Emily didn't know in Paris. Ethan's old movie studio sent an enormous wreath in the shape of California, and there were perhaps a dozen smaller ones from colleagues in Hollywood. Maggie sent all of the flowers to the nearest children's hospital.

After the first week, everyone but Maggie went home. Emily sat on the deck for much of each day, or at the front window seat, watching the ocean for hours on end. Maggie left her alone for the most part, trying not to intrude. But when two weeks had passed and Emily showed no sign of emerging from the silent, walled-in place she'd created for herself, Maggie intervened. When she insisted that Emily eat, Emily ate, and when she was asked to help around the house, she obeyed, moving about in a waxen manner that alarmed Maggie and prompted her to call Matthew O'Con-nell.

Matt arrived with Kate in tow, and immediately took

over. While Kate bustled around, opening windows and laundering everything in sight, he forced Emily to walk with him on the beach, then stuck her in the car and went for a long drive up the coast. During the drive, he said what he'd come to say.

"What's happened to you is bad, Emily. It stinks, and it's not fair, and there's not a damned thing in the world me or anyone else can do or say to make it any better or any easier—except this. If Ethan was here, he wouldn't stand for any of this crap you're pulling. He'd haul you up out of that chair and drag you outside into the fresh air. He'd make you comb your hair and wash it once in a while, and make you put on something besides that frumpy robe you've been walking around in. And there'd be hell to pay if you didn't!

"Okay. He's not here, but I am, and if he was here he'd be mad as hell at *me* for letting you get away with it for this long. So listen up, 'cause here's what's going to happen now. First, you're going to go home and take a bath. And then you're going to call your mother, and start keeping in touch with the people who care about you—like me and Kate. And after that, you're going to get up off your butt and start helping poor Maggie, who's been making herself sick worrying about you for weeks. And if you *don't* straighten up, I'm getting ready to put you in the damned hospital, strap you to a bed and feed you through a tube if I have to."

Matthew O'Connell mad was not a man to ignore, nor to take lightly, and Emily knew very well that if he deemed it necessary, she would be in that hospital within the hour, just as he'd promised.

* * *

The next day, Emily got out of bed early and showered, and before anyone could stop her, she took the car and headed for town.

Matthew decided not to follow her, nor would he permit anyone else to do so, and an hour and a half later, Emily arrived safely back at the cottage.

"I needed some air," she explained. "And to do a little shopping. I'm going to take a nap now, if it's all right with everyone."

She appeared at dinner, looking weak but smiling wanly.

"I've been a pain and a nuisance," she announced. "And I'm sorry. You've all been wonderful, and I'll never be able to thank you enough for being here and for putting up with me. But I'm all right now, and I want you to go home. I'll be fine, I swear, and I won't be any more trouble." She turned to Matt. "Matthew, before you go, can I see you alone in the bedroom?"

As Matthew followed Emily into the bedroom, Maggie and Kate exchanged worried glances.

They came out a few minutes later and stood in the hallway, talking quietly. Matt took a pen and pad from his jacket pocket and wrote something on a prescription pad.

"You get in there as quick as you can," he said, handing the slip of paper to Emily. "I'll call him as soon as I get home, and let him know you're coming. You have Maggie drive you in the first time, you hear me?"

Emily nodded, and smiled. Matthew turned to the nervous bystanders.

"What are you both gawking at? The damned stick turned blue, that's all. It looks like this girl just might be pregnant."

The next morning, with the cottage all to herself, Emily wandered around, touching something now and then—Ethan's things, mostly. She would sell the cottage as quickly as she could, of course, but it was still desperately in need of repairs, and that would slow any potential sale. As difficult as it was for her to think of other people living here, the idea of spending each day among so many lingering memories of Ethan seemed unimaginable. When Maggie insisted that Emily stay with her until the cottage was sold, she accepted the invitation gratefully, hoping to find a place closer to her best friend. But first, she would have to face the painful task of clearing away what remained of her life here, and of Ethan's life—and of everything they'd shared in the little beach house.

She'd found his wallet and a scattering of change on the dresser and the unfinished model ship he'd been working on sat on the desk by the window, half-masted. The pipe he'd given up smoking years earlier rested on the mantel, and the book he was reading the night before he died lay open on the small table by the fireplace. Not now, but someday very soon, she would have to go through everything in the house, deciding what to keep, what to give away and what to discard entirely. It wasn't a task she could face immediately, but it would have to be done.

When she picked up Ethan's book, several photographs fell from between the pages. She bent down and carefully collected them, then sat in the rocker and spread them on her lap. The photos were old, their fragile corners yellowed with age, and at first, she didn't recognize anyone in them. But as she studied the pictures more closely, she realized that the boy in the largest photograph had to be Ethan. He was perhaps nine or ten, sitting cross-legged in deep grass with a mixed-breed dog over his lap. Emily smiled and turned the picture over to look at the back, where someone had written in a neat, teacherly hand: *Ethan Andrew Douglas, Rockland, summer, 1938.*

He had told her about Kathleen, the dog in the picture, shortly after they moved into the house. A dog he'd loved dearly that had died of cancer. She couldn't recall now exactly why the subject of memories had come up that day, but she remembered the story clearly, and if Emily had believed in such things, she would have sworn that Ethan had purposely left these pictures for her to find.

"We called her Kathleen because we found her on St. Patrick's Day," he'd told her. "She was just a pup, and nothing but skin and bones. She was always my dog, right from the start. Four years later, when I was around ten, she got sick. We did everything we could to save her, but my mom sat me down one day and explained that soon Kathleen was going to be in terrible pain, and then I'd have to let her go. It was the first time I had to watch something I loved die, and I was taking it pretty bad, so Mom told me to try to memorize Kathleen while she was still with us— everything that I loved, down to the last detail. That way, I'd always be able to bring her back when I needed to."

He chuckled. "All that summer, I nearly drove the poor

dog nuts—touching her, burying my face in her coat to remember how she always smelled dusty, like the grass in the front yard. I wanted to remember the rough feel of her paws, and how silky her ears were, and how one of them never stood up right, and how she sat under my feet and howled whenever Mom made me practice the piano. She died that fall, and I learned that Mom was right. For years after she was gone I could still remember every single thing about her, and that felt good. It still does. Sad sometimes, but good."

Emily slipped the old photographs back into the book and closed it. She picked up the pipe from the mantel and held it closer to smell the faint aroma of charred wood and good tobacco, thinking back to that first day in the cottage. It had never occurred to her that Ethan smoked, since he'd never done so in her presence.

"I quit smoking twenty years ago, but I carried it around with me for a couple of years after that, like a prop. This pipe used to be a very large part of my persona. The studio thought it gave me a romantic air, like a country gentleman or maybe a salty sea captain. Remember Rex Harrison in *The Ghost and Mrs. Muir?* What do you think?" He stuck the pipe in the corner of his mouth at a rakish angle.

Emily had taken the pipe and sniffed it. She wrinkled her nose and placed it back on the mantel.

"Sorry, Rex. It still stinks."

Alongside the pipe were two additional photographs, but both of these were already familiar to Emily. They'd been in the same spot when she moved in, and she'd looked at them every time she dusted the room. The

first, very old and badly cracked, showed the cottage
when it was new. An improbably tall, bearded old man
in a frock coat and celluloid collar posed stiff and un-
smiling on the deck. The retired whaling Captain Enoch
Birdsong, presumably. He held a small American flag
and stood behind an Adirondack chair in which sat a
rather stout, dour-faced woman. The woman, probably
Mrs. Enoch Birdsong, was some years younger, and
dressed in an extravagantly crimped and pleated dress
with leg-o-mutton sleeves. She wore a ridiculously
small, flat straw hat adorned with artificial cherries.
Surrounding her chair were several young girls of
varying ages, each in the modest and primly flounced
bathing costumes of the period. Along the edge of the
picture was written the simple phrase: E.B. and
Family—July 4,1899.

Next to this photo was another—a younger Ethan on the
same deck in a pair of ragged cutoff jeans and a sweatshirt
that read *UCB*. He was smiling broadly into the sun, bran-
dishing a hammer in one hand and a bottle of beer in the
other. On the back of the photo, he had written, Herb and
me, attempting the impossible—Summer 1968. Ethan was
the only figure in the photo, and Emily assumed that the
unseen Herb Denning had taken it—possibly seconds
before he fell through the rotting planks of the deck.

Emily went outside and sat on the steps for a long time,
watching the ocean and the gulls. Finally, she got up and
went back into the house, picked up the picture of Ethan
from the mantel and dusted it with her sleeve. Then, she
rolled up her shirtsleeves and began to remove things from

the large cardboard box she'd just finished packing. She didn't need to move. She was already home.

Maggie, of course, threw a fit.

"You're not going to stay out here, all alone?" she cried when Emily delivered the news over coffee one morning.

Emily nodded stubbornly. "It's my house, and Ethan wouldn't have wanted it sold."

"Emily, this stupid house is not exactly the Douglas ancestral estate. He told me he bought it fifteen years ago from Walt Thornberry over at Surf Realty. Some yuppie couple from Connecticut was unloading it because the roof had blown away, and because they were fed up with living at the edge of the known world, without even *cable,* for God's sake! Before that, who knows who..."

"He bought it for me, Maggie," Emily said quietly.

Maggie stared. "He what?"

"It's a long story."

"Okay." Maggie tried again. "Overlooking the obvious fact that Ethan Douglas didn't even know you existed when he bought this dump, how about this? Don't sell the thing, just rent it out, if you can find some idiot dumb enough to risk his life living out here. Then buy a nice little condo in town, or near me—something modern, with central heating and a few bloody neighbors? Ethan left you very well fixed, sweetie, and I'm sure he didn't plan for you to spend the rest of your life waiting to be washed out to sea like a damned beachball."

"The cottage has been here for a hundred years," Emily pointed out.

"That is *not* a good argument, Emily Anne. All that means is the place is even closer to death than I thought. Houses don't live forever."

Emily smiled. "That's what Ethan always said. But this one's still alive, and Sam and I are going to live in it. I have the studio, and work to do and Sarah for company."

"Who the hell is Sam?" Maggie interrupted, eyeing her friend with interest.

"Samuel Ethan Douglas—what we decided to call the baby."

"You don't even know if it's a boy."

"It had better be a boy, because its…*his* name is going to be Samuel."

Maggie grinned and shook her head. "Samantha, maybe?"

"There will be no negative thinking, here, my friend. The name is Samuel Ethan, and that's that."

"What's wrong with girls, anyway?" Maggie protested. "What happened to all that women's liberation stuff you've always spouted?"

"There's nothing wrong with girls, but you can't go around naming them Samuel Ethan, now can you?"

"Samuel means 'gift of God,' right?" Maggie asked. When Emily looked surprised, Maggie sighed. "Hey, I didn't spend six years in Hebrew school for nothing."

"I think it's more like *'asked of God,'*" Emily said.

"I thought you didn't believe in God."

"I may be rethinking my position. Anyway, Ethan believed, sort of."

"So, you're going to camp out here like an Old Testament prophet and what? Contemplate your navel? You and

Ethan had each other, sweetie. You'll be lonely as hell out here by yourself."

"I'll have work to do, and Sam to take care of. And since Ethan died, poor Sarah won't let me out of her sight. For the first two weeks, she lay on his side of the bed every night and whined. Now she's started sleeping under the covers with me."

Maggie hesitated before bringing up the next subject. "Well, I know it's too early to start thinking about this now, and I'm really not as insensitive as this is probably going to sound, but what about men—eventually?"

"What about them?"

"Don't be coy. Ethan Douglas was a hot property, in more ways than one, if you'll pardon my being crude, and he brought you back from that self-enforced spinsterhood you'd fallen into. I hate to tell you this, Em, but take it from an expert. Good sex is addictive. You can't go back to living like a nun."

"Fine," Emily snapped. "When I'm ready, I'll call you, and we can hit all the scummy biker bars out on the highway." She regretted the words instantly and plopped down on the couch with her head in her hands. "That was really low, Maggie. I'm sorry. I didn't mean…"

Maggie sat down next to her friend and patted her hand. "No offense taken, but mostly, I'm into line-dancing and cowboys, not bikers." She poked Emily playfully in the ribs. "Anyway, just ignore me. I always talk too much. Besides, do you really think I want to drag some waddling, whining pregnant nun around with me, cramping my style? Now, are you really, *really* sure about this—staying here?"

Emily nodded. "I'm sure. I don't think I've ever been so sure of anything in my life, except for marrying Ethan. This is my home, and his, and it's going to be Sam's home, too—until it blows away, anyway." She winked.

Emily left the last thing until Maggie had gone. Ethan would want her to do this alone.

She sat by the window and waited until the sun was almost gone, then took the small white box and made her way barefoot across the dunes, through the tall grass, and down to the beach. She walked slowly, shivering in the autumn chill, then sat down and buried her feet in the sand to wait for the tide. The shallow ripples swept farther up the beach with each incoming wave, each one depositing its gleaming arc of foam closer to where she sat. She remembered a line from a poem by Rupert Brooke that described "the little dulling edge of foam that browns and dwindles as the wave goes home," but when she tried to remember the rest of the words, they eluded her.

When the first ripples of foam touched her feet, Emily reached down to open the box. Closing her eyes, she placed her fingertips very gently on the surface of the ashes inside, then slid her hand deeper, rolling the coarse grains between her fingers. They didn't feel like sand, as she had expected, but like what? Pebbles? No, more like crushed oyster shells. She smiled, knowing somehow that Ethan would have liked that.

With the light fading quickly now, Emily knew it was time. The water was bitterly cold as she walked out into the surf, and the strong bottom current swirled about her legs, stealing away the sand from underfoot and making it difficult to stand. She held the box tightly to her breast and tried to ignore the cold, concentrating instead on keeping her footing until she was farther from the beach.

Her legs were numb by the time she stood waist-deep in the incoming surf with the waves lapping gently at her upper body. With great care, Emily opened the box and took some of the contents into her right hand.

She cast the first of Ethan's ashes to the east, using all her strength to fling them in a wide arc over the water. Then, turning slightly, she threw several handfuls in a direction she imagined as west. In the pale moonlight, the ashes formed a ghostlike mist as they drifted back down, floating on the swell of the ocean for a moment before slipping beneath the surface. She continued until the box was more than half empty, then closed it, careful not to let the tide take it from her stiff fingers.

Slipping one hand under the water, she reached into the pocket of her long skirt to locate the small shell Ethan had found on the beach all those months before—on the night he asked her to marry him. It had lain on her bedside table since that night, and now it would go with Ethan.

When her fingers curled around the shell, she had to fight back a sudden flood of tears that threatened to interfere with the task she had yet to finish. She drew the shell out of the water, and opened her hand, watching it shimmer in the moonlight the way it had that first night, a tiny rainbow of delicate, translucent colors.

Emily closed her eyes again and pressed the shell briefly to her lips. Then, before she could change her mind, she hurled it as far out across the incoming waves as she could, and turned quickly back to the beach.

As she emerged from the ocean, she opened the box once more and walked along the beach to the spot where Ethan had proposed, allowing the remaining ashes to slip slowly through her fingers onto the sand. She knelt then, and filled the box with sand before continuing down the beach, spilling the mixture of sand and ash behind her. Later, she would start a fire in the living-room fireplace, place the box in the flames, and watch until it burned to nothing.

It was done now, and life would go on—a different life than she had dreamed of, but life nonetheless. A life no longer for Ethan, but for the child sleeping warm and safe inside her. For Sam.

Emily went to the beach again at dawn, trying not to think about the small part of Ethan that still lingered on the sand. The tide had swept the beach clean, of course, but somehow, the sand felt different beneath her bare feet. As she turned to go back to the house, her toe struck something hard, and Emily smiled, already knowing what it was.

She bent down to pull the little shell from the sand, closing her eyes as she felt for the two chipped spots she knew would be there. Then, slipping the rainbow shell into her pocket, she walked on. She had things to do at home.

Chapter 10

Josh

The Douglas cottage was located more than a half mile off the county highway, on Cooper's Island, which wasn't an island at all, but a narrow spit of land jutting out into the channel. The area was isolated, reachable only by the rutted dirt road that meandered between the dunes until it intersected with a two-lane strip of pavement named—rather grandly—Ocean Boulevard. Once at the crossroads, one could turn either left or right—with the same result. The road began in the outskirts of Dunlin Cove, made a five-mile loop of the "island," and ended back where it started.

The village consisted of perhaps a dozen year-round businesses and a somewhat larger number that opened in the late spring—for the tourists—and closed again in the fall. These seasonal shops were mainly of the arts-and-crafts variety, and when they were shuttered, the clapboard buildings gave the village the sort of rustic, unprosperous appearance that visitors found quaint.

Dunlin Cove's year-rounders bought their basic groceries and provisions at Kerrigan's Mini-Market and their immediate household needs at Duff's Hardware. There were a couple of stores that serviced the few fishermen who still worked the local waters, but for a substantial shopping excursion, it was necessary to cross the bridge into the modern portion of the island, that area usually called simply "town." Here, once could find a national chain supermarket, banks and a fair-size department store. Four restaurants did good business, there were two car dealerships just outside town and a couple of boatwrights still made a respectable living down by the water. Up the street from the boat builders was the small lumberyard belonging to Lundgren and Son General Contracting.

Lundgren General Contracting wasn't a big business by off-island standards, but it had been here for more than fifty years and enjoyed a reputation for doing quality work at a fair price.

Joshua Lundgren had been running the business since his father, George, was forced to retire. Josh ran the business with two regulars now, hiring what seasonal help he needed, while his mother, Grace, handled the office. Grace juggled her time making appointments, doing the books and spending as much time as she could at the nursing home where her husband had lived for three years, fading from Alzheimer's.

Josh Lundgren had inherited his father's tall, blond good looks and his mother's quiet, steady manner. Raised by devout Lutheran parents, he had stopped going to church years earlier, but he'd been left with a profound unspoken faith in God that he rarely thought about and couldn't have explained. An unassuming but steadfast and able craftsman, Josh took the same stubborn pride in his work that his father had—seeing to it that every job he took on was done as well he could do it. His true love was carpentry and cabinetry and he left as many of the business details to his mother as he reasonably could, preferring to be at every work site rather than in the office with a calculator in hand and a telephone at his ear. This attitude pleased his mother more than Josh knew. She had seen the same drive for perfection in Josh's father. Her son looked amazingly like his father, and as Grace Lundgren watched her only child laboring with such passion and intensity at his chosen trade, it was like watching her own husband as a young man.

Josh used what little spare time he had designing and building furniture, and what pieces didn't fill his own or Grace's home, he sold to quality decorators in Boston. But Joshua Lundgren's truest passion was building homes—houses for families. As a child, he'd wanted to be both a stonemason and a sailor, and he loved studying the countless old stone walls that seemed to be everywhere in New England. Stones dug out of the hard, uncompromising earth through backbreaking labor and transformed into sturdy structures that would last a lifetime and beyond.

Today, no one could remember who'd built most of these

walls, and it was almost certain that the stonemasons had not fancied themselves artists. But when he passed these rugged old walls, Josh Lundgren marveled at the unknown craftsmen's mastery of their art. Employing simple tools, and working with difficult and cumbersome materials, they'd managed to create something graceful and enduring—things that served a homely but vital purpose. Beauty, form and function all in one place—like a well-built house, Josh believed. A praiseworthy house. An admirable house.

Josh was happy in his work and in his life. Almost two years earlier, he'd married Annie, whom he'd met when they were both nine years old, digging clams at Shell Beach. He'd fallen instantly in love with her, even when she pelted him with mud, wet sand and at least one good-size clam. By junior high, they were "going steady," and even got briefly engaged while Annie was away at nursing school in New Hampshire. Josh made the twelve-hour round trip there every weekend for three years, creeping into her dorm at night while her roommate considerately slipped away to her own boyfriend's room.

Succumbing to his second great passion—the sea— Josh had left college in his second year to join the Coast Guard. Annie went on with nursing school, and though they continued to write, life took Josh and Annie in very different directions for a while, and it seemed their separation would be permanent. But then George Lundgren fell ill and Josh Lundgren came home to Dunlin Cove.

Shortly after he came back to help Grace with the business, Josh ran into Annie downtown, Christmas shopping, and the years seemed to drop away. In March of the following year, they married and moved into the two-bedroom bungalow Josh had built with his own hands. The house had a view of the sea and a low stone wall around the tiny yard, and with Annie there, it was everything Josh had ever wanted.

Now Annie was pregnant. "Big with child," Annie called it, after reading the phrase in one of the medieval romance novels she kept piled by the bed. "I am grown large in girth with milord's child and heir." She took his hand and pressed it to her stomach. "I fear milord's heir may emerge a football punter rather than a poet, as I wished."

Even as a boy, Josh's sense of right and wrong had caused him to be troubled by the problem of pain—why good people were so often struck down by tragedy, while others, good *and* bad, were spared. His parents had always led decent, charitable lives, only to lose what should have been their best years to a devastating illness that had made his mother old before her time. Josh had that curious Scandinavian tendency to melancholy and introspection, and he sometimes struggled with the guilty question of what he had done to deserve the happiness he'd found with Annie.

Annie was at the end of her sixth month now, just beginning to walk with the slightly awkward gait of a pregnant woman. Four days earlier, at Josh's insistence, she'd left her job to wait for the baby at home.

"I don't knit," she'd complained. "And we both know my sentiments about being a happy homemaker. What am I supposed to do all day?"

Josh had smiled and handed her a magazine. "Walk, read, sleep, take it easy and keep your feet up. Doctor Edgars says they're swelling too much."

"That's because I'm already a big, fat cow," Annie said glumly. "And now you want me to sit here on my big, fat cow's rear end and do nothing but read magazines for three solid months?"

"He says you were working too hard," Josh said firmly.

"Well, he ought to know," she grumbled. "I see more of him than I do of you. You've been so busy since I quit the hospital, I *never* see you. I may have to get myself a hard hat and start going to work with you every day."

Josh laughed. "Sounds great to me. Of course, you'd have to get up at four in the morning."

"Never mind." She leafed idly through a pile of papers on Josh's desk and picked up a small sketch. "This one looks new. Are you building it?"

Josh shook his head. "No, it's one of those old summer places out on the end of the island. I went out there a couple of months back and gave the owner an estimate on remodeling it. I'm going to get started with it come spring. The house is over a hundred years old, so it's going to be a pretty big job. The good news is, it could make the down payment on that bigger house you want."

"Like I don't know *that's* a big fat lie! You love playing around with those old beach places. You probably tried to talk the poor man out of modern plumbing and electricity! And I'll bet you ten bucks the wife, if there is one, doesn't even have a washer and dryer."

"I don't know about that," Josh said. "This guy's got

money. He used to be in the movies. Anyway, he gave me a nice deposit. So, sit down, put your feet up and think about where you want the kitchen in the new house. I'll be back later."

That evening after dinner, Josh described the cottage project to Annie as they watched a football game. Football bored Annie, and before long, she was expressing an overwhelming need for fudge brownie ice cream.

Josh raised an eyebrow. "Is that on the diet?"

Annie scowled at him. "I've been good all week, stuck in this house all day, and I want ice cream. Besides, we need a couple of other things, too—milk, bread, etc. I've got a whole list. My car's still in the garage, so hand over the keys to the truck, or I leave you for the first Good Humor man that drives by."

Josh stretched his arms above his head and yawned. "I'll go," he said. "It's getting dark. Just give me a second to get my boots back on."

Annie snatched at the keys on the table, but missed. "You know I hate football, and besides, you've been up since five this morning and all I've done today is vegetate. Put your feet up and watch the game, and I'll be back in a few minutes. And yes, sire, I'll use my seat belt, drive carefully, lock the car doors, and watch out for all the idiot drivers on the road. Anything else, or did I remember all the usual instructions?"

Josh grinned. "Okay, catch." He tossed her the keys, and looked at his watch. "In fifteen minutes, though, I call the cops and report the truck stolen. And don't back into the mailbox on your way out. If I find even one scratch on the new paint job tomorrow morning, you're in big trouble."

"I think you like that stupid truck better than me," she said sweetly, kissing the top of his head.

"No, but the new fender and paint job on *your* car is costing us almost as much as the obstetrician. One more flattened mailbox and we may have to sell the kid when it gets here."

"Very funny. Anyway, it wasn't my fault. The mailbox was leaning out into the driveway."

"And why was that?" he asked, laughing. "Maybe because you ran over it the day before?"

"If you start making women driver jokes, it's over between us, Joshua Lundgren," Annie threatened.

"Okay. No women driver jokes. Make sure to get back in time for the news, so I don't start worrying."

"I love you, even if you are a male chauvinist," she said.

"I love you, too, but I'm missing the game. Go!"

Annie waved goodbye, grabbed her sweater and rushed out the front door, leaving her list behind on the hall table where Josh would find it three days later.

After Annie left, Josh watched the game while finishing his beer. He woke up to the sound of the front doorbell, unaware that he'd been sleeping for over an hour. As he got up to go to the door, his first thought was that Annie had forgotten her wallet again.

When he opened the door, two state policemen were standing there. There'd been a robbery at the StopQuik— and a shooting.

* * *

The baby girl had died instantly when the teenage thief's first bullet penetrated Annie's abdomen. Annie struggled to hold on to her own life for three more days, and then simply stopped breathing while Josh was holding her hand and talking to her. When she died, a beeper sounded and a large green question mark appeared on the screen above her bed. Two nurses and a doctor hurried Josh and his mother from the room and worked for twenty minutes to bring Annie back, but failed. It was ten days before Christmas.

Josh and Grace drove back to the house in silence, and while Grace went inside, Josh locked the car and walked up the driveway to straighten the mailbox. It hadn't been quite right since the last time Annie backed over it. He knelt down to check the wooden post and saw it needed fresh concrete. Josh shoved the post in as deep as he could with his bare hands, then tried to stand up. When his legs went weak, he collapsed on his knees in the damp earth, weeping helplessly. Inside the house, a heartbroken Grace heard the wrenching sounds of her son's grief, but she knew not to go to him. Like his father before him, Josh would do his mourning alone. Grace also knew that after tonight, she would never see him cry again.

She sat on the couch by the front window and watched until his shoulders stopped heaving, and after a while, saw him get to his feet and walk stiffly to the garage. Soon, she heard the faucet running at the side of the house. In the freezing weather and almost total darkness, Josh was mixing cement.

Three months later, Josh's truck was traveling on a narrow county road when it careered off a bridge, overturned and came to rest in a deep, half-frozen creek ten miles from town. The state troopers who dragged him from the stream, barely alive, his skull fractured, were puzzled how an excellent driver like Josh Lundgren, cold sober and in broad daylight, could have misjudged a turn he'd made almost every day of his adult life.

Chapter 11

By the end of March, Maggie was calling Emily every day to insist she move in with her, or into town, or closer to Matthew and Kate—anywhere but in the isolated cottage. Emily was getting the same advice from her doctor, and from Matt and Kate, and had promised each of them—on different occasions and with slightly different lies—that she would make such a move "when the time was right."

Maggie took matters into her own hands by arriving at the cottage every weekend, uninvited. On one of these visits, she walked in on Emily's newest obsession—encouraging in Sam an appreciation for the music of his father's ancestors. She found Emily lying flat on her back with a portable tape player resting on her stomach. She was singing, and pressing the earphones against her abdomen.

"Folk songs," Emily explained. "Scottish, mostly."

Maggie sat on the edge of the bed. "You're nuts, of course. The kid will still probably pop out a fan of acid rock and martial-arts movies."

Emily grinned and shrugged. "It can't hurt. I've shown him all of Ethan's movies, too."

"Does he have a favorite?"

"He has very discriminating taste, actually. He agrees with me—*The Trail Home,* hands down."

"Yeah, well, this is all great fun, sweetie, but when are you moving to town? You're getting pretty close to blast-off, you know. What if you go into labor early? I can only drive so fast, and what happens if there's another bad storm, like the one last week?"

But Emily had no intention of moving anywhere. Not now. Something had happened during that storm that she couldn't explain, and that she didn't want to talk about yet. For the second time in her life, an unexpected storm had changed everything.

The storm had come up suddenly that morning, and after watching the weather report, Emily had decided against trying to reach Kate and Matt's. Matt wasn't happy, but he finally agreed that staying inside was better than being caught on the road during the worst of it. At that point, there seemed nothing to worry about other than the line of dark clouds far over the water. She would sit it out.

By early afternoon, though, she was regretting that decision. The clouds changed to a dense fog that hung low on the beach, a wall of cold, steady rain. The beach had disappeared into the fog, but she could hear the muffled boom of each incoming breaker, and feel the worn pilings shudder beneath the deck as the waves broke higher up the beach—edging closer to the cottage.

Emily knew that the surf wasn't the only problem. The rising wind was already strong enough to threaten both her and the cottage. Wind-driven patches of ugly brown foam had begun to float through the air, tumbling across the deck and splattering against the trembling glass of the picture window like bugs on a windshield.

When she stepped onto the deck, the wind was whistling around the corners of the house, slamming the shutters back and forth with a deafening clatter. The aging plywood had begun to warp and splinter, and the blue paint she and Ethan had applied months earlier peeled off in big chalky flakes as she struggled to close the heavy old shutters.

Emily had never been through a hurricane or a gale, but she knew without being told that getting the shutters closed was urgent. The wind was so strong that standing was difficult, and she slipped and fell several times on the wet deck. Flying sand stung her hands and face, making it nearly impossible to see what she was doing.

When the wind gusted, it slapped branches and slick tangles of uprooted kelp across the deck, till even walking was hazardous. She was getting nowhere, and the wind was increasing steadily. Each time she grasped a shutter, the wind ripped it from her hands. Finally, wet, cold and exhausted, Emily stumbled back inside, slumped to the floor and sat with her back against the door in a puddle of water, breathing hard and stroking her stomach to comfort Sam.

Emily knew she wouldn't be able to secure the shutters by herself, and as she visualized the rain coming through the broken window and wreaking havoc on the room she and Ethan had loved so much, she broke into tears, then fell asleep, too tired to care any longer.

She woke after a few minutes, dazed and sore, but feeling stronger and more determined. She got to her feet and went outside again, equipped this time with an enormous pipe wrench she'd found under the kitchen sink. The shutters were still flailing wildly, crashing against the house, in imminent danger of tearing loose. She grabbed the edge of the shutter and turned around to get her back against it, but the wind threw her forward into the deck railing. She held on, terrified of toppling over the edge. Being dumped repeatedly on her backside probably wouldn't harm the baby, but plummeting to the beach below was something she didn't want to risk.

But as she clung to the railing, afraid to let go, the impossible happened. The shutters began to close by themselves, edging slowly on their rusted moorings back toward the window. Mystified, Emily watched in disbelief for several seconds, then rushed across the deck and shoved the L-shaped bolts into their slots. She hammered each of the bolts firmly into place with the old wrench and had no sooner finished securing the large window when the flapping shutters on the smaller kitchen window performed the same astonishing feat, closing of their own accord. When the kitchen shutters were closed, Emily stood with the wind shrieking around her and stared, unable to believe what she'd seen.

Ducking inside, she sank breathlessly to the floor again, her arms numb with cold and her hands scratched and bleeding. She was coated from head to toe in gritty sand and flaked paint, and brackish water streamed from her hair. Another shingle ripped loose from the roof, and even through her fatigue, Emily noticed with amusement that the sound was like a giant bag of potato chips being torn open.

The furnace had gone off earlier that afternoon, and now the lights flickered and dimmed, threatening to leave her without light. As the room grew steadily colder, Emily dragged every blanket in the house onto the couch, passing the remainder of the night huddled there, soothing Sam and sharing four cans of Vienna sausage with the always ravenous Sarah. She had discovered that she and Ethan's dog shared a personality quirk. When frightened, they ate.

She tried concentrating on what would need to be done when the storm had passed, and tried *not* to think about what had happened earlier. With Sarah snuggled against her stomach, Emily fell asleep and dreamed of Ethan and of summer.

By two that morning, the wind had subsided, but the downpour was still torrential. It was impossible to see the beach through the impenetrable curtain of rain, but from the sound, Emily knew that the water was coming dangerously close. She returned to the couch, pulled the several quilts and blankets over her own head and Sarah's and drifted back to sleep.

She was awakened by what she thought was Sarah nuzzling her cheek. "Go to sleep, baby," she murmured into the darkness. "It'll be over soon." When she sat up, though, she saw that Sarah wasn't on the couch, but across the room, cowering under the piano. Emily touched her cheek curiously and shook her head. All in all, it had been a very strange night.

It was another full day before the storm moved inland. The phone was still out, but late that morning, Matt managed to get down the beach road to the cottage, and together, he and Emily walked around the cottage to survey the damage. The dunes were stripped bare, and the water had come up under the house, leaving great swoops and arcs of slimy brown foam in the sand and piles of snarled kelp against the foundation. The beach was strewn with vegetation and bits of sodden wood, some of which Emily recognized as broken shingles from the roof. The strip of wood that held the old deck awning to the house had been torn away, and days later, she found it half-buried on the beach, with shreds of the faded canvas still attached. One less job to take care of, she thought wearily.

Yet, with all its fresh wounds, the sturdy little cottage had survived.

With the emergency over, Emily sat down and tried to recall every detail of what had happened to her on the deck. Unless she was ready to believe she was seeing things, she could think of only one other explanation for what she'd seen—or *thought* she'd seen. Two weeks earlier, this explanation would have seemed ridiculous. But the incident on the deck was only one of several puzzling things that had occurred.

And with each succeeding occurrence, Emily had become more convinced that she was not alone in the cottage.

Since Ethan's death, Emily had tried to be patient, because that was what Ethan would have wanted. Everything she'd read about grief promised that the worst of the pain would recede, given time. But as the days of her widowhood turned to weeks, everything became harder, not easier.

Each morning, she woke up exhausted, then struggled out of bed with only one thought—to somehow get through the long, lonely hours that stretched out before her. And at night, unable to sleep, she was often overwhelmed by despair, knowing that the next day would be the same, and the next, and the next. Maggie and the O'Connells were wonderful, and at least one of them called or visited every day. Helene phoned every evening without fail, begging her to come to Los Angeles. But Emily knew that if she was to recover, it would be here, where she was near Ethan.

She thought of suicide occasionally, especially in the long, quiet evenings, but the thought was always brief, and she pushed it from her mind by talking to Sam. She talked to the baby constantly now, telling him everything she could remember about Ethan—all the lovely and funny moments she had stored away. And as she described Ethan's smile or the color of his eyes or the way he had of tilting his head to one side to listen when she talked, she found herself awash in small memories she hadn't even known were there—textures and sounds, and the way the wind smelled the first time they walked along the beach together in the rain. Everything came back, just as Ethan had promised it would.

Like daydreams, though, the memories were ultimately unsatisfying, but they were better than the pain, and she began to spend more of each day in the old rocker, thinking and remembering. She found the key to the boathouse, still lying on the mantel where she'd left it, then walked through the weeds in the neglected yard to unlock the bright red door that Ethan had finished painting the day before he died.

Everything was where they'd left it that last day—her art materials still neatly arranged on the shelves and The Six-Hundred-Dollar Easel at the window. Emily smiled as she ran her hands over the easel's sleek walnut surface, remembering the day Ethan bought it over her objections. As she moved it closer to the window, she noticed a yellow-handled screwdriver on the floor near the wide wooden base—where Ethan had left it on the last day of his life.

Emily picked up the screwdriver and sat on the edge of the daybed, turning it over in her hands. She touched the yellow rubber handle to her lips and closed her eyes, and then, without warning, began to sob. Clutching the screwdriver to her breast, she threw herself facedown and surrendered to the wrenching, physically painful anguish that she'd held inside since Ethan's death. Here, in the silence of the boathouse, with no well-meaning friends or family to witness her grief, she finally wept for the loss she feared she couldn't survive—Ethan's love and his touch.

At last, the weeping required more strength than she had left, and she stopped crying. She lay with her cheek on the damp pillow, drained and breathing hard, and fell asleep.

When she woke up, the yellow screwdriver was still beside her, and Emily might have begun weeping again had her first thought not been that it would be bad for Sam. Dragging herself from the daybed, she locked the boathouse and made her way through the weeds to the house. Tomorrow, she'd call someone to cut the grass and clean the yard. Inside the house, she filled the tub almost to the rim, carefully avoiding a glance in the mirror. She could imagine what she must look like after an hour-long crying binge. She didn't need to see it.

The water felt wonderful, but she didn't allow herself the luxury of a lengthy soak. She was afraid of falling asleep again, and that interested her. The realization that she wasn't suicidal gave her an odd sense of pride. Unhappy, miserable and probably hallucinating, but not suicidal. She dug a warm flannel nightgown out of a bottom drawer and went to bed, patting first Sarah and then Sam goodnight. Tomorrow, after she arranged for the junk guy to come and clear the yard, she'd go back to the boathouse and start painting again.

Her first few days in the studio were spent arranging and rearranging—first the furniture, and then the materials. She brought out a dozen of the coffee cans she'd saved and organized her brushes by size and bristle shape, then did it again, dissatisfied with the result. At the end of the second day, she had the twelve cans full of brushes and pens and palette knives, and all the cans carefully labeled and neatly lined up on her worktable. Still nothing painted or even planned. Tomorrow, she decided. She'd would begin tomorrow.

The next day it rained, and there was a chill in the air, so she stayed inside the cottage to clean cabinets, and turned up several shoe boxes perfect for holding colored pens. On the third day, she drove into town and bought a collection of size-graduated and color-matched storage bins to keep the remainder of her art materials. On the fourth day, she spent the entire day arranging and rearranging the materials into the bins and shoe boxes.

"And on the seventh day," she said aloud when she looked at what she'd wrought, "I will rest."

Sunday morning was cool and damp again, and when she felt a headache coming on, Emily lounged on the couch and started watching the Marlon Brando version of *A Streetcar Named Desire.* She fell asleep after the first half hour, and when she woke, the set was off.

None of what happened to Emily was the way she'd seen such things depicted in movies, and the sense that something of Ethan remained in the cottage came to her in small, insignificant ways that she barely noticed at first, or brushed aside as exhaustion or imagination. It wasn't until there'd been several incidents that she began to wonder about them. On one day, sitting drowsily on the deck, she'd suddenly feel a lingering touch on her cheek, and raise her hand to find nothing there. The next day, she might walk through a room and reply to a remark she'd clearly heard addressed to her. Déjà vu, she decided, or perhaps a fragment of remembered conversation.

And often at night, as she prepared for bed, she was aware of a vague whisper of a breeze, as though someone had stepped out of her way as she passed. An open window somewhere or imagination or…?

One particular night, Emily finished the page she was reading, marked the place with a tissue as she always did, and laid the open book on her bedside table. But as she arranged her pillow, yawning sleepily, a small movement caught her eye. The tissue had fluttered off the book and onto the floor. She tilted her head to one side and regarded it quizzically. There were no windows open and she hadn't felt a draft all evening. Her own movements might have created a breeze, and yet…

She placed the tissue back in the book and waved her hands above it.

Nothing. The tissue lay perfectly still. Amused now, she tried once again to move the tissue. She lifted the pillow and dropped it on the edge of the bed near the table. One corner of the featherlight paper trembled and then lay still. Finally, she plumped the pillow, turned off the lamp and with a wide yawn, lay down. She was already half asleep when she felt a slight breeze against her cheek, and opened her eyes just in time to see the tissue float off the book, waft briefly upward into the pale moonlight, and drift languidly back to the table.

Emily sat up and flicked on the lamp. Somewhere, she *must* have left a window open. Sighing, she climbed out of bed and walked through the cottage, checking for open windows. Finding each of them securely closed and latched, she returned sleepily to bed.

When she reached once more for the lamp switch, she noticed the book again. It was closed. She hadn't remembered closing it, but…

"Go to sleep, Emily," she said aloud. "You're obviously losing your mind." She yawned again, and lay down. By morning, she'd almost forgotten what happened—almost, but not entirely.

Two days after the incident with the tissue, she went into the living room to remove a vase of dead flowers from the mantel, intending to take them to the kitchen and throw them away. As she leaned across the old birch rocker to pick up the vase, something stroked her thigh in what felt like a caress. When she whirled to look, the rocker was moving—very slightly, but definitely moving—as though someone had just stood up and left it.

The vase hit the floor and shattered, sending shards of glass skittering across the polished planks and forming a pool of water at her feet. Emily stood absolutely still, holding her breath, afraid to move. This time, there was no doubt about what she'd seen and felt. Emily remained there for a while, barefoot in the puddle of water, surrounded by broken glass and wilted roses.

Shortly after that, she came home from the grocery store, opened the door, and heard, quite distinctly, several notes being struck on the piano. She stood in the doorway, unsure of whether to go inside, and yet she wasn't afraid. The cottage was so far from town that they'd rarely bothered to lock the doors or windows. It was the middle of the afternoon, and she'd seen no sign of a car or even a bicycle along the beach road. Any would-be burglar or deranged musician would've had a very long walk merely to play a few idle notes on Ethan's elderly, scarred baby grand. There was a mild wind that day, ruffling through the tall weeds, and the sound could easily have been imagined—except for two odd details.

The melody she'd heard as she came into the house had been, without question, the familiar last bars of "Farewell, Spanish Ladies." She set the groceries on the table by the door, and went into the living room. Empty, of course. When she walked over to the piano and touched the lid, she noticed with a quick stab of guilt that it was covered with the gritty dust endemic in a house this close to the beach. The piano had been Ethan's, and she tended to avoid it when cleaning. It had probably been weeks since she'd dusted it, but as she ran her fingertips lightly down the keys, she saw that the dust had already been disturbed. On the black keys, the pattern was clear, with only small arcs of dust visible at the back of each, where it wouldn't customarily be touched while playing. The middle three octaves of the keyboard were virtually dust-free.

Emily pulled the bench out and sat down to study the keyboard, placing her fingers carefully on the keys required to play the old song Ethan had liked so well. She was not surprised to find these notes entirely free of dust. For a long while, she sat on the bench and rubbed one finger thoughtfully up and down middle C, not knowing what to make of it. The dust, or lack of it, could mean nothing—or everything.

But something had changed again. Emily could feel it in the air.

Chapter 12

A t the very edge of the cottage's small yard, some overly optimistic early tenant had planted two apple trees, neither of which had thrived in the poor soil and salt air. The trees reminded Emily of the tortured-looking fruit trees in Van Gogh's painted orchards. But despite their wizened appearance, they did occasionally bear fruit. "Whenever the mood strikes them and the planets line up just right," Ethan had described it. The afternoon following the curious incident with the piano was pleasant and sunny, and since she had nothing better to do, Emily succumbed to an inexplicable urge to bake a pie, using the few withered apples she'd harvested earlier that fall and stored in the chilly boathouse.

The pie would be Emily's first. In fact, she'd never

known a Porter woman who pretended either an interest or a talent at baking, and even as a child, the only pies she remembered had come from supermarkets, or been brought as gifts by visitors. But at this point in her pregnancy, Emily had begun to notice sporadic impulses to do things she'd never liked doing before. She'd become almost fanatical about dirt, and spent much of her day scrubbing, mopping and polishing until every surface in the cottage gleamed. Although she recognized these unexpected spurts of homeliness as a nest-building instinct engendered by hormones, they surprised her. Making her own pie from her very own apples would be fun and homey, even from apples as unpromising as these.

"You'd better watch carefully, kiddo," she gasped to Sam as she lugged the cumbersome wooden box of apples from the boathouse. "I can promise you this'll be the first and last time you ever see your mother bake a pie."

Once inside the cottage, already breathing heavily from hauling the loaded box this far, she dumped the fruit onto the counter. Seen more closely, the crop seemed even smaller and wormier than it had earlier. The apples had been on the tree long past their prime, and each of them had obviously been sampled by birds—and by something else. When the idea of an apple pie didn't seem as appealing as taking a nap, Emily yawned, and asked Sam his opinion.

"What do you say to a little nap first, kiddo? These things couldn't get any worse in an hour, right?" She shoved the withered fruit into a colander and wandered off to the bedroom.

She woke feeling headachy, but dragged herself to the kitchen to finish the pie, which now loomed as a chore rather than an amusing project. She set the apples under running water to rinse off the more obvious insects and found a paring knife to begin the distasteful job of removing the less visible ones. Her knife was poised to stab the first apple when she heard a noise behind her—a distinct chuckle.

When she turned to look, she dropped the knife, which slid across the floor and under the table. The room was empty, as she'd known it would be. Nerves, of course, or lack of sleep. Emily took a deep breath to calm herself, wiped her hands on her shirt, and got down on her hands and knees to retrieve the knife, which had somehow gotten stuck behind the farthest table leg. As she reached for it, the knife moved, sliding quickly across the floor and directly into her hand. Emily yelped, let go of the knife again, and scooted back out from under the table as rapidly as her present bulk permitted.

"I told you they've never been fit to eat." The voice was clear and unmistakable. Emily's hands flew to her mouth.

"Oh, my God! Now I'm hearing things," she whispered, pressing her back against the lower cupboard.

"No, you're not, darling. You've known I was here for the last week, at least."

Emily shook her head violently and covered her ears. "I don't believe in things like this," she groaned.

Again, the familiar chuckle. "Neither do I, Em, but it's true. Please, don't be scared."

"I'm not scared. I think I'm going to throw up, though."

In the empty kitchen, her voice sounded breathless and thin, and despite what she'd just said, she *was* scared. "Was that you in the bedroom?" she whispered. "And yesterday at the piano?"

"Yes. I didn't know how to… What to do, exactly, to announce myself."

Emily got clumsily to her feet. "I can't believe… Can I see you?" she pleaded. "Can I just see you, darling? Really *see* you, even for a moment?"

Her eyes filled with tears, and she stretched out her hand, feeling foolish. When something touched her, Emily cried out and pulled back, then wriggled her fingers and stared at them in disbelief.

"It's true," she breathed.

"It's true, and I'm about to touch you again, darling. Promise not to jump—or throw up?"

Emily laughed, trembling so badly she had to sit down on the floor again. "I promise, but I may wet my pants. Sorry. It's a pregnant-woman thing."

Another chuckle. "Not exactly the welcome I was hoping for." And then, she clearly felt a soft caress down the length of her arm.

Emily closed her eyes and sighed deeply as the touch moved up her arm, and then to her cheek. Finally, as it came to rest on her shoulder, the pressure was warm, solid and real. Emily sat quietly, breathing with difficulty. After a few minutes, she raised her hand to her shoulder and felt for what she prayed would be there.

She took Ethan's hand in hers and pressed it to her lips.

"I can barely feel you, Ethan. It's as though…"

Something touched her hair. "I know. Wait for a while. Just sit with your eyes closed, and wait."

"I don't want to wait," she murmured, turning to reach for his face with both her hands. "I want to touch you... To hold you against me. Is that possible?"

"I never thought *this* was possible." And somehow, Emily knew he was smiling. "I guess we'll have to learn what's possible, and what isn't."

Emily wiped away a tear. "And you, darling?" she whispered. "What do *you* feel? When you touch me, is it..."

There was a pause, and in the pause, she sensed sadness. "No. It's not the same, Em."

"What, then?"

Another pause.

"It's like flying, Em. The clouds below you seem tangible. Intellectually, you know they're nothing but vapor and mist, but the illusion of substance is so strong—as though you could walk on them. And a sunbeam? You can put your hand right through a sunbeam, but you can't touch it or hold it. You know it exists, because you can see it and feel it. What you're feeling is the essence of the sunbeam— the heat. I think this is like the cloud and the sunbeam. It's real, but first you have to ignore what your mind is saying, and accept the illusion as real."

"This will only be real if I believe it is?" she asked.

There was no answer. Ethan had gone again. Emily sat for a long while in the kitchen, trying to understand and wanting to believe. Needing to believe. But for her, understanding wasn't necessary. She'd felt something of Ethan in this room. Something essentially true and tangible, and something of what she'd lost. And for Emily, that was enough. It would have to be.

Ethan came often after that, without warning, and each visit was far too short for Emily. She had thousands of questions, but he didn't have all the answers, and many of the answers were vague and bewildering.

"I don't know, Em. I don't know why I'm here, or how, or where I go when I leave. Maybe we're both dreaming. There are aboriginal tribesmen who believe that the time a man spends dreaming is his real life, and the time he spends awake is nothing but a dream."

"But what does it feel like to you?" she pleaded, desperate to understand the boundaries of what they would have together.

"At first, I could see you," he said, "but not touch you or speak to you. Now, I can do that, but not always. It feels almost like…like memory, Em."

"Memory?"

For a while, he said nothing, and the only sound in the room was the crackling of the log in the fireplace. "Like a memory that's beginning to fade. Like something you're trying to remember in perfect detail, but can't. A day, a moment in time… The exact color or smell or texture of something you loved—of something you knew so well you thought you could never forget it. That sounds sad, but it isn't really. I guess all memories, even the good ones, are a little melancholy, because they've already gone and can't ever be recovered. But I don't feel sad, the way you do."

"And when you touch me?" she asked softly.

"I sense you. The way I remember you, but it's never exactly the same. Today, it was the scent of your skin that day last year when we got caught in the rain. Last night, you'd been in the yard and smelled of autumn—the way I remember that day in Yarmouth, with the wood smoke, the leaves burning and the wind off the water. Sometimes it's a texture, or a taste. The way your skin felt in the sun, or the way your tears tasted. The way you always smelled like lilacs and baby powder after you came out of the shower."

Then Emily asked the question that worried her most and that she understood least.

"How long will this last, Ethan? Will it… Will you go away eventually?"

"I don't know that, either, darling. Maybe it'll all go away tomorrow, or the day after. But it will end when you want it to."

"I'll never want that!" she cried.

"Of course you will. I hope you will, anyway. Not only for you, but for the baby."

"Let's not talk about it now," she said quickly. "Let me tell you about Sam. He's a big baby, darling. I *know* it's a boy, and I've got my fingers crossed for your genes, not mine. If poor Sam turns out to be a dumpy, chubby little beast like I was, I'll never forgive myself—or my genes."

Several nights later, Emily was still awake at three in the morning. The night was muggy and warm, so she kicked the sheet away, slipped off her damp nightgown and lay naked in the humid darkness, thinking of Ethan and overcome by an achingly painful, physical longing.

She'd told herself that it was enough that she could talk to Ethan and be with him, but now, she knew she'd been wrong. It wasn't enough. She wanted *him*—to touch the man she loved, to feel his warmth, his lips, the solid strength of him moving inside her. And more than anything else, she wanted to know he could feel her touch, as well.

For a long time, she lay still, willing him to come to her, listening to every night noise outside the open window, hoping it was him. By the time she fell asleep, dawn was beginning to break.

She woke slowly, sensing Ethan's presence near her on the bed—and since that seemed impossible, Emily lay quietly, unwilling to relinquish the feeling by moving, or even opening her eyes. But the longer she lay there, the stronger the sensation grew.

Finally, with her eyes still closed, she reached out her hand.

His hair beneath her fingertips was like water—soft and silken, but with little substance. She slipped her arms around him, and in her embrace, his body was warm, yet as insubstantial as a summer mist. She tried once again, pressing her face against his shoulder, breathing him in, remembering the feel and smell of his skin.

At first, she felt only warmth, and heard nothing other than her own breathing, but after a while, she began to be aware of a faint fragrance in the room, and recognized it as the aftershave lotion he'd always worn. Lime. She placed his hands tenderly on the swell of her abdomen, letting him feel the child to whom he would never toss a baseball or teach to ride a bicycle. His hands explored her belly, gently, tentatively, and a moment later, when Sam obliged by kicking her, Ethan laughed softly.

He cupped her breasts in his hands, and the heat and strength of his touch was real and undeniable. Emily lifted her head and touched her lips to his mouth, then moaned and opened herself to him, fighting back tears of joy.

When Emily awoke again, it was one in the afternoon, but she was still tired. Her arms and legs seemed limp and useless, her entire body enveloped by an oddly pleasant languor. She lay in bed for some minutes, resisting full consciousness and allowing herself the luxury of waking up utterly happy, a feeling she hadn't experienced since the last time Ethan made love to her—the night before he died. She enjoyed the memory for several minutes before reaching beneath the covers to caress her belly, whispering a soft good-morning to Sam, still sleeping quietly inside her.

When she crawled from the bed, she knew the baby would soon wake and begin to move, and she would be overwhelmed again by the desolation with which she began each new day. Turning her face into the pillow, she closed her eyes and tried to drift back to sleep, and suddenly remembered part of the dream she'd had last night. A dream about...*with* Ethan. Emily smiled almost wickedly. The dream had seemed so real, so very real!

Chapter 13

Emily's days took on a tranquil, almost dreamlike quality now, and she drifted pleasantly from morning to evening, barely noticing the passage of time. She spent hours sitting by the window watching the ocean, and attended to the basic requirements of her life and her home with a kind of incurious but dutiful routine. Mostly, though, she wandered about the cottage in an agreeable languor, waiting for Ethan. She had learned that there was no predictable time when he came, with one exception. Although she didn't understand how, he always appeared when she was in some difficulty, however small.

She didn't see Ethan in the way she'd always believed traditional "ghosts" were seen, and never thought of him as ghostly. After the first shock, she rarely even thought of what was happening to her as odd. In spite of the peculiarity of her situation and the questions—so many questions—she was simply happy. Ethan was here. It was all she had, and it was enough.

It never occurred to her to share her experiences with anyone—not even Maggie, who would've sworn she understood and then rushed her to a psychiatrist. Yet, it wasn't other people's reactions or their disbelief that Emily feared. It was their intrusion. This was hers alone, and she intended to keep it that way.

When Sam kicked her especially hard, she closed her eyes and wished for Ethan to appear, and like a genie she'd summoned, he usually did. Emily positioned his hands on her belly, and waited with delight for his reaction. As the days passed, it seemed to Emily that he was staying closer and appearing more frequently.

As the date of the baby's expected birth approached, Emily remained near the cottage, avoiding even short trips to town for fear of going into labor elsewhere. She had decided to have the baby in the cottage—alone. A few weeks before she was due, she informed her obstetrician, implying that she had found a licensed midwife instead. As she had expected, the doctor wasn't pleased.

Ten days later, she woke with a feeling of pressure and discomfort in her abdomen.

She knew something was happening, and leafed through the pages of the books on pregnancy and delivery she'd collected, searching for a description of the early signs of labor. Sam wasn't due for another three weeks, but everything she read seemed to indicate that she might be having contractions. There was no pain or blood, so she lay down, hoping it was only gas, or false labor. By midafternoon, the discomfort had increased. The pain was still tolerable, but she had begun to see traces of blood. She picked up the phone and called Kate, praying she was home—and alone. She got the answering machine and left a message she hoped sounded casual.

Half an hour later, Matthew appeared on her front step, holding what looked suspiciously like a pie wrapped in aluminum foil. It didn't escape Emily's notice that he carried a black leather medical bag in his other hand.

"I'm here on an errand of mercy. Kate says you called and asked her to drop by for a visit. She's still over at Janet Paulsen's, checking up on the new triplets, but she'll be along soon. Meanwhile, I brought this. According to Kate, you're too skinny for eight months. This is her antidote—a cherry pie—homemade. I've been eating Kate's pies for close to fifty years, so I brought along a pocketful of antacids, in case you decide to actually eat the thing."

Emily opened the screen door wide. "Come on in and sit down. You look tired."

Matt scowled and thrust the pie into her hands. "I'm old," he said. "I'm allowed." He took a seat at the kitchen table. "I'd appreciate a fresh cup of coffee. Can you make coffee yet?"

"I can follow the directions on the can," Emily offered. "That's all I can promise. I don't drink it anymore." She set the pie in the middle of the table to unwrap it. "You're a very bad liar, Dr. O'Connell. I've already gained twenty pounds more than I should have. And your pie is a fake. The artful little bit of aluminum foil didn't fool me. I used to do that myself. The pie looks terrific, though. You can have some with your coffee while you tell me why you're here lying to me."

Matt scowled again. "All right, then, smart-ass. The truth is Jacob Forrester asked me to drop by and talk to you."

Emily made a face. "Let me guess. He wants you to talk me out of having the baby here."

"Something like that. His exact words were 'make the damned little idiot get her butt back in my office before she makes a mess of things.' Why didn't you tell me you'd quit seeing him?"

She cut a thick slab of pie, plopped it on a plate and slid it across the table to him.

"Eat your pie. I'll make coffee."

"I don't want any damned coffee! Just set yourself down in that chair and tell me what the blazes is going on. Kate said you sounded scared."

Emily sat, trying not to wince. The pains were getting sharper. "Nothing's going on, and I'm not scared. I just wanted a little company."

"Jake Forrester's one of the best OBs in the country. Why are you trying to tell him how to do his job?"

"When Dr. Forrester has a baby, he can have it anywhere he wants to," she said firmly. "I want to have mine here, in this house."

"You're thirty miles from a hospital, and if anything goes wrong…"

"Nothing's going to go wrong."

"And you got your medical degrees from where? Forrester says it's going to be breech. Why the hell didn't you tell me?"

"I was a breech birth," Emily said smugly. "And my mother came through just fine."

"Yeah? Well, why don't you give me your mother's phone number, and let me hear what she has to say about that," he countered.

"Why is *my* doctor talking to you about it, anyway?" Emily demanded. "Without my permission. Isn't that unethical?"

"Probably. So sue us. But first, start doing what Forrester tells you. You're not all that young to be doing this for the first time."

"Thank you for reminding me. I counted six new gray hairs this morning. Do you want to see them?"

Matt's tone softened. "Things can go wrong fast, Emily—a lot faster than you know."

"You could help me," she said quietly. "You and Kate."

"I'm retired," Matt sighed wearily. "And she should be, too. Delivering Janet Paulsen's triplets last week nearly knocked the stuffing out of the old girl."

"I won't be any trouble, Matt. I'll do everything you tell me to."

"Like you did with Forrester?"

"Millions of women have babies at home."

"You're not millions of women. You're someone we love, and Ethan's wife. This baby you're so all-fired sure is a boy is going to be our grandkid, if you'll let him come into this world safely."

Emily smiled. "I couldn't ask for better grandparents. Ethan would be proud that you're—"

Matt cut her off. "Enough of this crap," he growled. "You think you're in labor, don't you?"

"No," Emily lied. "I just…just wanted to ask Kate a couple of questions."

"Get your coat," he ordered. "I'll take you into town to see Forrester."

"I'm not going anywhere," she said stubbornly. "So quit trying to boss me around!"

Matt began fiddling with the saltshaker, and Emily could tell he was choosing his next words carefully, but when he spoke, it wasn't what she expected.

"I'm an old man, Emily, but I'm not blind yet. And there are some things old men know about that a lot of younger people don't."

Emily said nothing.

"For one thing," he said quietly. "I know why you're so hell-bent on having this baby here in this house and screw the consequences."

Emily looked at him, but didn't speak. Somehow, though, even before Matthew opened his mouth, she knew what he was going to say.

"You want Ethan to see his child born—and don't bother lying to me. I could feel something the minute I set foot inside the house. I've been feeling it for the last six weeks, but I wasn't sure till now."

Emily grabbed the dishes from the table and slammed them into the sink. "I don't know what you're talking about!"

"Quit lying to me! I can't see him, but I know he's here,

and I knew Ethan Douglas well enough to know he wouldn't want you taking this kind of risk—not with your life *or* his baby's. Now, get your coat and let's see if we can get things straightened out with Forrester before he writes you off for the ungrateful moron you are. And then get you to a hospital if you need one."

"No!" Emily pointed to the door. "If you don't want to help me, then just go home, but *I'm* not leaving."

Matthew thought for a moment, then pushed her down in a chair, and placed one hand on her belly. "Damn it!" he roared. "When did this start?" A bit meekly, Emily told him. He opened his bag and took her blood pressure and pulse, then swore again and gestured toward the bedroom. "All right, get in there, strip the bed down to the one sheet, and then crawl in it and try to get some rest. You're going to need it. I'll call Kate and get her over here—and I *don't* want an argument!"

"I'm not arguing. Go ahead and call her." Emily reached up and took his hand. "And Matt," she said. "Thank you."

"Just try to do as you're told, for once," he said. "And don't thank me yet. You're in for a hell of a night, and so am I."

Matthew waved her away, then phoned his wife. Emily went to the bedroom and stripped the bed of everything but the fitted sheet. When that was done, she showered and changed into a lightweight nightgown, then sat on the edge of the bed and closed her eyes, waiting to feel Ethan near her.

"It's almost time, darling," she whispered. "I can feel the contractions getting stronger. And I'm not afraid, I promise." She put her hands on her abdomen and sang very softly, "Farewell and adieu, my fine Spanish ladies…"

Emily gasped and doubled over in pain. In the next room, Matthew O'Connell sighed, shook his head and began to unpack his bag. The long night had begun.

It was late afternoon the next day when Kate O'Connell finally laid the baby boy Emily had named Samuel Ethan into the arms of his exhausted mother. Emily looked up drowsily and smiled.

"I don't know how to thank you, Kate—both you and Matt. I've put you through a lot of trouble, and I'm sorry."

Kate patted Emily's arm. "Well, love, this is what we've been doing our whole lives, but you could've saved yourself a real bad time by listening to Matt and Jake Forrester and getting to the hospital when they told you to."

Emily sighed. "I know. I'm stubborn."

"You surely are." Kate smiled as she stroked the baby's hair. "But about now I figure you're thinking all that pain was worth it."

Emily nodded and pressed her lips to Sam's tiny wrist. "It was."

Kate tucked the covers under Emily's feet and started from the room. "You can try feeding him now, if you're up to it. I'll be in the kitchen if you need me."

Emily waited until Kate left the room before she spoke to Ethan.

"He's so beautiful, darling." She poked through the tightly swaddled bundle to complete the age-old ritual of counting fingers and toes. "I can't believe how perfect he is. Your son is an admirable and praiseworthy baby. Come touch him."

There was a slight movement as the blanket fell away to one side, and for several minutes, while Ethan Douglas explored the perfect body and limbs of his newborn son, the only sound was Samuel's quiet mewling. Ethan kissed her very gently on the mouth, and when she felt the soft touch of his fingers on her shoulder, Emily reached up to lay her hand on his. Sam nuzzled against her and she opened the top of her gown to put their son to her breast for the very first time.

Emily was up and moving about the next morning, feeling tired but wonderful. By now, Maggie had arrived, and both she and Kate were insisting on staying for the next two weeks to help out. Kate slept on the living-room couch, where she could hear if Emily called, and cooked three hearty meals a day for her reluctant patient. Maggie would be sharing the smaller bedroom with Helene, who was already on her way from California.

"Why didn't you have someone call me when you went into labor?" Helene demanded within minutes of arriving. "I could have been there with you."

"It happened too quickly," Emily lied, casting a quick warning glance at Kate and Maggie. Kate merely raised an eyebrow at the deception and went back to cooking dinner. "Besides, Mom, everything went perfectly. The baby's healthy and I'm fine. Kate's husband Matthew is a doctor— my doctor, now. Maggie's here for two weeks, and Matt drops by every day to check on me. I'm being watched like a hawk!"

"You want me to leave, is that what you're saying?"

Emily sighed. "No, Mom. I want you to go in the bedroom and get to know your impossibly handsome, gifted grandson while I shower."

Helene frowned. "Should you be bathing so soon?"

"Yes. Now, go in there and take care of Sam—if you can beat Maggie and Kate to it. The diapers are in the bottom drawer. It's almost his lunchtime, so he's about to start squawking again. Sam seems to thinks it's *always* lunchtime!"

"Breast-feeding will make your breasts droop, darling," Helene advised, shaking her head in disapproval as she left the room.

"Then I'll droop," Emily called after her. "I doubt Sam will care."

Helene returned holding Sam, and crying. "He's the most beautiful baby I've ever seen," she sniffled.

Emily smiled and kissed both of them. "Of course he is. He looks just like his father."

After two hectic weeks of houseguests and chatter, Emily was finally alone again in the cottage with the baby—and with Ethan. On that first night of peace and quiet, she pulled Sam's cradle next to the bed and lay for a long time, watching him sleep. She yawned, ready for sleep herself. Soon, she felt Ethan next to her, and reached for his hand.

"Isn't it funny, darling?" she asked as his arms encircled her. "I never thought I'd like him so much."

Ethan chuckled.

"Don't laugh. I knew I'd love him, of course, but I actually like Sam as a person. He doesn't have a lot to say yet, but he's always so happy and easygoing. He doesn't seem to mind that I don't have a clue what I'm doing or that his diaper always falls off the minute I get it on. He's a very patient, nonjudgmental sort of baby, and brilliant, of course." She rolled over and slipped her arms around Ethan's neck, waiting to be kissed. "I should have known you'd make the perfect baby."

"I had some help." He stroked her cheek.

"Maybe, but he's not at all like me, thankfully. He's going to look like you. Tall. I can tell that, even now. Well, he's not *exactly* like you. He doesn't snore, but then, he's still very young."

When Sam was six weeks old, Matt drove her to see the still-annoyed Dr. Forrester, who pronounced her healthy and "progressing nicely." From there, they went to the new medical center, where Sam's pediatrician had an office.

When Emily and the baby were called in to an examination room, Matt touched Emily briefly on the arm.

"I'm going across the street to the hospital to check on a patient. I'll probably be back before she's done prodding and poking poor Sam, but if I'm not, you wait right here for me, you hear?"

"I won't move a muscle," Emily swore, raising her right hand. "I'll sit right there by the door, and eat my lollipop if I get one, until you come for us."

Matt walked across the street to the new extended-care

wing of the medical center. He found Grace Lundgren in her son's room, arranging a fresh bunch of daisies in a blue ceramic vase.

"How are you today, Matthew?" She rearranged a pillow under Josh's head and straightened the sheet. "I've missed you on my last few trips."

"Doing fine, Grace. How's our boy today?"

"No change, the staff tells me, but he seems a bit more alert to me. Is that possible?"

"It's always possible, Grace, but you know better than to see things that aren't there, right?"

Grace sighed. "I know."

Josh had been in and out of consciousness since the day he was pulled from the creek months earlier, but though he was still unresponsive, Grace Lundgren had been by his bedside every day of those long, weary weeks. When she finished at the office each afternoon, she came here, bringing flowers and cards, and things from home to make the room more cheerful. Josh's high-school football helmet sat on a shelf, alongside a track trophy he'd won in the eighth grade. There were photos of family vacations, taken before George Lundgren became ill, and an eight-by-ten portrait of Annie and Josh on their wedding day. The bed was covered with a quilt Annie and Grace had sewn together, and Josh's own robe and slippers were by the bed—never worn, but waiting.

Grace was a patient woman. Two months after Josh's accident, she had laid her husband to rest. It was a merciful rest, she believed, after the terrible lost years in a nursing home. He hadn't known her when he finally passed away, and had no memory of his only child, hospitalized only a few miles away. Now, everything in Grace's life that she still cared about lay under a handmade quilt in a metal hospital bed. A hospital bed she had been told he might never leave. Deep in her heart, though, Grace knew differently, and she was patient enough to wait.

When Matthew returned to pick her up at the pediatrician's half an hour late, Emily could see that he was in a foul mood, and as she strapped Sam into his car seat, something told her not to complain about the delay. She got into the front seat prepared for a long, silent ride home.

"Sorry I was late getting back," Matt said. "Poor Sam's probably wet and hungry."

Emily smiled. "Nope. He's dry and filled to the brim. I fed him while I waited, and changed him, too. But I didn't get my lollipop."

"You don't deserve a lollipop. Forrester says you're not eating right."

"Forrester talks too much. Don't I have any privacy? What are you, his paid consultant?"

"Professional courtesy, one physician to another. That means I get to trample all over your privacy. Get used to it and start taking those vitamins he prescribed. You're low on iron."

"Why are you in such a grouchy mood?" she asked.

Matthew shook his head. "Sad case. A car accident a few months back. Real nice young man ran off the road and hasn't really come to since. And it's about to kill his mother."

"Will he get better?"

"Maybe, with a little luck. He's strong, and he was healthy before it happened. I've seen worse cases come out of something like this. Of course, even if he does, he's going to have a hard row to hoe before he makes it back. The boy racked himself up pretty good."

"How old is he?"

"About your age. A carpenter. He spent a few years in the Coast Guard then went to work with his dad, right here in town. He's not my patient, but I treated his ma and pa for years until George came down with Alzheimer's. You probably read about the boy's wife. Ann Lundgren? She got killed in that quick-shop robbery some time back?"

Emily nodded. "I read about it. Awful. She was pregnant, wasn't she?"

"Yeah. That's what's stuck in my craw so bad this afternoon, I guess. You and Ethan, and this boy? Sometimes, nothing in life seems fair."

Emily reached back to fondle Sam's fat toes. "I know."

Matthew and Kate, and Emily and Sam were all fast asleep by the time Grace Lundgren locked her desk drawer and quit work for the night. She got out of her chair, stiff and aching after a long evening of doing the books. Grace had closed the business for several months after Josh's accident, unable to handle the construction end without him. When money became short, though, she'd hired a foreman and reopened. But staying ahead of the paperwork was hard, and she worried that the patience of many of their best customers and suppliers was wearing thin. She had hired the best workmen she could find, but most people wanted Josh's skills and expertise, not assistants, and she worried how much longer they would wait.

She'd been glad to see Matthew O'Connell that afternoon. Matt kept her feet on the ground without stealing her hope, and that made her trust him. Matt didn't deal in false promises or nonsense, and while his bedside manner was often gruff, it was honest and straightforward. If Matt O'Connell thought there was hope, that was enough for her to hold on to.

Grace went to bed, unaware of the flurry of activity that was going on twelve miles away in her son's hospital room. She wouldn't hear until morning, when the hospital staff felt that what had happened at 1:38 that morning was significant and not just a fluke or a reflex.

At precisely that minute, Joshua Lundgren had moved his fingers, opened his eyes, and asked about his mother.

Chapter 14

Three years later

The years following Sam's birth passed quickly for Emily, and her life seemed full and gratifying, if at times odd. Motherhood was even more enjoyable than she had expected, and as Sam grew older—past the "terrible twos" and into a charming companion—she found more time to work. Her confidence in her craft had grown, as well, and her work was in a number of excellent galleries along the coast. She was finally making a comfortable living at her chosen trade. Her work was usually judged to be technically excellent, but was often dismissed by serious critics as "nostalgic" or "sentimental." At first, she found these reviews insulting, but at the same time, she understood the truth of them.

It was difficult for her to paint anything else at this time in her life, when she considered herself totally fulfilled and content, and she believed it was this happiness that showed in her work.

"Fulfilled, my ass," Maggie said one afternoon as they sat in the yard watching Sam build a sand castle. "You live like a hermit out here, with a three-year-old munchkin— an admittedly brilliant and adorable munchkin, of course, but still three years old. I love your kid like crazy, Em, but his major topics of conversation are garbage trucks and Winnie the Pooh."

"And what have you got against Winnie the Pooh, or garbage trucks for that matter?" Emily asked with a laugh.

"Nothing, Emily. I dote on Winnie the Pooh. Am I not personally guilty of buying most of the hundreds of dollars' worth of Winnie the Pooh stuff in this house? Your son is probably the most enchanting, clever, entertaining little chap I've ever known, but he's a kid, and I hate to break it to you, sweetie, but sometimes he's *boring!*"

"Okay," Emily said menacingly. "Now you've gone too far, Aunt Maggie. Boring! And he speaks so highly of you."

"I'll tell you what," Maggie suggested. "Why don't we choose a night soon, drop the little charmer off at Grandma Kate's and have dinner and drinks somewhere, alone, without booster seats and bibs. We'll talk about adult women things—just for one night."

"What things?" asked Emily suspiciously. "As if I didn't know."

"Yes, you guessed my secret! I want to talk about men, and maybe even sex. You remember sex, don't you? Or have you already settled into the midlife doldrums—spending your evenings with erotic novels?" She kicked off her shoes and flopped down on the grass. "Besides, I want you to meet Gary."

"What's a Gary? Is it new or recycled?"

"New. And gorgeous, and what's more, he's asked me to marry him."

Emily leaped up and hugged her friend. "That's wonderful! Why haven't you told me about him before?"

"You've been busy being fulfilled, and I wanted to be sure and not jinx it. I've had more near misses than an international airport. This time, though, it looks like the real thing."

"Good. Now I can give *you* that wedding shower you were always trying to throw for me. I've got half a ton of pots and pans, only slightly used. A couple of male strippers and we're set."

Maggie shook her head. "Nope. Gary and I are going to do what you and Ethan did. Elope, and then get me knocked up before the ink is dry on the marriage certificate. Sam needs a playmate, and I feel it's my duty as a good auntie to fill that void."

"I'm really happy for you, Maggie, and of course I'll go to dinner with you. You think I'd let you marry some guy I've never even met?"

"There's only one problem," Maggie said hesitantly.

Emily frowned. "What is it? He's married? A chest full of tattoos with other women's names? What?"

"He's a Republican. A moderate, but still a Republican."

Emily giggled. "Okay, that's it! Dump the son of a bitch! Wait! Does he have his own hair? Does he play golf?"

"Uh. Yes and no, in that order."

"All right, then. That's two out of three. You can keep him. Remember our college vow? No Republicans, no golf fanatics and no fake hair?"

Maggie sighed. "Ah, yes. Our peacenik standards were unrealistically high, weren't they? You forgot one, though. No stockbrokers—greedy Wall Street enablers of the war-machine? You want to guess what Gary does for a living?"

"Well, time *does* move on," Emily agreed. "Why don't you invite your stockbroker to dinner here this weekend. I'll make a pot roast. It's a long drive back, so you guys can spend the night, if you want. I know it'll be a terrible inconvenience to have to share a bed with him, but we're fresh out of rooms. Sarah and I'll bunk in Sam's and you two can have the Bridal Suite—my bedroom. I'll even vacuum."

Maggie shook her head. "Thanks. We'll take the sleeping accommodations, but I'd rather not feed him your pot roast. It took a long time to bag this guy, and I'd like to keep him healthy. We'll take you out to dinner. There must be at least one decent restaurant somewhere in this outpost of civilization. Get a sitter for tomorrow night, and wear something other than jeans and a sweatshirt. You do own something else, right?"

"I'll check my closet. Just watch the dress code where you make reservations. I can only do so much about my wardrobe on short notice."

When Maggie had left, Emily fed and bathed Sam and put him down for the night, then went back to the living room to watch the news. After a few minutes, she dozed off, only to wake at the sound of Ethan's voice.

"Maggie's good for you," he said from the vicinity of the fireplace. "I haven't heard you giggle in three years."

"Did I giggle?" Emily asked, flushing.

"You giggled. And she's right. You need to go out more. I'm glad you're getting out of the house for one night, at least."

Emily sighed. "She's planning some kind of fix-up, you know. A last-minute blind date."

"Good. You need that, too."

Emily's temper flared. "You could at least *try* to sound a little jealous."

Ethan chuckled. "That's a luxury I don't have."

She leaned back against the cushions and reached for him. "You'll never need to be jealous, darling. You know that."

"I want you to be happy, Em."

She smiled. "But I *am* happy."

"And Sam?" Ethan asked gently.

"Sam's happy when he's got all eight colors of Play-Doh. And when I don't make him wash his hair at night. He's not exactly a social butterfly."

"No, he's not," Ethan agreed. "He's quiet for his age, Em."

"Now you're a child psychologist?" Emily snapped, then regretted it. "I'm sorry, darling. I didn't mean to sound bitchy. But believe me, Sam's a very happy little boy."

There was a long silence before Ethan spoke again. "He knows I'm here, Em."

"Ethan," she argued, "Sam's only three years old. He can't possibly—"

"Kids are perceptive. He doesn't understand it, but he knows when I'm here. I can see him trying to figure it out. Yesterday, he even talked to me."

"What!"

"I don't know how it happened. I've been careful not to say anything when he's in the room, but he was sitting on the floor playing with his trucks and I was watching him. I don't think he actually saw me, and he didn't seem scared, but he spoke to me."

"What did he say?" she asked nervously.

"He said, 'I know you're there.'"

"That's it?"

"That's it."

"But I don't even see you—not really. I mean, I see *something,* or *feel* something, but…"

"Is it like a stone at the bottom of a clear stream?" Ethan asked. "Where the image is distorted by the ripples and the current, but you can still tell what it is?"

"Yes," she breathed. "That's it exactly!"

"I think that's a dream, Em—with memory filling in the blanks. I'm not sure, but I think maybe that's why this happens. I remember everything from the moment I met you. How you always trembled when I lifted your hair to kiss the back of your neck. Your laugh. The fullness of your breast in my hand while we slept. That may be what we're doing—remembering. But with Sam it's different. It can't be memory, because he has none of me. It's something else."

"What?"

"I can't be certain, but I think he's picking it up from you."

"But that's not a bad thing, is it?" Emily pleaded. "How could it be?"

"Sam doesn't need an imaginary friend, or the memory of a father he's never known. He needs real friends, and someday soon, he'll need a father."

"He *has* a father."

"No, he doesn't, Emily."

"Well, anyway," she reasoned, "he has Matt. Sam adores Matt and Kate, and Matt does everything a father would do. They play ball and go to the zoo, and next year they're planning a vacation to Disney World, and…"

"Matt O'Connell is eighty years old, darling. There's not a better human being anywhere, and I loved him like a father, but Matt may not be around when Sam needs him most."

"Matt knows about you," Emily said quietly. "We've never talked about it since he first mentioned it—the day Sam was born—but he knows."

"He suspected long before that," Ethan said. "I could feel it. But stop trying to change the subject, Em. We—"

"I can't go out and look for a father for Sam like I'm going shopping, Ethan. Not now. Not until…"

"Until what?" Ethan asked softly.

Emily began to cry. "I love you, Ethan. I couldn't love you more if you were…"

Ethan finished her sentence. "If I were real?"

"Stop saying that! You *are* real. I get better at it every day, Ethan. I can feel you, darling, at night. When you…"

"Memory, Em, and maybe a dream. Try to remember that."

"No!" she cried. "I can feel you with me, when you kiss me, touch me… When you make love to me, for God's sake! How is that possible if… Oh, Ethan, please! Just hold me now! Hold me, and don't say anything else!"

She fell into his arms, surrendering completely to whatever it was she felt there—memory or dream, or the man she loved and needed. To Emily, it was all the same now, and too bewildering to try to separate.

Emily woke to the sound of Sam's humming. She sat up and discovered him on the end of her bed, playing with a headless plastic figure that had once been Batman.

"Good morning, sweetheart," she said, and Sam piled cheerfully onto her stomach, disrupting Sarah's peaceful slumber. "What happened to poor Batman's head?"

Sam shrugged, not especially interested in the superhero's maimed condition. "It fell off," he explained. "Sarah ate it."

"Do you remember where you're going tonight?"

"Disney World?" Sam suggested.

"No. You're going to Grandma's and Grampa's house to sleep over so Mommy can go out and have dinner with Aunt Maggie and her friend."

"I can stay with Sarah," he said.

"No, sweetheart. Just think how lonely you'd be here, with no one to play with."

"The man is here," he said matter-of-factly, pulling Batman's left arm off at the shoulder.

Emily tried not to show her shock as she helped Sam to reattach the severed limb.

"What man?"

Sam deftly removed Batman's right arm and offered it to Sarah, who declined the gift and went back to sleep. "The tall man you talk to."

Emily reached over and stroked Sam's blond hair. "Sweetie, there's no man here."

Sam pointed to the photo of Ethan on the bedside table. "Daddy," he said, looking directly at her. "The man is Daddy." And then, with his own eccentric and colorful pronunciations, he began to sing—perfectly in tune— "Farewell, Spanish Ladies."

That afternoon, Emily dropped Sam off at the O'Connells' for the two-night sleepover they had arranged, then went home to dress for dinner with Maggie and Gary. She had been anxious all day to talk to Ethan about the startling things Sam had said, but he wasn't around. By the time Maggie arrived, Emily was a nervous wreck.

They went to dinner at a Japanese steakhouse twenty miles down the coast, and on the drive there, Emily decided that the fabled Gary was probably a winner. Paul, Emily's own date for the evening, was already holding a table when they arrived. He was attractive, of medium height and wore glasses. He lived in Bangor, where he worked as a textbook editor.

After dinner, they went dancing, and as the evening wore on, Emily had to admit that Paul was witty, intelligent and an excellent conversationalist. He seemed to enjoy all her jokes, liked the same books she did and shared her political viewpoint. He complimented what she was wearing, asked with genuine interest about Sam, and when they danced, he held her with precisely the right degree of intimacy. He was the perfect date—and Emily couldn't remember when she'd spent a more miserable evening.

Back at the house, Emily said good-night to her guests as soon as she could without being rude and retired to Sam's room, where she tried to ignore the laughter and whispering coming from hers. She burrowed under Sam's Winnie the Pooh bedspread, crushed a well-worn Eeyore to her chest and cried into his soft gray neck for an hour. She wanted Ethan.

Where was he? She was awake most of the night, wandering the house and whispering for him, but Ethan never came.

Maggie and Gary, looking sleepless and haggard, stayed for a quick breakfast, and then left for home. Maggie glanced at Emily curiously as she and Gary went out the door, and promised to call the moment she got home. When they had gone, Emily walked around the cottage for a while, calling Ethan's name, and when there was still no answer, she collapsed on the couch and cried herself to sleep. Sometime later, Ethan touched her shoulder softly to wake her.

"Where have you been?" she demanded. "I needed to talk to you!"

"I thought it would confuse things if I was here," he apologized. "With other people in the house. Did you have a good time?"

She ignored the question. "You're right, Ethan. Sam knows. I heard him singing that stupid song. Where could he have…"

"It doesn't matter." Ethan's voice sounded tired and sad. "Em, it's time to talk about—"

"Don't start that!" she said obstinately. "Don't even start! I can't go on without you here, Ethan. I can't!"

"But you already have, Em. You've done wonderfully without me, whatever you think. Now it's time for you to take the next step, and let go. You need to do what's right for you and for Sam. I won't be coming back after tonight, darling, and I want you to—"

"No, Ethan, please!" she cried. "Please, listen to me! Stay! I'll go out more, I swear. I'll put Sam in nursery school. I'll do whatever you want, but you can't go! This house is yours! It always will be. Every time I touch anything in it—see where you've sat, or slept, or… Oh, God, please!"

"It won't work, Em. You have to leave. Maybe move near Maggie or into town. Sell the cottage and—"

"What will happen to you?"

There was a soft chuckle. "Nothing can happen to me, darling. It's already happened."

"But if I leave, will you still… Will you be here?"

"I don't know the answer to that, Em. I don't know why I'm here, now. Maybe it's the cottage, or maybe it's you. But I do know that it's time to go on with your life, and Sam's."

"My life is here. With you, Ethan," she implored breathlessly. "It's all I want. It's enough!"

"No, Em. It's not enough. Not for either of you. All this time I thought I was helping you, but I was wrong. You need to start over, with someone who loves you. Maybe even have more children when you're ready. And Sam needs a father."

Emily clapped her hands over her ears. "Stop trying to plan my life! I am so *sick* of people planning my life! I won't listen to this! I'm happy here with you, the way we are."

"Emily, darling," Ethan said softly. "Can't you see that I'm *not* with you? Not really. Not the way you need. And someday soon, that's going to break your heart. And as much as I'm capable of feeling sorrow, Em, it's breaking mine already."

They talked for the remainder of the day and most of the night, and when Emily fell asleep in his arms, she dreamed of a bright, sunlit beach where the three of them were collecting shells.

The last thing she said to Ethan before she slept was what she'd been saying all evening. But this time she tried to make her arguments firmly and calmly, without tears.

"I can't leave, Ethan. Not ever. Not this house, and not you. I love you, and if you love me, you'll never ask me to do that."

She got up the next morning and searched the house for her car keys, then stuffed Sarah in the backseat for the ride to Matt and Kate's to bring Sam home. Tonight, when she was calmer, she and Ethan would talk again. They would work something out. They had to.

When she got to the O'Connells' place, Matt was in the yard, watching Sam play a complicated game of hide-and-seek with the two little girls from next door.

"The Maxwells' grandkids," Matt explained. "The younger one's already set her cap for poor old Sam. Would you look at the little redheaded hussy? The kid doesn't have a chance. What's for lunch, wife?" he shouted into the kitchen. "Emily looks hungry enough to eat a horse."

"No, thanks, Matt. I'm running late. I need to collect Sam and get back."

"Eat, or we keep the kid," he said. "It's that simple. I hold all the cards."

Emily laughed. "You're a pain in the ass, Dr. O'Connell."

"I'm old," he grinned. "I get to be a pain in the ass."

After they'd eaten and she'd been loaded down with a basket of leftovers, Emily packed Sam and Sarah into the car and headed for home. It had turned cool, so Emily turned on the heat, slipped a tape in the player and she and Sam sang funny songs all the way to their turnoff. They were barely on the beach road when Sarah began to whine and Emily knew to stop the car at once. While Sarah searched high and low for the proper place to attend to her needs, Sam prowled the sand for interesting bugs and Emily leaned against the car and watched clouds gathering in the west. A storm was on its way.

"Come on, Sam, it's about to rain. We need to go," she called, then gave a whistle for Sarah, who had found a rabbit hole to investigate. As she lifted Sam into the car, Emily glanced down the beach toward the cottage. A cloud of gray smoke was rising above the dunes.

By the time she swung the car into the driveway, the house was fully engulfed in flames. Two fire trucks were on either side of the yard, pumping water in great silvery arcs onto the tiny cottage, which seemed even smaller in distress. Emily stopped well behind the trucks, locked a shrieking Sam in the car with Sarah, and ran to the back of the house.

She had almost reached the steps when a strong arm prevented her from getting any closer.

"This is my house!" she screamed, clawing at the fireman's arm to get free. "Please! Let me go!"

"There's nothing left, lady!" he shouted over the noise of the pumps. "Nothing! It went up like a torch. Try to calm down, and back off. Was there anybody inside? Any pets or anything?"

"My husband," she shrieked. "Oh, my God!"

"Your husband!" He whirled around and waved to another fireman. "Jimmy! She says there's a guy still inside!"

Suddenly, Emily realized what she'd said. "No!" she shouted. "I'm sorry! I didn't mean to say… No! There's no one inside!"

The fireman looked at her as though she were crazy. "Come on, lady, which is it? I'm not about to risk my men's lives if…"

Emily shook her head miserably. "There's no one left inside. No one." Numb with grief, she staggered back to the car, unlocked it, and took the terrified Sam into her arms. She crushed him to her, burying her face against his damp neck. He'd been crying hard, but now his fascination with the fire trucks began to distract him, and he settled into hiccups and sniffles, straining to escape his mother's grasp long enough to peek over her shoulder. Seconds later—with one deafening clap of thunder—the storm broke, and a torrential downpour swept over them.

It was two days before the fire department would allow her access to the cottage. Matt drove her, while Sam stayed at home with Kate and Sarah. Maggie came up to join the search for whatever might have survived the flames.

Emily was astonished to find the old bow-back rocker safe in the yard, sopping wet, but only a little singed, and when she saw it, she cried with relief. She had nursed Sam in that chair almost every day of his first year. But nothing else from the house had survived, beyond some dishes and a few of Sam's favorite toys. The toys, including the ubiquitous giant Winnie the Pooh, were found—unaccountably—many yards from the house.

In a curious but lucky coincidence, Emily had moved most of the photo albums and Sam's baby pictures to the boathouse several days earlier—at Ethan's suggestion. The bedroom closets were so crowded, he'd joked, there was no room for his shirts. Her own wardrobe was no loss, and Sam's grief at the loss of his truck collection was remedied with a quick trip to Toys "R" Us and the expenditure of a small fortune.

All that remained of the cottage was the charred framework and foundation, the flagstone floors in the kitchen and the massive fireplace. The lovely old wooden planking was badly scorched and the deck had been reduced to pilings and steps going nowhere. She found the burnt remains of a faded blue storm shutter lying on the sand, and under the house, the red flower pots she'd painted and then forgotten on the day Ethan died.

Within days, she was contacted by an investigator looking into the possibility of arson. The fire had started, they believed, with an antique oil lantern that had fallen from a windowsill. Did Emily know anything about it? It was daylight, she explained, and in any case, the lamp was purely decorative and had rarely been lit. No one had been home, and there was no trace of either footprints or tire prints, although the rain might well have washed them away.

Emily knew what had happened, or thought she did, although she couldn't explain how Ethan could have set a fire. Sam nearly created a problem by wondering out loud how all his favorite toys got outside by themselves. When she was questioned about this, she scolded Sam in front of the investigator, then told him, over Sam's howls of protest, that Sam had left them in the yard himself, like the careless little brat he was. It was obvious that the investigators weren't satisfied, but when it turned out that the cottage was woefully underinsured, she was eliminated as a suspect.

When Matt drove her home from the investigator's office, he put one hand on her shoulder and said simply, "He did this for you and Sam. You know that, don't you?" Emily didn't answer. She was thinking about fate, and remembering the unexpected rainstorm that had brought Ethan and her together. The fire department had told her that if *this* storm had arrived even fifteen minutes earlier, the cottage could have been saved.

Chapter 15

"You're coming home with me," Maggie said firmly, making it more an order than a statement. "Sam can start at the play school down the block, and I've got plenty of room for your art stuff, and—"

"Thanks, Maggie, but I'm thinking of staying in the boathouse for a while," Emily said.

"You can't be serious, Em! It's the size of my closet. And think about it. You'd have to be looking at what's left of the cottage all day. How depressing is *that* going to be?"

"It's big enough for Sam and me. He'll be with Kate a lot, and I'll have a chance to get back to work. I need that more than space, right now. As far as the cottage goes, I'm going to get someone to clear everything away as soon as I can."

"That's crazy," Maggie said bluntly.

"Maybe. But it's what I'm going to do."

"If you sell that oceanfront lot to some sucker, you'll be a rich woman," Maggie teased.

"I already am, it seems. I got a call from the lawyer. Ethan must've had the first penny he ever made."

"So you're going to live in a nasty, falling-down shed with no heat and a bathroom the size of a postage stamp—with no toilet?"

"It has a toilet," Emily said smugly. "It works with a chain. You pull the chain, water rushes down a pipe from a big wooden tank on the wall above your head, and there you are. Modern plumbing, circa 1906."

Emily had no real interest in toilets, showers or the relative comfort of the boathouse. What she wanted was to be alone to think, and to explore the remains of the cottage by herself. And she wanted to be able to cry without witnesses—to weep, to scream out loud the silent grief she was still holding inside. Most of all, she wanted Ethan, and this was the only place she knew to look for him.

Matthew and Kate were even more unhappy than Maggie with the idea of Emily taking up residence in the boathouse, and Matt had a considerably more colorful manner of expressing his disapproval.

"If you think I'm going to stand by while you lock yourself and my grandson up in that moldy, nineteenth-century meat locker, you're just plain barking up the wrong tree. That's the most dim-witted idea you've ever had, and you've had your share of them, that's for sure! Ethan would give your stubborn rump a good swat or two if he knew you were doing something this stupid.

"If you don't want to live with us, that's all right. I wouldn't, either, if I wasn't stuck with it. We'll find you a nice little house or an apartment near here, and Kate and me can watch Sam while you're working. Or you can get him in some sort of nursery school for a few hours each day. But you're not moving into that molding hovel, and that's the end of the discussion!"

It might have been the end of the discussion, but two days later, Emily and Sam and Sarah moved into the boathouse, along with several new pieces of furniture for Sam and three boxes of newly purchased Winnie the Pooh merchandise. A great deal had happened to Emily over the years, and she'd learned certain lessons better than others, but she was no longer about to be pushed around by any man, even the bombastic, well-meaning Matthew O'Connell.

She arranged for Sam to go to a small preschool in the village three mornings a week, and set about making the studio livable for the two of them and one giant dog. The boathouse was still without proper heat, but until she could think of a better living arrangement, staying here would keep them near Ethan, and near the place she'd been the happiest.

Emily spent the first few days combing through the wreckage of the cottage, searching for anything of Ethan's. She found the barely recognizable remains of his pipe by the fireplace, and the twisted metal frames of several of the photos that had been on the mantel. She knelt in the ashes and sifted for hours looking for the lovely little shell, but it, too, was gone.

Mainly, she sat on a stepladder in the gaunt husk of the cottage, pleading with Ethan to speak to her if he could. She did this every day for a week, while Sam played contentedly in the yard. If he thought it odd that Mommy spent her time sitting amidst a pile of burnt wood and rubble, he didn't show it. Sam had recently discovered that Sarah would chase a stick or a ball as many times as he cared to throw it, maybe thousands of times in a row, without complaint. And now, with a determination bordering on scientific investigation, he was testing the limits of her patience. Finally, after watching for a half an hour, Emily came to the exhausted dog's rescue.

"That's not nice, Sam. You're teasing Sarah."

"She likes it," he answered, quite reasonably.

"No, she doesn't, sweetheart. She's only doing it to make you happy, and to make you like her."

Emily smiled to herself, remembering her life with Dennis. Another life lesson, she thought.

By the end of that week, she knew that Ethan wasn't there. It was quite simple, really. He had been part of the cottage, and the cottage was gone. She'd never known him to appear anywhere else—not in the boathouse or even in the yard—only within the four walls of the cottage, and once on the deck. The realization that there was probably no further hope came over her suddenly, and for the rest of that day, she struggled to control her panic and fear and to get Sam to bed before giving way to her grief. At four in the morning, after alternately crying and sleeping fitfully for hours, she got up, clamped a fresh canvas on The Six-Hundred-Dollar Easel, and began to paint the cottage as she remembered it.

Though the new, proudly independent Emily would not have readily admitted it, the boathouse turned out to be a very bad idea. It was too small, of course, and damp. Even with the weather still warm, it was often chilly inside its thick stone walls, and the space heaters she had once used seemed unsafe with Sam around. The boathouse needed work. Emily pulled out a pad of paper and a drawing pencil and designed a room addition that would make the building roughly L-shaped. Someday, she would have a new house built on their beach—one with three spacious bedrooms, an extra bathroom and an enormous picture window with the same spectacular view of the ocean, But for now, this addition, along with a heating system and a bit of modern plumbing, would make her little studio into a practical apartment for her and Sam.

After prowling every inch of the boathouse with pen and paper in hand, Emily catalogued everything that needed repair, but when she began to reexamine the eight pages of closely lined notebook paper, she concluded that it would be easier to list what *didn't* need fixing. Assuming a day or two for each trifling repair and a week for more substantial ones, her initial calculations indicated that the boathouse might be habitable shortly before her seventy-eighth birthday. To make matters worse, she knew that if Ethan were here, he'd tell her it was a waste of money.

Emily sat on the floor, itself drastically in need of re-placing, and edited her list to include only those items that seemed life-threatening.

The boathouse was really only one large room, divided now into a tiny kitchen area and the living room/studio, where she'd had partitioned off one corner as a bedroom for Sam. Emily slept on a blue gingham fold-out couch that had been a gift from Ethan for the new studio. The building had been through several incarnations, as an office, a garage, and a guesthouse, and was equipped with a small refrigerator, a 1940s-era apartment-size gas stove that worked erratically, and an old porcelain sink from which Ethan had scraped enough dried paint, motor oil and rust to make it usable. Aside from the large front window that had faced the cottage, there were only two other windows—one of bottle-bottom glass set in the upper half of the door, and a second in the tiny bathroom that Ethan had laughingly referred to as the "head."

Her immediate problem, though, was heat. She asked Matthew, and after delivering a ten-minute rant about "obstinate females" he suggested a plumber named Harry Jarvis for the job.

Sam was at preschool a few days later, and Emily was working when she heard a car drive up.

"It's about time," she complained irritably, going to the door to greet the plumber, who was already two hours late. A dark green pickup truck was parked at the edge of the yard, and as she watched, a tall, well-built man got out and started for the boathouse. He wore a blue baseball hat over a heavy shock of white-blonde hair, and she noticed that he walked with a pronounced limp.

"You must be Mr. Jarvis," she said, opening the door to greet him.

"No-o-o," he replied slowly. "I'm afraid there's been a mix-up. My name is—"

"You're not Harry Jarvis?" she interrupted.

"No, ma'am. Harry Jarvis is a plumber. My name is Joshua Lundgren. Carpentry, general construction. I talked to your husband around three and a half years ago about a remodeling job." He nodded toward the remains of the burnt cottage. "That's a real shame. It was a great house."

"Yes, it was," Emily said sadly. "My husband passed away three years ago, Mr. Lundgren."

"Oh, I'm sorry to hear that, Mrs…?"

"Douglas," Emily said.

Josh shook his head. "Douglas! That's it, of course!" When he looked up and saw Emily staring at him, he apologized. "I'm sorry. I've been away for a while, and my records got in a real mess. If you've got a minute, I'll explain." He reached into his shirt pocket and pulled out a folded check. "When your husband and I talked, he gave me a deposit on the work we agreed to, and I'd like to return it, now, along with my apologies for the delay."

"I lost most of our papers in the fire, Mr. Lundgren," Emily told him. "I have no records or receipts, so there's no way I can insist on a return of…"

"Your husband seemed like a decent person, Mrs. Douglas. I'm not about to cheat his widow. What records I've got show he gave me a check for fifteen hundred dollars." He handed her the check. "That should be right. I've added thirty-eight months' interest, if that seems fair to you. There's no payee on it, so you can just fill in your own name on that line, I guess."

Emily glanced at the check and smiled. "More than fair, Mr. Lundgren. I appreciate it. I would never have known about this if you hadn't shown up. May I ask what Ethan… What my husband had planned? Not that it matters any longer, I suppose."

Lundgren looked embarrassed. "Well, that's the thing, Mrs. Douglas. I had an accident around that time, and don't remember much. I came out okay, but it left me with a few problems. A fuzzy memory, mostly. I was never much good at record-keeping, and usually just shook hands with clients and kept everything else in my head." He laughed. "Not a great idea, now that I think about it. I wasn't even sure of where to find you till my mom—she does the bookkeeping—went through the files and found a note I'd written back then. It's funny, though. I remember a lot about that cottage and talking to your husband. I'm sorry it took me so long to find you and return the money, but…"

"There's no apology necessary. Thank you."

"That's all right," he said. "I'm glad to finally get it straightened out. I'll be getting back to work now, I guess." He turned to leave, took a few steps and came back. "You didn't say what it was you needed done, but I might be able to help. I'm not a licensed plumber, but since Jarvis didn't show and I'm already here, I can at least take a look, if you'd like."

Emily didn't hesitate. "Thanks. That would be great. What I need is heat, a functioning bathroom and a room addition, and I need it all in a hurry. Please, come in." When Emily opened the door wider, he stepped inside, removing his cap and wiping his feet carefully on the mat. He was neatly dressed in a dark green flannel shirt and a pair of paint-spattered jeans that appeared freshly laundered, and he wore tan hiking boots. Like a workman should look, she thought, a neat, clean, competent workman. So far, so good.

She trailed behind him patiently as he surveyed the interior of the boathouse with what she hoped was an expert's eye.

"Small," he commented.

"Intimate," Emily corrected him. "And cozy."

He grinned. "Okay, intimate and cozy. You're actually living here?"

Emily made a face. "Why does everyone keep asking me that?"

Lundgren dropped to one knee and peered under the sink, then rolled up his sleeves and poked mysteriously at the pipes underneath. As he stood up again, he took a small notepad and a pen from his hip pocket. "I'll look around outside in a minute," he said. "But, first, why don't you give me a quick idea of what you were looking to do here." Emily saw that he had blue eyes. Not Ethan's gray-blue, but an astonishingly clear ice-blue, like Paul Newman. Chiding herself for being distracted by something so irrelevant as the color of Joshua Lundgren's eyes, Emily handed her list to him and watched nervously while he read it. The blue eyes scanned the list quickly. Too quickly, she thought, with a tiny stab of dread.

"Mainly," she explained hastily, "it's the heating. I've got to get everything all wired or ducted or whatever you call it before it gets much colder—so I can manage through the winter. Do you… I mean, can you do that kind of thing?"

He leaned back against the counter and crossed his arms, and Emily noticed his hands for the first time—strong, callused workman's hands, and beneath the rolled up shirtsleeves, his forearms were muscled and tanned, the blond hair bleached white-gold by the sun.

"Sure, I can," he answered, with a smile. "If you've got money to burn."

"What does that have to do with it?" She bristled at the crack, suddenly annoyed. "Look around. Does it look like I've got money to burn?" Emily was oddly reluctant to admit that she could easily afford what she wanted. She'd just met this man, but suddenly, she wanted his respect—to be regarded as responsible and thrifty, not extravagant.

Josh nodded. "I'm sorry. I didn't mean to sound rude. I just want you to understand the kind of money we're talking about here. This building wasn't meant to be lived in. It's not even insulated. Even the cottage you lost was never meant to be occupied year-round, and I'll lay odds that this boathouse was built a long time before the cottage. People used to come from the city for the season and leave by Labor Day. They generally closed these places up till the next summer. Someone's made a stab or two at fixing this place up, but there's no way that…"

Emily held up her hand to stop him. "Okay, I get the picture, Mr. Lundgren." She sighed. "So, nothing can be done?"

"My name's Josh," he said. "And lots of things can be

done." His maddeningly affable tone was beginning to irritate her. "But that brings me back to money."

Emily frowned. "All right…Josh. Yes, I can afford it, if that's what you're worried about." She sat down at the small table, and motioned for Josh to take the other chair.

As he sat, Josh shook his head with regret. "I'm sorry to dump all this on you, and I want you to know I sympathize. I really do. It's your money, but if you're asking my opinion, I'd have to tell you honestly that you'd be throwing good money after bad to try to turn this place into something it's not. What is it my Mom's always saying? 'You can't make a silk purse out of a sow's ear.'"

Emily grimaced. "Sow's Ear Cottage. It has a nice ring to it, don't you think?"

"I don't want to pry," he said, "but can I ask you a question?"

"Is it going to make my day even worse?"

When Josh laughed, she noticed—for no particular reason—that he had a lovely, warm laugh. "I was wondering if you have anywhere else you can wait out the winter." He looked around. "It looks like there's a child living here, and that could be a real bad idea." He seemed sincere, but she still found his concern mildly annoying.

"I don't think you need to worry about that, Mr. Lundgren. If you don't want the job, just say so." The brief look of hurt on his face made her relent. "I'm sorry. I didn't mean that the way it sounded. You've been very kind to listen. Can I ask you another question before you go?"

"Sure."

"What if I decide to rough it here, despite your good

advice, and believe me, you're not the only one telling me how stupid I am. What's the worst that could happen? And, please, be absolutely honest."

His tone toughened when he answered, and this time he didn't smile.

"Okay, I'll be absolutely honest. To begin with, you're too close to the water, and you're out here all by yourself. Plus, you've got a child to worry about. The fact is, this whole place could come down, or be swept away with you in it. That's one possibility. The two of you could be trapped and die of exposure and nobody'd know about it until they came out to turn off the power for nonpayment. That's also a real possibility, if you're going to be that stubborn, or that stupid."

For a few moments, neither of them said anything. Finally, Emily summoned her courage and asked one last question. "So, what you're saying is, you *might* feel safe living here—not in the winter, of course—but for the rest of the year, with some repairs?" she pleaded, looking for some small hope.

"Sure," he conceded with a smile, "but I'd sure as hell sleep with my pants on."

Emily sighed. "Thanks. So, tell me, is there any good news here at all?"

"Yeah." Josh grinned. "I'm not going to send you a bill." He checked his watch and stood up, pushing the chair neatly under the table. "Right now, though, I've got to get going."

"Of course. I'm really sorry I kept you so long." She got up to see him out. "Tell me, is there anything *else* hideously wrong with my exclusive beachfront property I should know about? There must be something! Toxic waste, un-recovered land mines, territorial man-eating sharks?"

"Nope. It's a great beach. I used to come out here when I was a kid. We used to call it Shell Beach. Good fishing, clamming, shell-hunting. There were more houses then, if that tells you anything. The winter storms come down the coast and hit this place like a freight train." He grinned again. "But I guess you already know that. I noticed when I drove up that you're missing a lot of shingles."

Emily sighed. "Four years, one semi-hurricane." She walked him to the door, trying to hold back her tears until he'd gone. "Anyway, thanks again for your help, even the lecture. It was nice of you to tell me the truth, and I've used up a lot of your time. Please, go ahead and send me that bill."

She shook his hand when he offered it, and stood in the doorway as he walked toward his truck. He stopped abruptly, then turned on his heel and came back, as though he'd forgotten something.

"I was wondering," Josh began, readjusting the blue baseball cap a bit self-consciously, "if you'd like to go to dinner sometime, or a movie—with me? In town, or up the coast? I know we only met today, but…" His words trailed off.

Emily flushed and stammered an answer. "I'm sorry, Mr. Lundgren…Josh. I stay pretty busy with my work, and…with my little boy. It doesn't leave me much time for… Well, for going out."

"I understand," he said politely. "Some other time maybe."

"I'm sorry," she repeated lamely.

Josh smiled. "No problem. You take care, now, and watch out for those land mines."

He climbed into his truck, and Emily watched until he turned onto the beach road before going back inside. The boathouse seemed oddly quiet now, and she glanced at her watch. Kate and Matt were to pick Sam up at school and have him home in time for dinner. That wouldn't be for another two hours and suddenly, she missed him terribly. Her first one-woman show was to be held at a gallery in Bar Harbor in little more than three weeks, and she wasn't ready, so she picked up a sketch pad, hoping to get some work done. Sitting on the floor across from her was the small painting of the cottage, and as she looked at it, an idea came to her. She opened the sketch pad and began to draw.

The next morning, she called Joshua Lundgren and asked him to drop by as soon as he could. She had a job for him, after all. A big one.

Chapter 16

Josh spread the drawings out on Emily's kitchen table and studied each one carefully. "These are terrific," he said. "I didn't remember much about that house until I saw these. It looks like you've got every detail of it down."

"You can do it, then?" Emily asked hesitantly. "Rebuild the cottage exactly like it was? Using these drawings and my husband's photographs?"

"It won't be that easy. There's a lot we have to do before I can start building. First, I'll have to get a set of plans made. That means measurements and materials and..." He stopped. "Before we go any further, Mrs. Douglas, we need to talk about a couple of things."

"I don't care what it costs," Emily said firmly.

"Well, those words are always music to a contractor's

ears, but the fact is, doing what you're talking about is…well, just plain dumb, if you don't mind my saying so."

Emily minded very much. "And exactly why is the idea so 'dumb,' as you put it?"

"For the same reasons I gave you the other day, when you asked about the boathouse. This location is dangerous. The house was even closer to the water than the boathouse is, and less protected."

"That cottage stood here for over a hundred years," she said sullenly.

"Mrs. Douglas," Josh said patiently. "I've lived here all my life, and I remember at least eight other summer cottages along this beach when I was a kid. Even before it burned, yours was living on borrowed time." He pointed out the window to the higher ground beyond the yard. "If you'd let me move it back up the beach, that might be all right, but here, you're asking for trouble. And if you're going to rebuild it anyway, why not enlarge it at the same time? It'll be a lot more livable, and easier to sell, too."

Emily shook her head stubbornly. "I don't want to sell it. I want it exactly as it was. The foundation is still there, and I have lots of pictures taken inside. You can use those to get the window sizes right and all the other details. I can show you the rest. I remember it very well."

He looked at the sketches again. "I can see that, but…" At that moment, Sam stumbled out of his "room," with Sarah right behind him.

"This is my son, Sam. Sam, say hello to Mr. Lundgren. He's going to rebuild our house."

Sam rubbed his eyes and said a dutiful hello. "I can build houses," he added.

Josh smiled. "I'm sure you can, Sam. You'll be my number one helper." He picked up the sketches and turned to Emily. "I'll take these with me, and do some rough plans, get some estimates and all that. I'll get back to you this week."

"Then you'll do it?"

"I'd like to think about it until tomorrow, if that's okay. I'll see what I can find out about the tides, things like that."

Emily thought for a moment. "All right," she agreed. "I'll be here all day."

As Josh drove away, Emily found herself hoping he'd agree. She hadn't bothered getting references or talking to other contractors. There was something about Joshua Lundgren she liked—and trusted.

But one thing was certain. She *would* have her way. Ethan's cottage would be rebuilt, exactly as it had stood for more than a hundred years.

Josh delivered the bad news in person. He wouldn't rebuild the cottage. It wasn't safe.

"And why isn't that my business?" Emily demanded.

"It is your business, but I don't have to cooperate in it. That's *my* business. Aside from everything else, I don't like seeing all my hard work get washed away. I'm proud of what I do, Mrs. Douglas, and I like to think that I build homes, not death traps."

Emily glared at him. "That's your final word?"

"Yes, it is. I'm sorry."

"Well, then, I guess that's it," she said. "Thank you for your time. Please send me a bill for what I owe you."

"You don't owe me anything,"

"Of course I do. Just send me the bill."

"Suit yourself." Josh stood up, put on his blue baseball cap and walked out the door, slamming it behind him. Emily sat down at the kitchen table, trembling with frustration.

That night, after Sam was asleep, Emily walked round the ruins of the cottage once again, turning over pieces of rubble with the toe of her shoe and looking at the moon. She perched on Sam's swing and let herself drift idly back and forth, thinking. She knew Josh was right, and what was worse, she knew Ethan would have agreed with him.

"What do you want me to do, Ethan?" she asked softly. "Please tell me, darling, if you can."

There was no answer, and Emily went inside to bed, but she didn't sleep. During the night, it turned colder, and when she got up to put another blanket on Sam's bed, she looked down at her sleeping child. Sam was the most important thing in her life, and she saw more of Ethan in him every day. Outside, the wind whipped around the corners of the boathouse with an eerie wail. Emily pushed Sam over in the narrow bed and crawled in next to him. He was still wetting the bed at night, and she knew she'd wake up soaked to the skin, but tonight, she needed to feel him close to her. She pulled up the covers and lay for a long time, listening to his soft breathing.

Early the next morning, she woke to the sound of a car

in the drive and leapt out of bed to see Josh Lundgren's
truck in the yard. As she'd expected, she was damp, and
smelled like Sam. When Josh knocked, she poked her head
out the door and asked brusquely what he wanted.

"I have an idea," he said.

"So do I," Emily responded. "Go home. I'm not up yet."

Josh looked at his watch, and slapped his head. "I'm
sorry. I can never remember that not everyone keeps my
hours. Can I come back later?"

"I thought you said everything you needed to yesterday.
Have you decided to bill me, after all?"

"Can I come in for a minute?"

Emily lost her patience. "Look, Mr. Lundgren. I just
climbed out of bed after sleeping all night with an un-
housebroken three-year-old. I smell like a wet little boy,
and I need a shower."

"Hey, I used to be a little boy," he said cheerfully. "It
won't bother me. It'll only take five minutes, I promise."

Emily groaned, but opened the door a crack. "All right,
enter at your own risk. Keep an eye on Sam, please. I'm
going to shower, if I can get the stupid thing to work."

She came out of the bathroom in one of Ethan's old
flannel robes to find Sam at the table, munching a piece
of toast and a scrambled egg.

"Sam doesn't like eggs," Emily said, watching Sam
scoop up the last bite of egg.

Josh set a plate and a cup of steaming coffee down in
front of her. "Do you like eggs?"

"I eat anything that doesn't eat me first," she said
grumpily. "What is this?"

"Eggs Benedict—sort of."

"Eggs Benedict," she repeated. "Okay, so you've tricked your way in here with exotic food. Now, what's this great idea of yours?"

"A seawall."

"A seawall where?"

"Between the last dune and the cottage. You said cost was no object, and I'm warning you right now. It *will* be expensive."

"And this seawall will keep the cottage from being washed away?"

"No. If Mother Nature wants to take out that cottage, it's history. But a seawall might give you a few minutes to get away."

"That's not very comforting."

"You're the one who was willing to live in it with no changes at all."

"When can you begin?"

"We'll need a good engineer first, to show me where to build it."

"Tomorrow?"

"Bright and early."

Emily beamed. "We're going to have our house again, Sam." Sam burped in appreciation, and reached over to steal one of her eggs.

Emily found Josh Lundgren to be a meticulous worker, who studied her sketches and turned them into a set of plans faster than she'd thought possible.

"You should have been an architect," she told him.

"Thanks, but I've wanted to be a carpenter since I was six."

Emily flushed. "I'm sorry. I didn't mean to suggest that being a carpenter was less—"

"No, that's okay. I can see why an artist like you would think that."

"But I don't," Emily protested. "I can't think of anything more wonderful than making homes for people to live in, to be happy in. With your own hands. Things that last. That's the best kind of art, Josh. Something that's useful *and* beautiful." Without knowing it, Emily had paid Joshua Lundgren the highest compliment he could have asked for.

He arrived on Wednesday with two other men and the heavy equipment required to dig the trenches for the seawall, which would go up at the same time as the new cottage. The timing would have to be perfect, Josh explained, but if the weather held, the entire project would be done before the worst of the winter storms hit them.

The next day, they began tearing down what remained of the cottage. Emily stayed inside, preferring not to watch as the frail remaining timbers crumbled. Josh had helped her comb through the rubble for scraps of molding and woodwork to get the measurements and details of each room right. Later, while Josh scribbled down figures, Emily rummaged through Ethan's photos, looking for interior shots.

They were able to save much of the original plank flooring, ripping the old boards out and stacking them under a canvas tarp until they could be refinished. The charming old flagstones in the kitchen and the mudroom were unscathed, and the stone fireplace had come through the fire with nothing more than a heavy coat of soot.

Two weeks later, while the foundations of the long seawall were curing, Josh turned his attention to the cottage. Once the debris was cleared away, the plans completed and the building permits were in hand, Josh and a helper began the framing, and within three days, the skeleton of the cottage began to reappear.

Emily's biggest challenge was keeping Sam out of the way. Having abandoned his aspirations to drive a garbage truck, he had decided to be a carpenter and a stonemason. To Sam's delight, Josh let him try his hand at both, never seeming to mind the endless questions and constant tug at his pant leg.

"I'm sorry," she apologized again, dragging Sam away from the pile of lumber he was clambering over.

"Don't worry about it." Josh tousled Sam's hair. "He's no trouble, really. He's a great kid. You're a lucky lady."

"You want to buy him?" Emily asked cheerfully. "Stick around till bedtime some night and make me an offer. Sam thinks bedtime is for sissies."

Josh laughed. "I never liked to go to bed when I was a kid, either. I was always afraid I'd miss something."

Emily gave him a curious look. "That's exactly what Sam says. He told me he's afraid good stuff will happen while he's asleep and he'll miss it. I think he's gotten life mixed up with Santa Claus coming."

"Well, I guess it's a great thing to get up every morning thinking something terrific has happened while you were sleeping," Josh said. "It'd be great to look forward to every day like a kid does, instead of like we…"

He stopped without finishing the thought. "I'm sorry, I didn't mean to get philosophical, if that's what it was. Maybe it was just whining."

Though she wasn't doing the physical work of rebuilding the cottage, Emily still felt drained at the end of every workday. When the workers had left for the day, and Sam was finally in bed, there was little time or energy left for grieving, and she was grateful for that. Even as she recognized the irrationality of worrying about the well-being and happiness of the dead, she thought about Ethan every day—and worried about him. She was tormented by what he had once told her—that in some way, he was capable of feeling loss. The sooner the cottage was finished, the sooner she'd know where he was, and *how* he was.

Sam talked incessantly about Josh now, and after Josh brought him a miniature yellow hard hat and a fully equipped tool belt of his own, Winnie the Pooh slipped several notches in her son's affections. Before long, Pooh and Piglet were sleeping in the toy box, replaced in Sam's bed by the beloved tool belt. He'd never spoken about the "tall man" again, and Emily began to accept that Ethan had been right. Sam *had* needed someone else in his life. What was harder to accept was that with each day that passed, she realized more clearly that *she* had needed someone else, as well.

Josh hadn't asked her out again, but she knew it was only a matter of time. She'd seen the way he looked up when she walked by, and noticed how often he sought her company or her advice about some unimportant detail.

She'd learned about Josh's own tragedy from Kate,

right after she hired him. Kate was in the middle of baking when Emily dropped by with the news.

"Actually," Emily explained, nibbling on a burned cookie, "Ethan had already contracted this guy several years ago, so I guess he's good. His name is Lundgren."

Kate stopped what she was doing. "Not *Josh* Lundgren?"

"That's him. Why? Do you know him?"

"Of course." Kate's face suddenly went sad. "Josh's wife, Annie, was killed in that terrible robbery a few years back. At that minimarket out on highway four?"

Emily remembered the story Matthew had told her about the shooting. "I didn't make the connection," she said softly. "How awful."

Kate shook her head sorrowfully. "He's such a nice young man, too. And his mother, Grace, is as good a soul as you'll find on this earth. For a while, it looked like losing Annie and the baby was going to kill poor Josh, too. A lot of people still think he didn't go off that bridge by accident. It was months before he could go back to work, and even longer to really get his memory back."

Kate wiped her hands on her apron and sat down at the table across from Emily. "You know how Matt and I feel about your building that house again, but since you're set on it, you've certainly found yourself a good carpenter—probably the best in the state. You know, it's a funny thing, but I even thought about introducing the two of you a while back. I thought you might hit it off, but Matthew told me to butt out, like he always says to my matchmaking. But I still think it's a good idea."

"I'm not ready for that, Kate—not yet."

"And when will you be ready? Seems to me you've already grieved more than is healthy."

"Ethan wasn't just my husband, Kate. He was my life."

"Nonsense! You loved him and he loved you, but now he's gone and you've got your whole life ahead of you. And Sam's life. I can just imagine what Ethan would say to that kind of foolishness."

Emily didn't have to imagine it. "And when we die, all's over that is ours; and life burns on, through other lovers, other lips…" she said softly.

"That's pretty. What is it?"

"A line from a poem. I found it inside a book—after Ethan died." Emily didn't mention that Ethan had left the poem in her book *two years* after he died.

"You know, Emily," Kate said. "When I was a girl, all I ever wanted was to be a nurse, a missionary, and have kids—six, at least. So, after nursing school, I spent fifteen years in a Brazilian jungle trying to bring a group of Guarani Indians to the Lord, only to find out that they were already better Christians that most people I knew. Then I got real sick and the church sent me home. It was a year before I was up and around, and that's when Matthew came along. We tried for a while to get me pregnant and then found out that all the drugs I took during my illness had left me sterile. By that time we were too old to adopt. For a while, it was real hard for me to bring babies into the world for other women when I couldn't have one of my own, and I almost quit."

Emily reached across the table and grasped Kate's hand. "I never knew, Kate. I'm so sorry."

Kate brushed away a tear. "But then, when I was feeling really low, Ethan came to us. We were lucky. Emily, honey, I know it sounds cruel—me sitting here telling you how lucky you are—but I'm going to say it, anyway. You and Ethan were both wounded, unhappy people, but by luck or the grace of God you found each other. You thought you couldn't have Sam, and you did. And now, Josh Lundgren walks into your life, like…"

"Oh, for heaven's sake, Kate, don't turn this into a big romance. I hardly know the man!"

"Has he asked you out?"

Emily stared. "How did you know that?"

Kate went to the stove to get the last batch of cookies. "Just a guess. Are you going?"

"Of course not! I told you, I barely know him."

"You'd better do something about that quick. Josh has had a hard time of it, grieving for his wife and baby and getting over his injuries. Now he's ready to start over and you can bet he didn't just pick you out of some hat. Josh is a real careful fella."

"And you are a hopeless romantic, Kate O'Connell." Emily took one last cookie for the road, and went home.

The walls were framed and the roof timbers were going up when Josh asked her out to dinner again. And once again, Emily declined.

"It's only dinner," he said. "We don't have to call it a date."

"It wouldn't be fair to you, Josh. Please understand."

"Okay, then. I'll wait awhile, but I *will* ask again, if it's all right. I'm not in a hurry. All the best things take time to build, you know. But they last." He grinned. "Sorry, I didn't mean to make you sound like a contracting job."

Emily laughed. "It sounded fine. I think I even feel complimented. That's how I felt when I first saw the cottage, actually. It was so sturdy, I knew it would always be here—be ours." She looked across the yard and sighed. "My husband told me then that nothing lasts forever, no matter how much you want…" Emily didn't finish the sentence, but motioned toward the kitchen. "Would you like a cup of coffee, Josh? Sam's napping, so I might even be able to get a word in edgewise. I make rotten coffee, but it's hot."

"Good enough. I've never found a cup of coffee I couldn't drink. When you get up at five o'clock every day, you learn not to be picky." He flushed again. "That didn't come out like I wanted, either. Sorry."

They ended up spending two hours over coffee, one without Sam and one with, and when Josh left, Emily stood with her son in the doorway and waved, already anticipating his next visit with pleasure. Kate was right. Josh Lundgren was a very nice young man.

Chapter 17

"**O**kay," Maggie said, peering out the boathouse window at the workmen in the yard. "Who's the hunk?"

"Get away from there!" Emily cried. "They'll think you're checking them out."

"I *am*. I ask again. Who's the hunk? The tall, blond Viking—with the great biceps and tight buns?"

"Give it a rest, Maggie." Emily laughed. "How would Gary like it if he knew you were shopping for a replacement?"

Maggie moved the edge of the curtain so her view was unimpaired. "Window-shopping doesn't count. Gary's position is secure, and he knows it. Is the blond one Josh by any chance?"

"Yes. How did you know?"

"Gee, do you think it might be because you've said his name at least a hundred and fifty-eight times since I got here?"

"I talk about him because he's the one doing most of the real work—the planning, designing, all that," Emily said huffily. "He's a very nice young man."

"Well said, Grandma Moses. How nice and how young?"

"Very nice and probably about my age, maybe a couple of years one way or the other. I never asked."

"Has he asked you out yet?"

"No," Emily lied. "I'm his employer, nothing else."

Maggie shook her head. "How can such a bright girl be so dumb and so blind? Even your kid's in love with him."

Emily looked out the window and saw Josh carrying Sam around on his shoulders. "Yeah, they're a team, all right. Josh is great with Sam. He got him completely toilet trained, in one day, by telling him that real carpenters aren't allowed to wear training pants on the job, and…" She giggled. "*And* by showing him how to pee against a wall—'like a real construction worker,' Sam says. I told Josh that as long as Sam doesn't start guzzling six-packs and getting tattoos of naked ladies, I'm okay with it. What the hell, it worked."

For Josh Lundgren, the third try was the charm. Emily finally agreed to have dinner with him after he managed to talk Sam out of sucking his thumb.

"I'm afraid to ask how you did it," she said. "I've tried everything but duct tape."

Josh laughed. "I didn't think of that. I gave him a bag

full of metal slugs off the junction boxes. I told him every time I saw him sucking his thumb he had to pay me back two slugs. Your kid's got a real greedy streak. He wasn't about to end up with an empty bag. After a couple of days it began to work. He must have five pounds of them."

She nodded. "He even sleeps with them. The ones he didn't stuff in his piggy bank. I offered to change them for nickels but he wouldn't go for the deal. Sam may be greedy but he's no financial wizard."

They shared more Sam stories and then Josh asked her again to have dinner with him the following night. "I promise it'll just be dinner, and nothing fancy, at that. Maybe a sandwich or a burger at McGinnis's? Or there're a couple of places up the coast I thought you might like."

Emily started to utter the familiar refusal, but then she hesitated. And while she thought about it, Josh stood and waited politely for her decision. He probably asked women out all the time, she realized, a bit surprised by the twinge of jealousy she felt.

"That sounds very nice," she said finally, cringing inwardly at her clumsy choice of words.

Josh smiled. "Great. I'll call you tonight."

Emily watched him drive away, then walked slowly back to the boathouse, trying to decide if she was pleased or terrified by the idea of having dinner with Josh Lundgren—and why a simple "date" was so unnerving.

That evening, Emily tried not to focus on Josh's promised call, and when the phone finally rang at a quarter to nine, she didn't answer immediately. She was still having difficulty with the concept of a date, and had spent the past two hours thinking about how to politely escape from her rash promise. She'd practiced several conversations—sensitive, considerate ways of backing out without injuring his feelings. After letting the phone ring seven times, she picked up the receiver.

The problem was resolved when she discovered that the caller wasn't Josh at all, but a robotic voice offering her an excellent deal on vinyl siding. After hanging up, she opened the book she had been pretending to read, oddly annoyed that the invitation she was so smugly preparing to reject didn't seem to be coming, after all. When the phone didn't ring again for two hours, Emily concentrated resolutely on her book, struggling with the impulse to check and see if the phone was out of order. At eleven-thirty, she conceded defeat and picked up the receiver, only to hear the whine of a healthy dial tone. She slammed the phone down again and swore aloud.

"Damn! It's like being in high school again."

After her divorce, Emily had also resisted dating, and her first experiences had only made her more wary of her own judgment. In the first year, she'd accepted a blind date with a "real great guy" recommended to her by a coworker. Aaron, the real great guy, turned out to be an insurance salesman who owned a very pretty little house, a pool and a dog. Since she liked Aaron and the dog and wanted them to like her, Emily eased into the familiar pattern of doing everything she could to please Aaron. Agreeing to Aaron's wishes and everything Aaron said in order to keep him in a good mood was an easy regression for Emily, but it wasn't long before his wishes began to sound like orders, and before Emily realized that Aaron had begun to remind her of Dennis.

After she said goodbye to Aaron, she missed the dog a lot.

Aaron had been her last date—until Ethan swept into her life.

Just after midnight, when Josh still hadn't called, Emily kissed her sleeping son, turned off the lamp and made her way to the couch in the dark. Framed by the large front window, the beach glowed clean and white, and Emily lay for close to an hour, watching the blue-green ocean and feeling lonelier than she had since Ethan left.

Sam was already at his new play school when Josh pulled into the yard the following morning. Emily threw a light jacket over her flannel nightgown and straightened her hair, and went to the door. A cold wind was blowing, but she found Josh kneeling at the bottom of the steps.

He glanced up from what he was doing. "Hi. What's up?"

"I was about to ask you the same thing," she said, hoping to sound cool and indifferent.

"What are you doing?"

Josh pried up a splintered board from the bottom step with a crowbar. "I'm fixing your steps. They're rotten. Someone could get hurt."

"Don't bother. I'm running way over budget, as it is. Besides, I'm the only one who ever uses them. Your friend Sam usually jumps off the top step into the mud."

He began loosening the next stair. "That's okay. I work cheap."

Against her will, Emily softened. Josh was hatless in the cold but wearing a heavy denim jacket, a grim reminder of the approaching winter. His hands looked red and roughened by the biting wind, and when it gusted and blew his hair off his face, she noticed a thin scar on his forehead.

"You've got to be really cold. Coffee?"

"Sure. I'll be inside in a couple of minutes. You'd better get out of the wind."

She went inside and started a pot of coffee, swearing again at the ancient stove. She'd opened the oven door to warm the room, but it was barely taking the edge off the morning chill. Emily watched through the small window as Josh carefully measured and then sawed off the end of several boards, and she noticed for the first time that he had a habit of biting his lower lip when he concentrated. She also noticed that Josh was still wearing a wedding ring.

A minute later, he closed the toolbox, brushed the sawdust from his pants and came up the new steps. He knocked once, then opened the door and looked in, rubbing his hands briskly. "Hello again," he called, before entering.

Emily motioned for him to sit down at the table and poured two mugs of coffee. "I forget. Do you like sugar or cream?"

"No, thanks. This is good." He pulled the cup across the table to him, warming his hands on the hot mug and looked out the front window toward the beach.

"About the steps," she said. "I appreciate the thought but you didn't have to do that—especially in this weather."

"It's the windchill that makes it seem colder than it is," he said. He nodded toward the open stove, and frowned.

"The new furnace should be in by this weekend, but until then, stop using that stove for heat. It's not safe."

"I'll add that to my list of code violations," Emily snapped.

"Sorry, I didn't mean to sound…" He put down his coffee and looked at her. "I wanted to apologize for last night, too."

Emily tried her best to seem confused. "Last night?"

"I was supposed to call," he reminded her. "About dinner tonight?"

"Oh, yes. That's right. I'd forgotten," she lied.

"I was tied up at a work site," he explained, "and by the time I got to a phone, I figured Sam would probably be asleep—maybe you, too. Anyway, I'm really sorry. Are we still on for tonight?"

Emily hesitated.

"What time?" she asked, finally.

"Seven, if that's okay?"

When they had agreed on the time, Josh stood up and walked to the door. "I'm just going to finish those steps then I'll take off. I'll see you tonight—at seven."

He closed the door behind him and went down the steps to his toolbox. A few minutes later, Emily saw him drive away, leaving behind four new steps. In addition to the repair, he had taken the rotten boards with him and cleaned up all the scraps of wood he'd created. Emily sighed. It seemed that everything about Joshua Lundgren was perfect.

After she picked Sam up at school, Emily dropped by Kate's to ask if he could spend the night, then casually mentioned that she was having dinner with Josh. Kate's reaction was enthusiastic.

"I just knew you two would finally get together." She beamed with pride.

"We're not together. It's just dinner," Emily reminded her. "I'm not looking for anything else, Kate. Not yet."

"Not yet, my eye!" Kate chided. "It seems to me you're trying to make it not *ever*. If Ethan knew you'd try to turn that place into some kind of shrine to his memory, he'd have burned it down himself, even if he had to come back from heaven to do it."

Emily paled, but tried not to react any further. "I know Josh is a good man, Kate," she said quickly, "but he's been hurt in the past, and I don't want to be the one to hurt him again."

Kate laughed. "Well now, don't get so high and mighty about it, like you're doing the man a favor. Josh was quite the heartthrob in high school—captain of the football team, with every cheerleader and homecoming queen in two counties after him." She winked slyly. "And I wouldn't be surprised to hear that one or two of those old flames of his are at loose ends these days."

"Okay, so I was never a cheerleader," Emily said, scowling. "I was a hall monitor once, until I got canned for smoking in the faculty bathroom. Does that count?"

"Joke as much as you want," Kate said. "But be sure you know what you're throwing away. Now, go on home, take a long, hot shower and for goodness' sake, darling, do *something* about that hair!"

Chapter 18

Emily briefly considered a last-minute cancellation, but then her curiosity and growing interest in Josh triumphed over her panic. Now, as she sat at the dresser brushing her hair, she added up what she actually knew about him, other than what she'd heard from Kate. He was an excellent carpenter, had the good taste to adore Sam and he wasn't a known felon. On the negative side, there was that cheerleader thing, and Emily had noticed that certain tastes never seemed to change where men were concerned.

Since Ethan's death, Emily had given up looking at herself naked, seeing it as pointless, emotionally destructive and masochistic. But now, she stood before the mirror in nothing but her underwear and studied her body carefully. She held her breath and drew in her stomach, then turned slowly from side to side, trying to see herself as Josh might, if it should come to that. Sex wasn't something she wanted now, and Josh seemed ready to follow her lead. Still, for the first time in years, she was about to undergo appraisal from a man's point of view—an attractive man's point of view. A man whose point of view had likely been skewed, according to Kate, by past familiarities with the cellulite-free bottoms and perky breasts of homecoming queens and cheerleaders. She hadn't thought to ask Kate what Annie Lundgren had looked like, but it had also been Emily's experience that captains of football teams and high-school heartthrobs rarely married plump, frumpy women.

Starting at her ankles and progressing slowly upward, Emily confronted each flaw or blemish that might come under scrutiny. The body in her mirror was not that of a cheerleader. Some of the pounds that she had battled most of her life had sneaked back since Sam was born, bringing with them a few new ones. She was relieved to see that her breasts were still satisfactory—nothing spectacular, but firm, with a barely discernible droop even after a year of breast-feeding Sam. Ethan had always expressed high praise for her bottom portions, and she smiled at the memory and turned to inspect the area in question, wondering if his opinion had been sincere or another of his loving attempts to boost her fragile ego.

And then Emily sat down on the floor and began to weep.

* * *

Emily had her hand on the phone to call Josh and cancel when she heard his car in the driveway, precisely at seven. She greeted him at the door, then kept him waiting while she ran to the bathroom and swallowed a handful of antacids to quell the rumbling in her stomach. She had started a new diet, and since yesterday, had consumed nothing but six cups of black coffee. Her nausea increased as they drove for almost thirty minutes along a winding coastal road. Finally, Josh turned onto a narrow lane that led down to the water's edge, where an old wooden building perched at the end of its own pier.

Emily stepped out of the car and breathed deeply to calm her nerves and her roiling stomach. Josh took her arm and looked at her closely.

"Are you feeling okay?" he asked. "You look a little shaky."

Emily smiled faintly and nodded. "I'm fine," she lied. "Really. It's just…the car, you know?"

"Yeah, that road can be kind of rough. You'll feel better when we get inside and sit down." Josh held her elbow firmly as they crossed a small footbridge that led inside.

The interior of the restaurant was simple and cheerful, with perhaps ten tables, and tall windows overlooking the ocean. An enormous open fireplace dominated one end of the room, and several people talked quietly at a small bar at the other end. Most of the tables were occupied by couples listening to a guitarist who sat on a stool before the fireplace, singing softly in Portuguese. Josh gave his name to the maître d', and they were shown to a window table.

As he took her coat and pulled out her chair, Josh's hand brushed the back of her neck, and Emily was conscious of a quick involuntary leap in what novels always referred to as her "loins." It was the first time she'd reacted physically to another man since Ethan, and it surprised her. She was grateful for the dim light, knowing that she had blushed at his touch.

"Feeling better?"

"Much better," she lied again.

"Good. Would you like a cocktail? Or wine?"

"Just wine, I guess… White."

A waiter appeared quickly, bearing menus and a wine list, and when they had ordered, Josh and Emily chatted about the cottage, and about Sam, and about Josh's work and hers. But while she admired the warmth and apparent ease with which Josh spoke about his wife—how they met and even about her death—Emily avoided any mention of Ethan.

After a few awkward moments in the car, Josh had visibly relaxed, and now seemed fully at ease, yet Emily remained uncomfortable. This situation, with its as-yet-undetermined boundaries and romantic potential, felt dangerous to her. She realized that dating was probably a regular event for Josh now, and she resented him slightly for it. She also resented that he had managed something she hadn't. He had crossed the bridge across the chasm of his grief and arrived on the other side, prepared to go on with his life.

It would be some time before Emily understood that her inability to talk about Ethan was because she felt guilty. She was enjoying Josh's company when she hadn't wanted or expected to. Midway through dinner, Emily glanced down and saw that Josh was no longer wearing his wedding band.

When they finished dinner and stepped out into the bitingly cold air, Emily felt briefly dizzy again, and appreciated Josh's steadying arm as she climbed into the car. He switched the heat on immediately, then reached behind her and took a plaid blanket from the backseat.

"There's some kind of glitch with this heater. It may be a while before it warms up in here, so you might need this." He placed the blanket in her lap.

She pulled the blanket gratefully up around her shoulders as he exited the parking lot. The radio was playing softly and she pretended to listen to the music, suddenly unable to think of anything else to say.

"I want to thank you for tonight, Josh," she said finally. "It was really nice." Emily winced at the sound of her own words, and began to count the number of times she had used the word *nice* since they left the cottage. *Please, God,* she thought, *don't let him notice.*

"Yes," he said, smiling across at her. "It was very nice. Unusually nice."

She groaned. "I'm sorry. I promise you that I'm not always such an imbecile. My friend Maggie says I'm losing the ability to make intelligent conversation. I live with a three-year-old and a dog, out there in what you tell me is a godforsaken death trap, and until you started work on the cottage, I talked more to seagulls than to adults."

A few minutes later, Josh slowed the car and pulled off the road. Emily knew they were almost home. In the foggy distance, she saw the street lights of Dunlin Cove.

"If you look real close, down there," he said, "you can just see your place—the death trap." He pointed toward a long, dark stretch of beach, and Emily finally made out a tiny dot of light. She took his word that it was the boathouse.

"See what I mean?" she laughed. "I told you I live in a very exclusive neighborhood. No neighbors at all!"

"Are you sorry you started this project of ours?" he asked. "Considering everything?"

Emily sighed. "No, I needed to do it. The reasons are a little complicated, but they're important to me. I know it's taken up a lot of time you could have used elsewhere. I guess the real question is, are *you* sorry you got involved? I know I haven't been the easiest client you've ever had."

"I like clients who know what they want—usually."

"Usually?" Emily asked.

Suddenly, Josh's voice became more serious.

"I guess I'm having a little trouble understanding what it is about this house that's so important to you—getting every detail the way it was."

"It was the first house I ever owned, that's all. My friend Matt says that—" Emily saw a chance to change the subject and grabbed at it. "Oh! I keep meaning to tell you.

We have a mutual friend—friends, actually. The O'Connells, Kate and Matthew?"

Josh smiled. "I know. Kate was Annie's midwife, or would have been, if… Matt's an old friend of my mother's. He helped her through a lot while I was sick."

"Kate gave me quite a sales pitch about you," Emily said. "She says you're a real catch."

He laughed. "Don't believe everything you hear. Kate's a notorious matchmaker. She may even be working on commission from my mom. They've both been trying to palm me off on somebody for the past year."

"I'm crazy about Matt and Kate," Emily said. "They've been Sam's grandparents—his only real family, actually. My mother and I aren't particularly close and she's out in California, anyway."

"That sounds pretty lonely," he said.

"You get used to it after a while. I want you to know how grateful I am to you, Josh, for being so sweet to Sam. He needs people in his life—especially a man."

"And what about your life?"

In the darkness, Emily blushed. "My life is…sort of at a standstill, Josh, until…"

"It doesn't have to be," he said quietly. "I've been where you are now, Emily, but at least Annie and I had more time together. We started dating in junior high school, the same year she got her braces. When I joined the Coast Guard, we kind of drifted apart, but then, one day, I ran into her again, shopping. After that…"

"That sounds like fate," Emily observed.

"That's what I said, but Annie always said it was the two-for-one shoe sale at Sears." Suddenly, Josh took a corner of the blanket, pulled Emily closer to him and tilted her face up to kiss her, very gently. It might have been the wine, but without actually thinking about it, Emily returned his kiss, and when he slipped one hand inside her coat to caress her breasts, she put her lips to his neck and breathed in the pleasant essence of warm male skin and the faint trace of his aftershave.

Josh opened her blouse and Emily helped him to remove her bra, moaning softly as he took her breasts in his hands and kissed her shoulder.

Suddenly, he swore and pulled away. "My God, Emily, you're freezing! Your shoulders are like ice!" He sat up quickly, closed her coat in one motion, and started the car. Dazed, Emily pulled herself upright and began straightening her clothes. She was breathing hard, and while her face was unbelievably hot, her feet were so cold she could barely feel them.

"What the hell was *that* all about?" she demanded, making no attempt to mask her indignation.

Josh shook his head. "I'm sorry. I guess that sort of wrecked the mood."

Emily scowled, tucking her blouse back into her rumpled skirt. "Could we just go now, please? Now that you bring it up, I *am* getting cold."

"Okay. I'm sure the car will warm up in a minute."

Emily said nothing, feeling too foolish to respond. Instead, she glared out the window, wondering how far they were from home.

They had gone no more than half a mile when he glanced across at her and asked. "Are you really that mad?"

Emily's reply was cool. "I'm not mad. I'm cold. Just forget it, all right? It's not you. I should never have agreed to go out like this. We don't even know each other. And I'm out of practice."

"Look," Josh pleaded. "I wasn't trying to rush you into anything back there…this soon, but you… Oh, hell! I'm making it worse! I'm lousy at this kind of thing."

"That makes two of us," Emily snapped.

He stopped the car again. "Emily, I'm sorry. My timing was rotten. I was just… I just didn't want you to get a case of frostbite on our very first date."

Emily stared down at her hands, feeling her anger dissolve. "It's all right, really. I was only…" She drew in a deep breath and looked up at him. "If you're not still chicken about drowning or being carried off in a hurricane, we could always go back to the death trap," she suggested, trying to sound more casual than she felt. "And talk for a while, maybe?"

Josh smiled. "I'm willing to risk it."

By the time they got back to the boathouse, though, Emily's nerves were on edge again. While Josh used the bathroom, she turned on the two electric heaters and closed the curtains to conserve what heat there was. The mood had definitely passed and she felt like a scared teenager. She wished fervently that they had remained in the darkened car, even if she lost all her toes to frostbite.

When he came out of the bathroom, Josh had combed his hair, but he looked as flustered as she felt.

"Would you like something to drink?" she offered.

"A beer, thanks, if you've got one."

She opened the little refrigerator hopefully. A single bottle of beer stood at the very back, a souvenir of the last time she had entertained Maggie and Gary.

"As a matter of fact, that's exactly what I've got. One lonely bottle. I'm not the world's best hostess, as you've probably already noticed. Or the best supplied. I think I've got potato chips somewhere."

"We can split the beer." He smiled, and Emily knew he was trying to put her at ease, but that made her feel even more foolish.

"I don't really like beer. It's all yours." She handed him the bottle and reached to the small shelf above the sink for one of her three glasses.

He glanced inside the tiny fridge.

"What *are* you in the mood for?" he asked.

Emily blushed, struggling not to laugh at the unintended humor, but couldn't help herself.

"Sorry," Josh apologized, grinning sheepishly. "I'm having a little trouble keeping my foot out of my mouth tonight. Like I said, I'm kind of out of practice." They exchanged embarrassed smiles. The ice had been broken.

As it turned out, they didn't sleep together that night. After several hours of quiet conversation and some restrained necking on the couch, Josh went home, lingering at the door long enough to deliver an extremely passionate final kiss and a promise to call the next day. Then he walked back to the car, motioning for her to go into the house and lock the door before he drove away. Emily obeyed, then stood in the middle of the room, feeling aroused but perplexed. In the car, she had very much wanted this awkward evening to end in bed, and it was obvious that Josh had felt the same. But for some reason, he had backed off, leaving her to wonder why.

So, Emily went to bed alone, and woke just before dawn in tears. Confused and frightened, she lay for a long time, trying to understand what was wrong. The truth came as a shock. In the hours since Josh Lundgren had first kissed her, she hadn't thought of Ethan once.

Chapter 19

Every evening that week, Emily and Josh talked on the phone late into the night. He began staying at the end of each workday, fixing small things around the house and ignoring Emily's protests that he was doing too much. He kissed her when he arrived, when he left, and several times in between. On Sunday night, they went to the cinema in town, held hands during the movie, and then necked rather intensely in the car before he walked her to the door and kissed her good-night. When he still hadn't tried to make love to her after two weeks, Emily finally realized that Josh Lundgren was courting her—in a rather old-fashioned and gentlemanly manner, but definitely courting her.

Saturday dawned warm and sunny, in astonishing contrast to the recent weather, and Emily spent the morning outside with Sam, basking in the unexpected sunshine and the almost humid breeze. Josh called at ten from a work site forty miles down the coast, suggesting a drive and lunch at a local inn. He arrived with a picnic basket, blankets and a cooler on the backseat of the car.

"It's such a great day, so I sort of preempted the plan. Okay with you?"

"I'm with you," she said cheerfully.

He looked around. "Where's Sam?"

"I prevailed upon Kate. This is your only day off. You don't need to entertain Sam again. You and your crew are already my unpaid babysitters."

Josh grinned. "You think we're a bad influence on him, right? Slipping him old *Playboys* when you're not looking?"

"It's not his morals I'm worried about." Emily sighed. "With all you guys around, he's turning into a football fan. Before you know it, it'll be hockey. Personally, I was hoping he'd grow up to be a poet."

"No money in it," Josh said. "Now, a plumber, that's different." He nodded toward the car. "My pal Sam the Spy tells me you don't like to cook, so I made sandwiches. Okay?"

"If I don't have to cook it, I love it."

Josh found a quiet stretch of beach a few miles from the cottage, and parked on the side of the road. Below them, Emily could see a lagoon, surrounded by a series of tide pools and protected on either side by large rock formations. Josh made his way down the steep, narrow pathway to the beach with the basket and cooler, while Emily followed with several blankets and a thermos of coffee.

"It's beautiful!" she cried. "Did you discover it?"

Josh grinned. "Sure. Just me and every tourist that's come through here for the past hundred years or so. It's even got some touristy name like 'Pirate's Cove,' but at this time of year we've got it all to ourselves."

"I hope you have a styrofoam cup or something on you," Emily said. "I'm a tide pool freak."

He held up a finger for her to wait, then climbed back up to the car, returning with a yellow plastic sand pail and matching shovel.

"How's that for prepared?" he asked.

"Amazing!"

"I got them for Sam, and if you should need a Donald Duck swim ring I'm the man to ask."

Emily removed her shoes and socks, dipped one foot in the water, and withdrew it quickly. "You know what? I think I'll skip the wading."

Josh tossed her a small towel. "The Labrador Currents. Very few people go wading in Maine in October. Which reminds me, guess what Sam told me when I showed him the swim ring."

Emily sighed. "I'm afraid to ask. Sam knows all my secrets, and apparently he can be bribed with a Donald Duck swim ring."

"He said you won't let him go in the ocean, even in the summer."

"Sam has a very big mouth for a little boy," she said grimly. "I may have to rethink my moral opposition to spanking." She sat down on a rock. "Sam is all I have, Josh, and he's my responsibility. Yes, I worry. Maybe too much sometimes. This motherhood business still feels new to me and I know I'm not always good at it but I'm the only parent Sam's got."

"It doesn't have to stay that way," Josh said quietly.

Abruptly, Emily changed the subject, stooping to roll up her pant legs. She grabbed the bucket and shovel.

"Am I going to find anything spiny or disgusting in there?" She made a face, and indicated the rocky tide pools. "You know, things that bite or sting?"

Josh shrugged. "Search me. You'll be the first to know. I'm planning to sit here, stay warm and see what happens. I think there's a snake-bite kit somewhere in the trunk, though." He began spreading a big plaid blanket on the sand. "Of course, it could be out of date."

Emily smiled sweetly. "I'd really hate to have to go back and tell Sam that his hero is a sissy. Scared of a few little creepy-crawlies."

Josh grinned, then took off his own shoes and socks and offered his hand for support as they climbed over the slippery rocks.

They explored the cove and nearby stretch of beach for almost two hours, holding hands and talking quietly, and ended the afternoon huddled together on a blanket, finishing the sandwiches and coffee. The fog came in, and they covered themselves with a second blanket, determined to make the day last despite the change in weather. When Josh unbuttoned her blouse and pressed his lips to her breasts, Emily let her fingers wander down his thigh and between his legs.

Finally, they shook the sand from the damp blankets,

gathered the picnic things and made their way back to the car in the descending twilight. Inside the car, Emily pressed as close as the bucket seats permitted, exploring his body tentatively at first, then with a growing urgency. After a few minutes, he kissed her one last time, then reached down and took her hand away. "We'd better go," he murmured.

"Why?" she whispered, trying to move close to him again.

He touched her face with his fingertips. "I love you, Emily."

Emily flushed. That word had never been spoken out loud before now. "But then…"

He smiled. "Not in the car. Not the first time."

As they drove back to Kate and Matt's to pick up Sam, Josh asked if she could get away for a couple of days. Emily promised to try.

But for the next few weeks, Emily found one reason after another not to get away for the planned weekend. First, Sam came down with a cold, and the next week, Sarah got a splinter in her paw that became infected. The following week, Emily had to finish a commissioned painting she'd simply forgotten about. The client was annoyed, she explained, and insisted on it being completed immediately.

Josh accepted the first few excuses with his usual good nature, but after the fourth cancellation, he stopped asking. He began to arrive at the cottage early, give orders to his crew about what had to be done that day and then drive off to another work site. When Emily asked why they had seen him so rarely, he remarked brusquely that it was the tail end of a busy season, and left again.

Josh's absence was hard on Sam, who asked about him every night at bedtime. Finally, Emily gathered her courage and called him at home, asking him to dinner. Josh declined politely, with no explanation.

The next time she saw Josh alone in the yard, Emily went out to talk to him. Sam was at Kate's and the work on the cottage was nearing completion. There would be few chances to be alone with him after this week. The cottage had turned out beautifully, and to Emily's eye, it looked perfect in every detail. It even had a slightly aged quality to it, and the same faded blue on the shutters. She'd avoided going inside since the interior work started for fear that it wouldn't look exactly right—or maybe because it would. She found Josh installing the same brass locks that had been removed from the cottage's burned doors.

"Will they still work?" she asked, trying to make conversation.

His reply was curt. "They work fine. I cleaned and oiled them. I still think it would've been better to get new locks, since you never did find out who torched the place. But it's your house and your money."

Emily touched his hand. "Sam misses you a lot, Josh."

"I miss him, too, but I'm about done here so I figured there was no point letting him get any more attached to me than he already is."

Emily sighed. "Are you that angry with me?"

Josh slammed the door hard. "I'm not angry, Emily. I'm confused."

"About what?" she demanded, annoyed by his tone.

He handed her the door keys and started for his truck. "Well, for one thing, about why you haven't even taken the time to look around inside this idiotic playhouse you've built for yourself after spending enough money on it to set yourself up in a damned castle."

"I will," she said sullenly. "I'm just not ready."

"Oh, I see," he said bitterly. "You're not ready for that, either. Now, let's see if I have this right. You're not ready to move back among the living. You're not ready to give your kid a normal life. And you're sure as hell not ready to have anything to do with *me!* Just what is it you *are* ready to do?"

"Go to hell!" Emily shouted, then whirled around and ran back for the boathouse. When Josh came after her and grabbed her arm, she shook herself loose, stormed up the steps and closed the door so hard she broke a bottle-glass window pane. Josh flung open the door and caught her as she tried to lock herself in the bathroom. He pulled her against him and crushed his mouth down on hers. Emily used all her strength to push him away and buried her face in her hands, moaning. "I can't do this, Josh. Not yet. You don't understand!"

Josh threw up his hands. "No, I *don't* understand, and since I'm obviously too dumb to get what's going on here, you're going to have to explain it to me. I know you loved your husband, but it's been four years!" He pushed her firmly down onto a kitchen chair, and knelt next to her. "Listen, Em, I know how hard it is to lose someone you love. After Annie and the baby were killed, I figured I'd never get over it." He rubbed his eyes wearily. "It's not something I talk about a lot, but ending up in that creek wasn't an accident—not completely, anyway. I closed my eyes, took my hands off the wheel and let God decide. And that was wrong, Em, because all I really did was make a mess of my mom's life and my own and nearly ruined the business.

"Maybe we're not supposed to 'get over' some things. Annie and I always shared everything—good and bad—and even the terrible way she died was part of that. I didn't have the right to avoid that just because it was hard for me. I know now that the only way to honor everything we had together is to use it for something worthwhile—to go on, and at least *try* to be happy.

"Maybe this isn't about your husband at all," he suggested wearily. "Maybe it's me. Maybe you don't feel about me the way I thought, and the way I feel about you. If that's it, tell me straight out and I won't keep trying. But I had begun to hope…"

Emily sighed. "It's not you, Josh. It's not even Ethan. It's… I'm sorry if I've hurt you, but there are things you don't understand about Ethan and me. Things I can't explain—that may not make sense."

"You don't think he's really dead, is that it?"

Emily gasped. "What?"

"It's that damned house. You think that by making it the way it used to be you'll feel closer to him—happier. You can sit in there night after night and pretend he's still alive. You think you owe him that kind of noble sacrifice—like some grieving widow in India, throwing herself on a funeral pyre. But it doesn't work that way, Em. That way everybody loses and everybody stays miserable. If you owe anybody in this world something, it's that kid of yours. You owe Sam a mother who's happy and there for him when he needs her, not off in some daydream. And the next person in that line is *you*. You owe yourself the chance to be happy, and to fall in love and maybe have more kids if you want them—and grandkids someday. And yeah, you even owe *me*, because I love you and that gives me some rights in all this."

"Do you think I don't know all that?" Emily said. "It's just not that easy. Ethan was more than just my husband. He saved my life. He gave me back what I'd lost—my self-respect, my confidence and a lot of other stuff. I let my first husband turn me into nothing, because that way I didn't have any responsibility for my own happiness. And Ethan made me see how wrong I'd been. He made me face it and go on."

Josh shook his head. "And now you're throwing all of that away—everything he gave you. If Ethan was everything you say he was he'd be the first one to push you back out into the world. He wouldn't try to keep you locked up so you could worship his memory!"

"I don't worship his memory! I love him!"

"He's dead, Emily! Just like Annie, and they're not coming back." Josh slumped in a chair next to her. "I know every day of my life that wherever she is, Annie's happy that I found you and Sam. If Ethan gave you something worthwhile, then you need to stop feeling sorry for yourself and pass it on! Because *that's* what it's all about."

"What do you want from me, Josh?" she asked softly. "Right now. Just tell me what you want and I'll try my best to make you happy and—"

"Cut the crap, Emily! I don't want your sacrifice! I want a woman and a wife. I want someone to laugh with, and to fight with. Someone I can take care of and who'll take care of me. I want someone to finish my sentences, and to watch old movies with and spend my life with. And maybe even a mother for my kid someday—a sister or brother for Sam."

He stopped to take a breath. "If what you're trying to do is keep Ethan alive by rebuilding that house into a shrine—by pretending he's still alive... That's not normal, Emily. It's sick and selfish, and... Oh, God, I'm sorry, Em."

Emily had begun to cry. Josh pulled her to him, and before he could stop himself, he kissed her. But this time, Emily didn't resist.

Later, they sat on the steps and talked, and Emily tried again to explain.

"I thought Ethan and I would always be together, Josh. Oh, I know everybody says that, but I believed it with all my heart. Just when I had given up on life, I got this wonderful, shiny second chance. I was convinced that my first marriage had failed because I was some kind of emotional misfit—one of those people not cut out to be happy. So when I promised to love Ethan forever and that he'd be the last man I ever loved, I meant it. It feels wrong to love anyone else as much as I did him. It feels...disloyal."

Josh smiled. "So love me just a little less if that's what it takes. Not too much less of course, but a little. And in the meantime, maybe I'll keep growing on you. I figure we'll get tired of each other after sixty or seventy years, anyway. You can go out and find yourself some other old guy—maybe a good plumber this time around, or a car mechanic. You could use both. And I'll find me some sexy old lady who *likes* to cook and darn socks."

Emily laid her head wearily against his knee. "I do love you, Josh," she said softly, saying it aloud for the first time. "But I need time. Not much—just until… Until I've worked some things out. I can't explain now, but it won't be long. In the meantime—could you stay here with me tonight and don't make me say any more? Just stay with me?"

They went inside the dark boathouse and Emily waited quietly while he opened the couch and turned down the covers. She closed her eyes as he undressed and began to touch her, reveling in the feel of his hands on her body and willing herself not to think of Ethan's hands. Afterward, as she lay in Josh's arms and listened to the rain, Emily began to understand what she needed. She needed to live with this man, raise Sam and be happy again. When she closed her eyes, she could see that shining future clearly. But what she *wanted* was a sign that would give her permission to step into that new happiness without guilt. Permission to love again—from Ethan or maybe from God. From anyone but herself, because Emily still didn't have the courage to take that chance by herself and risk the consequences. To marry Josh, she would have to abandon the lingering hope of Ethan—and she couldn't do that. Not yet.

Not until she had a sign that he was never coming back to her.

Not until the cottage was finished.

Two days later, Emily was sitting outside on the back steps, watching Sam measuring the lawn chairs, when Sam asked the question she had always feared he would ask. Several days earlier, Josh had presented her son with a retractable stainless-steel tape measure, and Sam had become obsessed with knowing how long and wide things were. His grasp of inches, feet, and yards wasn't good yet, but that hadn't stopped him from informing Emily solemnly of the height and width of everything inside the boathouse and out. The table was five, the swing set was eight, Sarah was three, and so on.

Sam shoved his tape measure in his pocket and came over to sit with her.

"Hi, kiddo. You all done measuring for today?"

He nodded, but said nothing. Sam was a child who was never without a question or an opinion on every issue, so his reluctance to talk was unusual.

Emily tried again. "Where's Sarah?"

Sam picked up a stick and drew in the sand. "She's there." He pointed to where Sarah lay napping under the picnic table.

Emily ruffled his hair. "You sound down in the dumps, sweetie. Hard day at school?"

No response. Sam tossed the stick away, and without

looking at her, asked the question she had known was coming someday.

"Is Josh going to be my daddy?"

Emily pulled him closer to her on the top step. "Would you like that?"

"Okay."

"I thought you really liked Josh," Emily said.

"Will Daddy ever come back?"

For a moment, Emily didn't know how to answer. She was still unsure of what Sam remembered of his "sightings" of Ethan while they were still in the cottage.

"No. Daddy is never coming back," she said finally.

"He's dead?"

"Yes, Sam. Do you know what that means?"

"Like my rabbit?"

"Yes, darling. Like your rabbit." Sam had found an injured baby rabbit in the grass that summer, and despite Matt's best medical efforts, it had survived for only two days. After an elaborate graveside ceremony, they had buried the little rabbit in the yard and for two weeks Sam sat by the grave for a while each day, obviously pondering what it all meant.

Once, he had asked Emily if they should dig it up, to see if the rabbit had already gone to heaven.

"Grandma Kate says my rabbit's in heaven, now," Sam said.

"Well, maybe Grandma Kate's right. Would it make you happy to think your rabbit is in heaven?"

Sam frowned. "Is Daddy in heaven?"

Emily hesitated. It would have been easy to say yes and give Sam that small comfort, but she couldn't. Her own feelings about death and a possible heaven were far too complicated for a yes or no answer. Fortunately, Sam went on without waiting.

"When you're dead, you're all gone?" Sam asked. Another hard one. Emily thought for a moment.

"You know when we watch the boats on the ocean," Emily asked. "When they get so far away we can't see them anymore?"

Sam nodded.

"Well, I think maybe it's like that, Sam. We know the boat is still there somewhere, but it's so far away our eyes can't see it any longer. It can't ever go away completely, because everything has to be *somewhere,* right?"

"A big wave could sink it and all the people could get drowned," he said.

Emily sighed. This mothering thing was sometimes harder than she had expected. "Maybe, but they'd still be somewhere, wouldn't they? In the water?"

Sam outwitted her again. "A big fish could eat them."

"Then they'd be a part of the big fish," she said. "And if another fish came along and swallowed *that* fish, they'd all be part of the even bigger fish."

Sam played with a hole in his jeans. "But the people wouldn't be real people anymore."

"No, maybe not the way we knew them, but some part of them would still be the same. The part we remember about them."

Suddenly, Emily had an idea and took him inside to the kitchen. She filled a large glass vase with water and rummaged through the drawer until she found a box of food coloring. She let Sam drip a single drop of blue coloring into the vase and they sat at the table and watched as it swirled around and finally disappeared.

"Okay, kiddo, where's the blue water now?"

"It's all gone."

"It can't be all gone, can it? Where would it go?"

"It mixed up with the other water," Sam concluded.

"Right. Now put in some more water." Sam poured another cup of water into the vase and pressed his nose against the side.

"I can't see it."

"But it's still there somewhere, isn't it?"

The little-boy logic came to the surface again. "I could pour it out on the grass."

"And what then?"

"It would be part of the grass and the dirt." He stopped and thought. "And the grass would grow bigger?"

Emily hugged him proudly. Her son was obviously brilliant—a scholar and a philosopher.

"You see, Sam? Nothing ever goes away completely—not the people we love or the good things that happen to us. Even if we can't see them or feel them or talk to them, they're always with us somewhere—for as long as we remember them, and want them there."

"Like Daddy?"

"Just like Daddy."

That night, after Sam was asleep, Emily called Josh and agreed to a three-day weekend at an oceanside resort not far from them, then called and arranged for Sam to stay with Maggie. The excursion was a romantic one, of course, but they both understood that there was much more at stake. Josh's reasons for going were fairly simple. He had bought a ring and intended to propose. Emily's reasons were more complicated. She badly needed to know what Josh expected from these few days, and when they had checked in and unpacked, she asked him.

"All I want is to be with you, Emily. No expectations and no strings, if that's the way you want it." His voice was calm, but Emily could hear the disappointment.

"And no promises?" she insisted.

Josh hesitated, but finally nodded in agreement. "No promises."

At dinner that night, Emily ordered two margaritas, finished them quickly, and asked for another as dinner was served. As she began the third glass, Josh took it from her hand and set it on the table. After a moment of considering the dripping glass, he looked up at her.

"Are you afraid of me?" he asked, twisting the base of the margarita glass around slowly on the damp tablecloth.

Emily was startled. "Am I what?"

"I asked you if you're afraid of me," he repeated, watching carefully for her reaction. "Afraid of being alone with me."

"Of course not!"

"Then why are you trying to get drunk?" There was no anger in his question, but only a kind of sad bewilderment.

"Are you hungry?" she asked suddenly. "I mean, really hungry?" Before he could answer, she rushed on. "If you're not literally starving, could we just skip dinner and go back to the room? Please? Right now?"

Josh signaled to cancel their dinner orders, apologized to the waiter and handed him a folded twenty-dollar bill as they left the table. In the several moments before the elevator arrived, Josh never took his eyes from her, obviously still puzzled. When they reached their room, Emily threw off most of her clothing before Josh could lock the door. Her cheeks were flushed and hot and her hands shook slightly as she kissed him hard. She fell back on the bed, pulling him down on top of her with an urgency that left little doubt as to what she wanted.

It was fast and feverish—far from the romantic candlelit encounter Josh had clearly planned for their first evening at the hotel. Afterward, they made love again, slowly and tenderly, and when it was over, Emily made an effort to explain. Josh lay propped on one elbow as she sat crosslegged on the bed in front of him, blushing and embarrassed. There was a noticeable quaver in her voice when she spoke.

"You were right, Josh," she confessed. "I *was* afraid. Not of you, but of this. Of taking this big step. It's been so long, since… Since I've been with a man. Oh, I don't mean sex. I mean…" She glanced up to gauge Josh's reaction to the garbled words that sounded nonsensical, even to her. "Coming here with you feels like it's my first time all over again, and I was scared. But now that we've gotten it over with, that awful feeling is gone. Does that make any sense, or do I sound totally nuts?"

For a moment, Josh was silent. "I'm not sure there's a right answer to that question," he said at last. "One that's not going to make me sound like a selfish, insensitive heel. Maybe it isn't nuts, but you'll have to pardon me if I don't find it particularly flattering, either. Getting it over with? Is that what you were doing just now?"

Emily looked stricken. "I didn't mean it that way. I meant…"

Josh shook his head. "I know what's going on, Emily, and so do you. What's bothering you is pretty simple, really. You feel guilty. Guilty about cheating on a dead husband."

Emily flushed in anger. "That's ridiculous! Besides, you and I already made love once—that night in the boathouse."

"I figure you chalked that one up to needing comfort. But this time is different. This time you're doing it on purpose. You planned to come up here with me, and that makes you feel guilty—like you're cheating on him."

Emily grabbed a pillow and hurled it at him. "That is the most stupid, unfair…"

Having ducked the thrown pillow, Josh calmly went on. "And you know how I know all this? Because that's how I felt the first time I asked you to dinner. I hadn't been with another woman since Annie died. That's why I tried to go slow. Because I didn't want us falling into bed just because we were lonely. I knew right then—the day I met you—that I had turned a corner. The big difference between us is I was *ready* to turn that corner, and you're not. I could do it because I already knew that Annie would have been cheering for it to happen. I already had permission, but you're still waiting for it. The go-ahead—some kind of sign that it's okay."

Emily closed her eyes and put her hands to her face.

"I'll take that to mean I'm right," Josh said quietly. "And I'll tell you something else you're not going to like. The second reason you agreed to come up here was to keep me happy—to tide me over and buy time until you got your head on straight about what's going on."

Emily snatched up a second pillow, preparing to throw it, but dropped suddenly into a chair, defeated.

Josh chuckled. "Another bull's-eye?"

Emily glared at him before quickly dressing and leaving the room without another word.

It was two hours before she returned. Josh had straightened the room, turned down the covers and was sitting on the bed watching the news. Emily came in silently and sat down next to him.

"Okay. No more histrionics or whining," she said softly. "You were right. Yes, I thought I needed a sign, and tonight I realized I was wrong. I've already had that sign. Ethan never asked me for eternity, Josh. I volunteered it. I don't need permission." She sighed. "But I do need to say goodbye."

For the next three days, Josh and Emily did exactly what they wanted. They took long showers together, ate greedily, shopped for souvenirs for Sam and slept blissfully late every morning after talking far into the night. They made love where and when the mood struck them, on the wide bed, in the bathtub or on the lush carpeting in front of the fireplace.

When Emily called home each night to talk to Sam, Josh lay on the floor or the bed and watched her face as she laughed at Sam's little stories.

Josh had intended to ask Emily to marry him on their last evening, but after she'd extracted his promise of no expectations, he'd wrapped the diamond solitaire in a pair of socks and hid it in the bottom of his suitcase. His proposal, and Emily's answer, would wait for another less stressful time.

On their final day, they walked around the harbor admiring the sleek white yachts that lined the docks, and when they came to a boat rental booth, Josh pointed to a small sailboat.

"You want to go out on the bay for a while?"

"You know how to do that?" she asked, somewhat surprised. "Sail a boat?"

Josh laughed. "I think I can handle it. I was born here, Em. I spent most of my summers when I was in school working as a sternman on lobster boats. My dad and I used to keep a small sloop. Nothing fancy, just for weekends."

"You are a constant source of amazement to me, Joshua Lundgren. I'd love it, but please don't mention this to Sam. He'll never forgive us."

They spent the remainder of their last afternoon on the boat, enjoying the sun, the smooth, easy sailing and quiet conversation.

"If it doesn't bother you to talk about it, Josh," Emily asked, "where is Annie buried?" Josh had taken in the sail a few minutes earlier, allowing the little boat to drift on the tranquil bay.

"You know the old Quaker cemetery?"

Emily smiled. "Oh, yes. It's beautiful there."

Josh gazed out over the water. "You probably noticed

that I don't wear my wedding ring anymore. A while back, I took it out there and left it with Annie and the baby. I dug a little hole right under the headstone and buried it there. It seemed like the right thing to do—and the right time. I knew I was falling in love with you, Emily."

Emily looked down at her own wide gold wedding band. After a moment or two, she slipped her hand inside her sweater and withdrew the long chain she had worn since the day Ethan died—the chain that held Ethan's matching wedding band. Joshua watched her, saying nothing.

She glanced up at the sky. "It'll be getting dark soon. Should we go back?"

Josh nodded and raised the sail.

As the boat began to move silently through the water, Emily looked up again at Josh.

"Do you know any verses from the Bible, Josh?" she asked softly.

"Not many, but don't tell my mom when I take you to meet her. I spent too many Sunday mornings not paying attention, I guess. I know the Twenty-Third Psalm, and part of that verse from Ecclesiastes, about a time to love and a time to die…"

"A time to weep, and a time to laugh…" Emily continued. "A time to mourn, and a time to…" She paused. "I can't remember the next line, but I'm sure it's something we've talked about. Something about getting beyond grief."

Josh nodded. "I guess that verse covers just about everything."

Emily slipped the ring from her finger and slid her wedding band down the delicate gold chain until it touched Ethan's. After closing the clasp, she folded the chain and the rings into her palm, leaned over the side of the boat and let her hand trail in the water.

"Are you sure you want to do that, Em?"

"It feels right, Josh, like you said. The right thing and the right time." She smiled. "Besides, it's kind of a tradition with me."

Emily opened her hand, allowing the joined rings to slip into the water.

The gold edges of both rings caught the last rays of the dying sun, glittered beneath the surface for a moment, then disappeared.

"Let's go home, Josh," Emily said. "I have something I need to finish."

Chapter 20

They arrived back at Dunlin Cove in the late afternoon, and as they came down the beach road and neared the last rise, Josh pulled to the side, stopped the car and got out.

"Now comes the unveiling," he said. "I told my guys to finish up the trim and install the shutters by the time we got back. Your part is to close your eyes, open them when I tell you to and scream with delight."

He opened her door, then took her hand and guided her up the last dune, while Emily kept her hands over her eyes.

"Okay. You can look."

The sight of the restored cottage took Emily's breath away. Every detail was as it had been that first day she came here with Ethan.

"Do you mind if we walk the rest of the way?" she asked.

Josh took her hand again as they walked up the wooden path, watching her face as she stopped on the walkway to look again.

Emily smiled. "Ethan said this was the cottage's best side—that she liked to be seen first from her best side, like a vain movie actress."

"Kind of a dowdy actress, I'd say," Josh said. "But he was right. You both were. It's a nice little house."

"Praiseworthy," she said.

"Well, since I'm the one who built it—almost by hand, as it turned out—I won't argue with that," he said. "When do you want to move in?"

"Let's wait and talk about it okay? All that's left of the furniture is the rocker. You did a beautiful job restoring it, Josh, and it means a lot to me. It belonged to Ethan's great-grandmother, and I nursed Sam in it."

"I have a table and some chairs I'd like you to have, if you want them," Josh said. "I made them a couple of years ago and I think they'll look good by that large front window."

"Thank you, Josh. I'd love that—something you made with your own hands."

"There's a Shaker cradle, too," he added, smiling. "Just in case you need it someday. I figured Sam could keep his stuffed animals in it for now—or his tools."

They stopped at the seawall and looked up at the cottage again. "I think I'm about ready to take the grand tour," Emily said quietly.

Josh reached in his pocket and pulled out the key to the back door. "Do you want company?"

"Not this trip, if you don't mind. I won't be long."

Josh kissed her one final time, then climbed the steps that went over the seawall. He looked up at the sky. "There's a storm brewing out there. We may have gotten that wall in place just in time."

Emily ran her hand along the top of the stones. "It's beautiful," she said. "Isn't that funny? I never thought of a wall as beautiful before."

Josh smiled. "I love you, Emily Douglas."

"I love you, too, Josh."

When Josh had gone, Emily walked up the beach to the cottage. As she unlocked the back door, she glanced down at the twin flower beds. On either side of the door was a rosebush, pruned for winter. She looked for the tag on the new plant and smiled. Josh had planted a second white rosebush across from the charred remains of the one Ethan had put in years earlier.

Inside the house, in the small entranceway window, she found a row of bright red flower pots—the pots she had painted the afternoon Ethan died. Each one was planted with a fresh geranium cutting.

Emily wandered slowly through the empty rooms, stepping carefully to avoid creaking planks and pausing now and then to listen to a small scraping noise from the living room. One of the workmen had opened a front window to rid the cottage of the faint odor of fresh paint, so it may have been the wind that was playing tricks with her hearing. She listened again. Maybe the slight rustle of leaves or the gentle thump of a branch against a windowpane?

When she had closed the living-room window, she

stood for a long while with her back to the room and watched the distant ocean. This room had been Ethan's favorite—the room where they had been happiest that cold winter, laughing, talking, making love by firelight.

Emily turned to look at the beautiful old rocker that had somehow survived the flames—restored now under Josh's touch. She ran her fingertips tenderly over its newly burnished surface, enjoying the satin finish of the birch, remembering Sam as a baby. She drew the chair before the stone fireplace and sat down.

The warm afternoon faded swiftly into an early dusk, turning the golden sunlight that filtered through the big front window a melancholy amber. In the deepening twilight, the familiar room seemed somber and damp. Somewhere out at sea, there was a low rumble of thunder and Emily shivered, closing her eyes to listen more intently. When she opened them, heavy clouds had drifted across the face of the rising moon, and soon, the room was dark except for stray beams of blue-white moonlight that slanted in through the window. As the wind rose, the undulating shadows of things heard but unseen crept along the walls. Emily closed her eyes again.

In the doorway, something moved.

It might have been the wind, of course, or her imagination. Emily took a deep breath, opened her eyes and spoke into the darkness.

"Ethan?" she asked softly.

Emily closed the back door of the cottage and walked up to the boathouse. The light shone from the big front window, and as she got nearer, she smelled the heavenly aroma of peppery clam chowder and baking bread. Josh had cooked dinner. Another of his many talents.

When she opened the door and came in, though, Josh was asleep on the couch. The pot of chowder was simmering, and a basket of biscuits had been set to warm on the stove. She knelt down next to the couch and kissed him.

At her kiss, he woke up and smiled. "Okay, what's the verdict? How do you like the finished product? Do I get paid for all my hard work or do I have to sue?"

"The finished product is perfect," she said, kissing him once more, "and the check is in the mail."

"Do you mind if I ask how it felt? Being in the house again after…"

Emily sighed. "It felt…empty."

"I'm sorry," he said.

Emily looked at him and smiled. "There's only one problem with it."

"What?"

"There's a couple of mice in the living room. Newly-weds, maybe."

Josh swore. "I told the guys to keep the damned doors closed. Where are they?"

"Right by the back door," she said cheerfully. "Under the radiator."

"I'll set traps tomorrow."

"No, you won't. Just catch them for me, if you can. Sam's crazy about rodents. He's been bugging me to get him a hamster, but he'll settle for mice."

* * *

Later that evening, after they had eaten the clam chowder and the biscuits, Josh went to the car and came back with the pair of socks he had a wrapped around the ring box, and then sat Emily down on the couch.

"I've got a couple of things I want to say before we go get Sam tomorrow. I know you'll probably tell me you're not still ready, and if you do, I'll have to live with it." He took a deep breath. "Okay, here it is. The proposal. I love you, Emily. I think I started loving you the first day I met you. I love you now, and I always will. I'll spend the rest of my life trying to make you happy, being the best husband I know how to be, and as good a father to Sam as my own father was to me. Will you marry me?" He smiled. "That's it. Sam's already said yes, by the way. We talked it over, man to man. Of course, I *did* bribe him a little. I promised we'd go to Disney World on our honeymoon and take him along. If that's not okay, *you* have to take the rap."

A large tear rolled down Emily's cheek.

"I don't know whether I can do this, Josh," she said, sniffing.

He took her hands in his. "Why, Em?"

She leaned over and kissed him, half laughing through her tears. "Because every time you open your damned mouth, you go and say something like that—that makes me cry. I've always hated women who cry all the time, and that's all I've been doing for months—no, *years!* I don't know about you, but I'm getting really sick of it."

Josh handed her the ring box. "Then you'll wear this?"

Emily looked down. "Your gym socks?"

He unwrapped the green velvet box and opened it. Emily touched the stone with her fingertips. "It's beautiful, Josh. I don't know why you still want me after what I've put you through but if you do, then yes, I'll marry you. I love you, Josh. I'll spend the rest of my life in love with you."

Josh slipped the ring on her finger then held her in his arms.

Emily slipped her arms around his neck. "Are you absolutely sure you want to take a three-and-a-half-year-old on our honeymoon?"

"Sure, now that he's housebroken. Which reminds me, I have something for him, too. I figured diamonds weren't his thing. I found this in the yard a couple of months ago, mixed in with all the building rubble we dumped. I know he likes shells, and it's kind of unusual."

Josh pulled a small shell out of his shirt pocket.

Emily smiled as she took the shell in her hand. "It was mine, actually. I found it on the beach a long time ago." She closed her eyes and ran her fingertips along the edge to feel for the two small chips. "I never knew what kind it was."

Josh took the shell back and turned it over in his hand. "It's not native to Maine, that's for sure."

"How did it get here, then?"

Josh shrugged. "Who knows? Maybe it was dropped off a boat? Or drifted here on a wayward current? You never know how things end up in the odd places they do." He smiled. "Or people, either, I guess."

"I've kept it for a very long time," she said quietly, brushing a bit of dust from her eye. "I'd like Sam to have it now. You know how he is about colors. In a certain light, it changes color—like a rainbow."

"You said you had something to do at the cottage, Em. Did you…do it?"

"Yes. I just needed to say goodbye to a lot of memories. I've got something to tell you, and you're going to get mad when I do."

"Tonight? Impossible. Unless you're going to tell me your check is no good."

"I don't want to live in the cottage. It's too small, and there's only one bathroom. It'll make a nice summer place, though. Don't you think?"

Josh grinned. "Twelve thousand bucks' worth of insulation down the toilet, but hey, lady, it's your house. Whatever you want."

California

May 2006

Emily slipped the shell back in her pocket and nudged Josh's arm.

"Wake up, darling. They're about to serve lunch."

Josh yawned and stretched as well as he could in the cramped seat. "Good. I'm starving."

He shook out the stiffness in his arm and glanced at his watch.

"When are your mother and the new husband due in from Florida?"

"Tomorrow morning, just in time for the ceremony, and please stop grinning like that. She's happier than I've seen her in years."

"Too bad she didn't find this guy a few years back, when both our kids were still in braces. An orthodontist could've come in handy."

Emily leaned against his shoulder. "Well, anyway, I'm glad Mom could get here. I was just sitting here thinking how proud and happy Matt and Kate would be…" Her voice trailed off.

Josh sighed. "Yeah. I thought about that a lot this morning at the house. I was wandering around Matt's old study, looking for something, and I began missing both of them again. Sam is working up a video for us to take back to Mom. She'll get a kick out of seeing it, even if she wasn't up to the plane trip out here." He yawned again. "Anyway, on to the next annoying subject. Where is it we're meeting Maggie and Gary for dinner tonight, to show off Katie and Whatshisname?"

"Some place called The Painted Oyster, down near Fisherman's Wharf, and you know perfectly well what his name is. It's Chuck, and he's a very nice guy."

Josh grinned. "Yeah? Well, as long as Chuck the Very Nice Guy is still living in sin with my daughter, I get to forget his name now and then, okay? In revenge for his robbing the cradle?"

"They're not living in sin. They're engaged, with a gorgeous ring and an apartment twenty minutes from us. In eight more weeks, Chuck will be *our* son-in-law, and *your* office manager. Besides, if Chuck hadn't insisted on it, Katie would never have agreed to go back to school this fall. She was happy as a clam being a carpenter."

"The best carpenter in two hundred miles, too," he reminded her. "Maybe in the state of Maine."

"Yes, and she's about to marry a graduate MBA. What more could you want in a team to take over the business now that you're thinking of retiring?"

"Just thinking, please. But you're right. I take it back. Chuck's a great guy, even if he can't tell a hammer from a chisel. But Katie's *still* too young to get married."

"Of course she is, but we both know she'll do exactly what she wants to do, just like she always has. And what she wants is to marry Chuck, run Lundgren and Sons, and be the best carpenter she can—just like her father."

He glanced out the window. "Is that California down there?"

Emily leaned over and looked where he was pointing. "No, darling. Too green. Look for something brown."

After the graduation ceremony, Sam dragged Josh off to meet one of his favorite professors—one coincidentally in need of advice from a good contractor. Emily sat on a low stone wall, tired and overheated, and waited for them to return. They would have to find a cab from here to meet the rest of the family at The Painted Oyster, and it was already getting late. It had been unusually hot for the end of May in Berkeley, and the afternoon heat was rising off the pavement in waves. It had been a busy day, and Emily was ready for a frozen margarita and a lobster dripping in drawn butter.

At last, Josh and Sam appeared in the distance and started across the wide lawn toward her. Josh's arm was draped across Sam's shoulder as they walked, and father and son were laughing together at some private joke. Emily smiled, wiping away one of the many tears she had vowed not to shed today. It had been hard on Josh when Sam decided to attend school in another state, and seeing them together was an emotional moment for her.

But as the two men came closer, another tall figure suddenly appeared, walking beside Sam, his hand resting on Sam's left shoulder. From this distance, it was impossible to make out his face, but the stranger's walk and general bearing were familiar. Emily shaded her eyes from the sun's glare and looked more closely. As the sun began to sink lower behind them, the three figures were momentarily silhouetted against a blaze of orange, and the mystery figure seemed to glow for several seconds with an almost incandescent shimmer. Then, as quickly as he had appeared, the tall figure faded away into the setting sun.

While Sam went to find a cab, Josh came over to Emily and slipped his arms around her. "Well, the deed is done. Our kid's a genius and he's got the paperwork to prove it. Proud?"

Emily was still staring off in the direction they had just come from. Josh brushed a wisp of hair from her brow. "You okay? You look a little dazed. Too much sun?"

Emily kissed him. "Just for a moment."

Something about her smile made Josh turn and look back across the lawn. He gave her a quizzical look.

"Somebody you used to know?"

"You saw him?"

Josh smiled. "No, but I knew he'd be here. Where else would a father be on the day his only son graduates *summa cum laude?*"

Later that evening, in the blessed quiet of their hotel room, Emily joined Josh in the enormous bed and asked him something she had wanted to ask for years.

"If I ask you a question, will you tell me the absolute truth, Josh?"

He leaned over and kissed her. "Yes. You look terrific in the new dress you bought. That shade of green complements your eyes, makes you look ten years younger and it definitely flatters your hips—not that they need flattering, of course. How's that?"

Emily rolled her eyes. "That wasn't the question, darling, but I compliment you on such a deeply sincere and intelligent answer."

He laughed. "Okay, then. What was the question?"

"Do you remember the night Katie was born? What we talked about?"

He nodded. "Sure. You had just promised God that if Katie came through all right, you'd tell me the whole truth about Ethan and the cottage. And you did."

"Did you believe everything I said that night?"

"Well, you *were* stoned out of your skull, as the kids would say. Floating on Demerol, if I remember correctly. But yes, I believed you, because I knew it long before you told me."

Emily stared at him. "Then why didn't you ever say anything?"

"Because I figured you'd tell me when you were ready."

She snuggled closer. "Weren't you ever jealous?"

Josh chuckled. "Maybe a little. Hell, when we first met, I didn't know how to compete with his memory, let alone his ghost."

"You always told me you didn't believe in ghosts."

"I didn't, but then I remembered something my great-grandmother from Sweden used to say. She told me once that people who didn't believe in ghosts just weren't paying attention."

"Isn't it nice not having a dog on the bed with us for a change?"

Josh laughed. "You bet. Why is it that all three dogs we've had since old Sarah died thought they had squatter's rights to our bed? You think she's keeping an eye on us from canine heaven?"

He patted her hip. "Well, it's been a big day. You about ready to get some sleep?"

Emily ran her hand down his thigh. "Sleep, my eye! This room cost us five hundred and eighty dollars, darling. We can *sleep* at home."

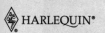

HARLEQUIN®

NIGHTS™

*Not everything is above board
on Alexandra's Dream!*

*Enjoy plenty of secrets, drama and sensuality
in the latest from Mediterranean Nights.*

Coming in November 2007...

BELOW DECK

by

Dorien Kelly

Determined to protect her young son,
widow Mei Lin Wang keeps him hidden
aboard *Alexandra's Dream* under cover of
her job. But life gets extremely complicated
when the ship's security officer, Gideon Dayan,
is piqued by the mystery surrounding this
beautiful, haunted woman....

HARLEQUIN Romance

New York Times bestselling author

DIANA PALMER

Handsome, eligible ranch owner Stuart York knew Ivy Conley was too young for him, so he closed his heart to her and sent her away—despite the fireworks between them. Now, years later, Ivy is determined not to be treated like a little girl anymore...but for some reason, Stuart is always fighting her battles for her. And safe in Stuart's arms makes Ivy feel like a woman...his woman.

Winter Roses

Available November.

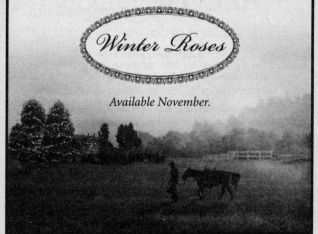

HRIBC03985

REQUEST YOUR FREE BOOKS!

2 FREE NOVELS PLUS 2 FREE GIFTS!

HARLEQUIN®

E V E R L A S T I N G   L O V E ™

Every great love has a story to tell™

YES! Please send me 2 FREE Harlequin® Everlasting Love™ novels and my 2 FREE gifts. After receiving them, if I don't wish to receive any more books, I can return the shipping statement marked "cancel." If I don't cancel, I will receive 4 brand-new novels every other month and be billed just $4.47 per book in the U.S. or $4.99 per book in Canada, plus 25¢ shipping and handling per book and applicable taxes, if any*. That's a savings of about 15% off the cover price! I understand that accepting the 2 free books and gifts places me under no obligation to buy anything. I can always return a shipment and cancel at any time. Even if I never buy another book from Harlequin, the two free books and gifts are mine to keep forever.

153 HDN ELX4   353 HDN ELYG

Name	(PLEASE PRINT)	
Address		Apt.
City	State/Prov.	Zip/Postal Code

Signature (if under 18, a parent or guardian must sign)

Mail to the **Harlequin Reader Service®**:
IN U.S.A.: P.O. Box 1867, Buffalo, NY 14240-1867
IN CANADA: P.O. Box 609, Fort Erie, Ontario L2A 5X3

Not valid to current Harlequin Everlasting Love subscribers.

Want to try two free books from another line?
Call 1-800-873-8635 or visit www.morefreebooks.com.

* Terms and prices subject to change without notice. NY residents add applicable sales tax. Canadian residents will be charged applicable provincial taxes and GST. This offer is limited to one order per household. All orders subject to approval. Credit or debit balances in a customer's account(s) may be offset by any other outstanding balance owed by or to the customer. Please allow 4 to 6 weeks for delivery.

Your Privacy: Harlequin is committed to protecting your privacy. Our Privacy Policy is available online at www.eHarlequin.com or upon request from the Reader Service. From time to time we make our lists of customers available to reputable firms who may have a product or service of interest to you. If you would prefer we not share your name and address, please check here. ☐

HEL07

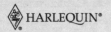

Cut from the soap opera that made her a star, America's TV goddess Gloria Hart heads back to her childhood home to regroup. But when a car crash maroons her in small-town Mississippi, it's local housewife Jenny Miller to the rescue. Soon these two very different women, together with Gloria's sassy assistant, become fast friends, realizing that they bring out a certain secret something in each other that men find irresistible!

Look for

THE SECRET GODDESS CODE

by

PEGGY WEBB

Available November wherever you buy books.

TheNextNovel.com

HN88146

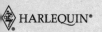

EVERLASTING LOVE™

Every great love has a story to tell™

Charlie fell in love with Rose Kaufman
before he even met her, through stories her
husband, Joe, used to tell. When Joe is killed
in the trenches, Charlie helps Rose through
her grief and they make a new life together.
But for Charlie, a question remains—can
love be as true the second time around?
Only one woman can answer that....

Look for

*The Soldier and
the Rose*

by
Linda Barrett

Available November wherever you buy books.

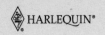

HARLEQUIN®

EVERLASTING LOVE™

Every great love has a story to tell™

COMING NEXT MONTH

#19 THE SOLDIER AND THE ROSE
by Linda Barrett

Charlie Shapiro fell in love with Rose Kaufman
before he ever met her, through the heartwarming stories
Joe used to tell his war buddies about his young wife. Then
Joe was killed in the trenches…while Charlie survived
World War II. Slowly he helped Rose through her grief and
they made a new life together. But for Charlie, now in his
eighties, the question remains: can love be as true the second
time around? Only one woman can answer that.…

Linda Barrett, a popular author with Harlequin
Superromance is known for her warmly appealing characters,
her realism and her ability to create a sense of community in
her writing.

#20 A RENDEZVOUS TO REMEMBER
by Geri Krotow

On the verge of divorce, Melinda Thompson comes home—
to her recently widowed grandfather and to her own empty
house. When Melinda reads her grandparents' journals, she
learns about their Resistance and wartime experiences. And
she learns why people like her grandparents have been called
"the Greatest Generation." And how her own life can begin
to measure up to theirs…

Geri Krotow's story is both thrilling and deeply moving—
truly a book you'll remember.

www.eHarlequin.com

HECNM1007